Wicked Games

Fallen Royals
Book 2

S. Massery

Introduction

Hello dear reader!

First and most importantly: this is **not** a standalone. Wicked Dreams must be read prior to this, as Wicked Games is a continuation of that storyline.

If you've read me before, you know my stories run quite dark. This book contains themes common to dark romance, including bullying, blackmail, stalking, and dubious consent. This story also includes mentions of childhood trauma.

Stay safe out there, friends, and happy reading!

xoxo,
Sara

P.S. This series was previously published (under the same title) in 2020, but has since been revised.

Chapter 1
Caleb

It's done.

I expect a weight to lift off my shoulders, the same as every other time I did this.

Over the years, I've systematically destroyed Margo's world. It's become something of a secret sport—me versus her. The game continued when she moved here, when she was suddenly in my path once again.

But the first time, we were twelve. It took me two years to stew, thinking she had just gotten away without retribution, to realize that if anyone was going to make her pay for her sins, it would be me.

Of course, at twelve I didn't think like that. I just wanted her to hurt.

I took a taxi. I'd overheard my uncle talking about her, where she was. He, too, kept tabs. But he didn't show up at her door like I was planning. I approached her foster mother with a rather twisted view of the truth. The woman just stared at me, her eyes round, as a kid laid out Margo's crimes.

I left their front porch but hung around for the fireworks.

I paid the taxi driver to park at the curb. His meter ticked onward, but I didn't give a shit. I was a *kid.* Money was a far-off concept, sure, but I also knew we had enough of it to cover this adventure. Her social worker arrived at the house, talked to the parents. She carried out a trash bag and set it in her trunk.

Margo came home from school only to meet the social worker. Hell, the foster mom had been so disgusted, she didn't even want to be there.

I leaned forward, wanting to soak up her every reaction. Her dark hair was in two braids that swung across her back. There were little pink bows in them. She seemed fine. So opposite of me. She was smiling, but it faded when she realized who was on the porch.

The social worker broke the news.

Margo didn't cry.

That was disappointing.

She didn't cry the next time either, when I found her again.

Each time she carted out her garbage bag, which I learned was full of her clothes, she kept her shoulders back. Her chin up. At fifteen, I sat in my uncle's car a house down from the fosters' and tried to suck an ounce of gratification out of it.

The game turned into: How far can I push until she breaks?

Ruin her in one way, and she might recover. Ruin her *every* way, and she'll crumble. Mind, body, and soul.

I began hanging around longer to see if she would lose control. Not close enough for her to see me—I'm not an idiot. In all the times I fucked with her, whether it be through the school she attended or the foster home, she only slipped once.

When she was torn away from siblings.

Once in seven fucking years.

It felt good to see her cry, but odd. Something cracked inside my chest. Her breaking was breaking me, too. I had let her stay at that home for a while. Two whole years of idyllic bliss while I tried to forget about Margo Wolfe.

I drowned myself in hockey. I even fucked her ex-best friends. But I couldn't shake her. She resided in the back of my head, popping up at the worst times.

Senior year was approaching, and it was time for Margo to return home.

The Bryans were perfect. It wasn't their fault I had that card up my sleeve. As I told the Bryans: they were a common subject of my aunt and her social circle right after the accident that stole their daughter's life. My aunt went to church and prayed for their family, but then she'd come back with her friends, gossiping like schoolgirls about where the drugs could've come from.

Was it true? Did Amber Wolfe, Margo's mother, kill their daughter?

Maybe.

Hell if I know.

This isn't about them—this is about Margo and her resilience. It's about ruining another good thing for her, while being up close and personal to watch the fallout.

I didn't expect Lenora Bryan to cry.

Or maybe I did. I tried to morph my face into a semblance of sympathy, but... it's sympathy I don't quite feel. Not for them anyway.

Will they kick Margo out? Or will their perception of her shift just enough that it becomes unbearable?

I guess we'll find out. I leave their house, trotting down the steps and to my car. Once in, I tip my head back and breathe a sigh of relief.

It's done. Whatever happens next is on them.

I scan my phone before I take off, clearing away messages from classmates and my mother. I pause on my best friend's latest text. It came in less than a half hour ago.

ELI

You schmoozing the Bryans? Freaked your girl out that you were there.

I pause.

Two things. *My girl?* She is mine—but to hear him acknowledge it is an entirely different beast. The second—

Margo saw my car?

I'd figured Eli would take his sweet time getting out of there. He was supposed to offer to take them to breakfast or some shit. Give me time to cause my mayhem and leave.

I type back.

ME

Dickhead.

But really, this is a bigger issue.

ELI

She got out of the car at the top of the street.

Did you see her?

No, no I didn't.

"Shit." I slam my hand against the steering wheel. I've never had her catch me before. I've never been this careless, though... Just hours ago, I was *inside* her. Making her scream and squirm under my touch, bringing her pleasure. And now, the opposite.

But what did she see? Or hear?

I dial her number and drum my fingers on the steering wheel. I need to drive away from the Bryans' house, but not until Margo answers me.

It goes to voicemail.

I dial again, just in case.

It must be off, because it barely rings once before it switches over to her breathy voice on the recording.

This plan... It was set in stone a while ago. Pulling her down piece by piece. But I'm not ready for her to fall—not yet. I'm not done with her.

This was supposed to be slow. A shift in their family dynamic. An unsettling.

Seven years ago, she broke me. Now I'm just showing her what she created.

A beast in my chest demands to be free—a beast that only wants Margo's blood.

I pound my hands on the steering wheel again, in rapid succession.

Slowly, I drop the walls around the demons I keep locked away. It's nice to let the darkness take over. Fury washes through me, but it's calm, liquid ice.

Margo Wolfe may have run away, but I'm going to find her and bring her back, even if it kills me.

We're not done.

Eventually, she'll shatter for me, and the game will finally be over.

Chapter 2
Margo

I couldn't go anywhere I knew he would find me.

Because he *would* find me.

I have no doubt that, as easily as he hurt the Bryans, he would come for me. Something broke him. Something fucked up in our past. For some reason, I can't fathom what it is. Whether I've been lied to, am misremembering things, or blocked it out of my memory...

The truth will set me free.

It tugs at my memory, but it's just out of reach.

I ring the doorbell and take a quick step back. A minute passes, then a voice shouts for me to hold on. The door swings open.

Ian Fletcher scowls down at me.

Honestly? This is the last place I want to go. My stomach still aches from the force of his kicks, and the bite mark has barely scabbed over. The idea that Ian has marked me permanently—because it will probably scar—turns my stomach.

And yet...

"You said you hated Caleb more than me." I'm not

going for subtlety here. I'm desperate, and I'm so out of options it isn't funny. It was never funny in the first place. "Well, now's your chance."

He raises his eyebrows. "My chance for what?"

"I hate him, too."

"And?"

"And..." I grimace. "I'm what he wants. What he's fixated on. So here's my one-time offer. Use me against him."

We watch each other for a moment while he thinks through what I just said. What I'm giving him on a silver fucking platter.

He could easily slam the door in my face, and I'd be screwed. I have no doubt Caleb would find me at Riley's house, and I don't know where else I could go. He'd find me anywhere else.

Ian pulls the door open wider.

I exhale, relief building, and I slip past him. I've been here before, but it looks different when it's not packed with students. The house is actually set up nicely, although it's pristine in the way showrooms are.

Does anyone actually live here?

He brushes past me, and I trail after him.

Is this madness? Probably. But what option do I have against Caleb?

In the end, Caleb hurt me, too. Ian's wounds have mostly healed, but I doubt Caleb's betrayal ever will. It burns under my skin like a living thing.

The house is nearly silent. Just our footsteps and my quiet breath.

He slides open a door and enters a home office. I pause in the doorway while he throws himself into the chair behind the huge oak desk.

"Why should I take you at your word?"

I'm numb to it at this point—happily so. "Caleb thinks I'm to blame for the video of me and him."

Ian snorts. "Impossible."

"Why?"

"Because I know who recorded it."

My mouth drops open.

He continues, "Did he blame you publicly? Honestly, I doubt anyone would believe it. You make some rather hot noises in it, but I didn't peg you to be an exhibitionist."

My face gets hot.

He tuts, leaning back and putting his feet up on the desk. "Why did you come here?"

"I had to go somewhere he wouldn't find me." I try to keep my voice from trembling. This was the harebrained part of my plan. It hinges on Ian being rational, and I'm pretty sure he's got a screw loose. "And I figured... here was good."

"After what I did to you."

I wince. "Especially after that."

He watches me for a long moment. "You don't have a stupid fucking crush on me, do you?"

"Not on your life."

He doesn't seem to believe me.

"I'll just go, then." I stand. "And that offer is off the table."

"No. Sit."

I grind my teeth and glare at him. "I'm really sick of people ordering me around."

I put my bag over my shoulder and find my way back to the front door, ignoring the way his attention stings.

When I was a kid, I fell into a bush of stinging nettle. It's a bit like that.

"Wait."

I glance back. He's in the hall, only a few feet away.

"I have a guest room," he says. "My parents go to Los Angeles for the winter, and they're already there. They'll never know."

"What's the catch?"

He rolls his eyes. "The catch is that you keep your promise."

Great.

"I'll let you stay... for a kiss." He circles me. "That's your offer, right? To get back at Caleb. Kiss me."

"Why did you kick me in the stomach?"

His eyes light up. "Ah. Do you still have bruises? Can I see?"

"This was a mistake." I can't get away from him fast enough. Really—what on earth was I thinking?

I try to step around him, but he blocks me. I step around him again, and he follows me down a hallway, into the kitchen. It's big and cold. There's a sliding door that leads out onto the porch. I got drunk in this house. It was here that Unknown got that damn video of me.

"Kiss me and you can stay, rent-free, for a month. If you aren't discovered before that."

He's standing right behind me, while I'm frozen with my hand on the glass.

"And I'll tell you who took that video," he adds.

"Tempting," I say.

"He kissed Savannah in front of you."

"How kind of you to bring that back up."

"Multiple times, if sources are correct." He sneers. "I'm not kind, Margo. I hope you didn't come here expecting *that*, of all things."

My gaze wanders over his backyard. If there was somewhere else I could go, I wouldn't be here. But I am. I haven't even begun to process what I overheard Caleb say. I shove those thoughts away as soon as they rise.

"I don't understand why you'd want to kiss me," I finally say.

I turn around, and he's *right there.*

He's not Caleb. He's intimidating, sure, and the fear that spikes through me is real. But he doesn't give me butterflies along with the fear. He crowds me, and all my body remembers is the pain.

He's close enough to touch me, but he doesn't. He stares into my eyes, a slight frown on his lips.

He leans into me. I put my hands on his chest and shove.

He catches my wrists, keeping my palms flat against him. His body heat seeps into my fingers.

"Let. Go."

He switches his grasp on my wrists, taking both in one of his hands. With his other, he yanks my shirt up. Not far—just to the lower edge of my bra.

My stomach is still a kaleidoscope of bruises. It was a vicious move on his part.

"Got what you wanted?" I yank again, but he holds fast.

He runs a finger over my abdomen.

I shut my eyes. "Stop."

"He calls you a lamb," he says. "But I think you're proving to be far from that."

I open my eyes.

His attention is fixated on the bruises. He has an odd expression—a split second of remorse maybe, and his damn finger on my skin.

"Stop touching me, Ian." My voice doesn't tremble like I thought it might.

He releases me like coming out of a trance.

"Payment accepted." He clears his throat. "Take the room, Wolfe. Upstairs, first one on the left. Don't ask me for anything else. I'll hide you until I figure out how to make Caleb burst with jealousy."

I don't push it, and I don't ask what that means. I said he could use me—but I didn't mean... I don't know what I meant.

How far would I go?

I slip past him and dart up the stairs, stepping into the room and closing the door behind me. I lean against it for good measure. My bag hits the floor next to me.

The room is huge. I mean, big surprise—the whole house is a freaking mansion. But it's *pink*. A girl's room, clearly, by the white-and-pink bedspread and the light-pink walls. The curtains on the two windows are white. A rug covers half of the hardwood floor, a low dresser in the corner... a vase of flowers on one nightstand and a lamp on the other.

Weird.

I'd imagine they must have a housekeeper, someone who keeps everything clean and fresh. The water in the vase is high and clear. So even though the room must not be occupied, *someone* changes out the flowers and water.

There's no lock on the door, but I can't be bothered to worry much about it. I inch toward the bed, and exhaustion crashes over me. It's not even ten o'clock in the morning. Was it only five hours ago that Caleb was inside me? He wasn't professing love—I'm not *that* daft—but our sex...

It felt real.

And I'm delusional. Clearly.

After a night of limited sleep, I could stay in bed for a

week. Even a frilly, girly, foreign bed like this one, in an unsafe house, with a potential psychopath downstairs.

The enemy of my enemy is my friend.

I lie down and stare at the tiled ceiling. My eyes won't close, even though they feel like sandpaper. I can't cry either. I spent most of the walk to Ian's house swinging between stoicism and sobbing. No in between.

How could he do this?

There are questions that need answering.

I hop up and pull a notebook out of my bag. The way to get organized is to make a list.

Who is Unknown?

Why is Caleb set on ruining my life?

Tobias—Dad's attorney?

When I try to remember my past, nothing happens. It's like there's a wall in my mind. It isn't active unless I try to access the few months before I entered into foster care. I remember being with my dad in the park, but that's because Caleb practically forced the memory out of me.

Maybe...

No.

I look down at my list again.

There's more.

Where are Caleb's parents?

Why is his house seemingly abandoned?

What happened in our past? Why can't I remember?

Who sent the video?

My head pounds. Ian told me he knew that. I'll have to ask him again.

I lie back down and force my eyes shut.

Today's been a clusterfuck. Being here... well, I can't say that makes it any better. My phone is off, at the bottom of my bag. I can only imagine the texts and calls piling up. Or maybe worst of all: no calls at all. The Bryans might call to inform me that Angela will be picking me up. I might come back and find my stuff on the curb.

That happened once.

Angela was waiting for me. A bag with my belongings—a few shirts, underwear, pants, and a toothbrush—was already in the car. The foster family hadn't even given me *toothpaste*. Not that it mattered.

I prided myself on not losing my shit. I'd learned the hard way that tears solved nothing. They *changed* nothing.

Twelve-year-old Margo learned that bad things would continually happen. It was her new reality. I went into the system when I was ten, but for that first year, I was optimistic. I thought I'd go back to my mom and dad, that life with the Ashers would return to normal.

I couldn't have been more wrong.

Chapter 3
Margo

Past

The detective took my dad away.

A lady sat next to me on the bench and smiled. Even though she looked nice, she wasn't particularly warm and fuzzy. Not like Dad when he held my hand on the way here.

"Ready to go, Margo?"

Dad struggled. He yelled my name, and officers were yelling back. I stared at him, not quite comprehending why they were dragging him away. Why his arms were behind his back, or the panicked look in his eye.

"Margo," the woman beside me said again.

I faced her. "Am I going with Dad?"

She frowned. "Your dad was just arrested. I'm with Social Services. We're going to try and locate your mom, okay?"

I didn't know what arrested meant. But at the mention of my mom, tears formed in my eyes, and my throat got all tight. My chin wobbled. "Mom? No, she..."

Blank.

"It's going to be okay." She introduced herself, shook my hand, and then wouldn't let go. She pulled me up and away. Down the path. It split, and we went a different way than my dad.

Are more police officers coming to arrest me, too?

"Come on, honey."

We were almost to her car.

Dad said never to get in the car with strangers.

I screamed.

Blank.

I screamed, didn't I?

Blank.

If I didn't scream, did I get in the car? Go with her willingly? Give up on my family?

Blank.

Blank.

Blank.

Present

I wake with a start. Pink walls. White curtains. Flowers a foot from my face. I'm not ten and scared—I'm seventeen, on the verge of eighteen, and in Ian's house. Not really any less scared, but still. Not in danger.

A dream—maybe more real than not?

There are gaps in my memory. I think they're bigger than I realized.

"Who is Unknown?"

I roll over with a gasp.

Ian sits on the edge of my bed, facing away from me. He

has my notebook open on his lap. He's reading from my list of questions.

"Well, I think the point of the name Unknown signifies your lack of knowing who they are. Unless they call themselves Unknown? Hmm." Pen scratches the paper as he writes something. "'Why is Caleb set on ruining my life?'"

"Why are you in my room?"

He glances back at me. "Technically it isn't *your* room."

"You're prying." I get off the bed and circle around it, stopping in front of him. "Give it back."

"I'm most curious about this question. Why is Caleb set on ruining your life?" He taps his pen on his lip. "Dare I answer?"

"Knock yourself out."

"You ruined his life first," he reasons. "At least, that's the way my parents explained it."

I stare at him. "What?"

"What part of that was confusing?"

"The part where your parents were talking about it."

He chuckles, setting the notebook down next to him. "Ah. Caleb's aunt and mine are second cousins."

"Holy shit. You're related? I didn't—"

"Distantly," he says in a tone that ends all of my other questions.

He stands, and I take a quick step backward.

That door really needs a lock.

"You think he won't come here searching for you?" Ian walks to the door.

Does he realize that by standing in the doorway, he cages me in? Boys like him have all the power. I shouldn't be taken aback by that.

He's still watching me, and I realize he asked me a question.

"He might," I admit. "He'll probably look high and low for me. Especially since I shut my phone off."

Ian scoffs. "Well, I guess that'll put you in a predicament tonight."

"What's tonight?"

"Party."

Of course. It's Saturday.

"We just had the ball last night," I protest. "And you're hosting a party? Here?"

He shrugs. "Yep. It's an after-party of sorts."

It must be a desperate bid to cure his loneliness. He's all alone in this big house for the whole winter. I'd get lonely, too. And lonely people do dangerous things.

Wait. No, I shouldn't be sympathizing with the enemy. Above all things, I cannot empathize with *Ian Fletcher*. I should've gone somewhere else. Even Amelie's house might've been a better option... one I didn't think of until right this moment.

"Is Caleb invited to your party?" I finally ask.

He smirks.

I groan, throwing my hands up. "You couldn't have warned me before—"

"Before what, Wolfe? Before you got settled?" He looks pointedly at my bag by the door. "You didn't even take off your shoes."

True. It's a runaway kid habit. Be ready to go in an instant.

I shake my head. "There's not even a lock on the door—"

"You can hide out in my room. There's not a lock on it, but just imagine if Caleb found you? How pissed he would be." He's positively gleeful.

I narrow my eyes. "You're not going to tell him?"

"Probably not."

I groan and leave the room. I don't trust Ian. Not that I particularly trust anyone at the moment, but Ian and Caleb are at the top of the shit list. Which furthers the point that it makes no sense why I would come here.

Is it too late to leave?

I was hoping to go to bed early tonight, sleep in, and then figure out how the hell my mother was involved with the Bryans' daughter. *If* she was involved. That would also include tracking her down. If I can find her, then I can prove her innocence—and in turn, *my* innocence.

The Bryans will take me back.

Ian follows me downstairs, into the kitchen. I open the fridge and lean in. My mind is still buzzing, and I need a distraction so I don't completely freak out about whose house I'm in.

A little nap made a world of difference in my thought process.

"By all means, make yourself at home," Ian intones. "There's enough meal-prepped shit between the fridge and freezer to last a month."

I straighten and face him. "What? Why?"

"Mother Dearest makes sure I'm taken care of over the winter." He leans against the island, watching me. "A chef comes in and prepares meals once a month. It's a big ordeal. Time consuming. The whole house stinks like a restaurant for at least three days after. Lucky for us, she was just here a few days ago."

A chef?

He pauses. "Margo?"

I blink and take a quick step back. I froze, I think.

"My mom is a personal chef."

I clear my throat. She *was* a personal chef. Is she still? Did she find work with some other rich family? Finding her couldn't be so easy... it would be laughable if she was employed by the Fletchers. That's right under the Ashers' noses. And mine, too.

"I'm familiar," he replies.

"Because she works for your family?"

"No."

"Then why say that part?"

He scowls. "I said it because it's the truth. Why? Do you need things sugarcoated? Should we never talk about chefs, or murder—"

"Stop." I decide on an apple out of the bottom drawer and take a bite. "It just took me by surprise, that's all."

"That we have a chef? To be fair, what we have is completely different from your mom. I mean, you guys lived in the Asher guest house. I've heard the stories. How she catered to Mr. Asher's every whim—"

I chuck the apple at him.

It hits him in the chest, juice splattering on his shirt. He catches it before it falls, then shakes his head at me.

"Where's your sense of self-preservation?" My face is getting hot.

"You just need a dose of reality, since Caleb refuses to acknowledge it." He takes a bite of the apple, winking at me. "So anytime you want to face the truth, let me know."

He tosses the apple back at me and strolls out of the kitchen.

"Wait," I blurt out. "My mom..."

He stops in the doorway. "Yes?"

"How much do you know?"

"Definitely not as much as you wish I did. I'd love to lie

and say I could tell you what's lost in your memory. But even I don't know exactly what happened in the Asher house."

My lips part. "How...?"

"Did I know you can't remember?"

The one thing I respect about Ian is that we can talk about this fucked-up situation without pity or sympathy. He doesn't show any emotion except faint amusement. Amusement doesn't bother me. It's everything else that tends to get...

Suffocating.

"You wouldn't let Caleb near you with a ten-foot pole if you knew the truth," he says, not waiting for my answer. "And as much as I hate him, I'm not willing to spoil it. The longer it goes, the better the fireworks will be."

He mimes explosions.

I don't have a reply. My mouth is dry, and I feel... off-kilter? The ground seems to be shifting under my feet constantly, not allowing me to get a grip.

He leaves, and I stare down at the apple in my hands. My appetite has fled, along with my sanity.

I don't know where the hell my mother is—but she has to have some answers.

Step one: find her.

Step two: hope she'll talk to me.

And there's Tobias, too...

So many freaking questions.

Plus, the leaked video, and Caleb's betrayal, and Ian decided to throw a party.

I set the bitten apple on the table and go back to the pink room. I flop on the bed and consider Ian's words. Slowly, I toe off my shoes, letting them fall to the floor. A sign that I'm not running... not quite yet.

You wouldn't let Caleb near you...

My head pounds. I drape my arm over my eyes, blocking out the light.

What's the truth?

What's a lie?

We may never know.

Chapter 4
Caleb

I stalk into Riley's house.

There's a commotion above my head, so I go to the stairs. The layout isn't rocket science. Half the homes in this part of town have something similar. I climb the stairs and stop in front of a door.

Her door.

Eli told me which bedroom is hers, and here I am. Except, the door is locked.

I could pick it if I wanted to—if I had the patience for it. But patience isn't something I'm known for. Not now, with intoxicating anger flowing through me. I take a step back and kick, smashing her door open.

Empty.

Who locks an empty room?

I consider that, going so far as to check the closet, then get the fuck out of there.

There are only a few places that Margo would go to avoid me. A few places she would either trust to hide her from me—big mistake—or that she'd think I wouldn't hunt for her.

Savannah or Amelie maybe.

Or Ian.

Riley was the obvious choice. I'm almost proud that Margo didn't run straight here. I check with Eli, confirming that he's with Margo's best friend, and he sends a selfie of the two of them.

My phone rings. I smother a groan, dropping into my car.

"You better be calling to tell me you left town," I say.

"Hello to you, too," Margo's mother says. "I just—"

"If you're about to ask for a favor, don't."

"Caleb, you don't understand."

I growl. Amber is a distraction and a drug addict. She had her uses, but her *calling* me? Absolutely not.

"Your mom is looking for me," she whispers.

I freeze. "What?"

"I don't know what to do. Somehow she got my number—"

"Then *change your number*." I stare straight ahead. My mother, Margo's mother, the fucking Bryans. This mess is snowballing.

This wasn't part of the game.

I hang up on her. Can't really do anything about Mother, since she's always been a wild card. Everyone else has a plan, motives, wants, and needs. She's just crazy.

I try calling Margo again, but it's still going straight to voicemail. If you had told me two months ago that the girl I had carried a grudge against for seven *fucking* years would change me, I would've punched you in the goddamn face.

She's under my skin. She found the cracks in my armor and slipped right in, and I loathe her for it.

Maybe that's why I went through with my decision to talk to the Bryans.

My next stop is Theo's house. As much as I'd love to barge into Amelie's home, it wouldn't do me any good. So I'm sending someone who can be a little more persuasive.

Theo and the Page girls have history. Amelie's sister goes to Lion's Head, our rival school in the neighboring town of Beacon. But because Amelie attends Emery-Rose... Lucille has always hung around. To say her and Theo somehow got off on the wrong foot would be putting it mildly.

But while there's no love lost between them, there's a weird sort of kinship, too.

I don't get it. I don't try to get it.

Theo meets me in the driveway, his eyebrow raised. Already expecting me to ask him something—because why else would I show up unannounced?

"Margo's missing," I tell him.

His expression doesn't change.

"She might be at the Page house."

He snorts. "She might decide to hide in a bed of vipers, too."

"You want to go find out or what?" I snap.

Time tugs on my skin.

Every second that passes, she's getting farther away from me. Every bone in my body needs to know where Margo is. She can't run away. She isn't in control. *I am.*

But right now, I don't think that's quite true. She got the upper hand on me.

"Where are you going?" Theo questions.

"Dunley's, then Fletcher." I shake my head, already mentally crossing off Savannah Dunley from my list. "Maybe straight to Ian's. The fucker deserves to be hit again."

I've already been suspended from hockey for six weeks.

I've got nothing left to lose, except perhaps the rest of my season. And there, my goal of playing hockey in college would most likely sputter out.

Nothing beats the impending doom of being forced into a job I don't want like hockey does.

Theo's eyes darken. "And the video?"

"Apparently it came from Savannah." I lift my shoulder. I don't know how much truth to put into that. Savannah holds grudges, sure, but I wouldn't have expected this from her.

It's a bit too conniving. More on Amelie's level...

"Another reason to visit her first," Theo reasons.

I sigh. Savannah and Amelie were Margo's best friends. Now, they're causing more trouble than they're worth. But unfortunately, we don't live in a society where I can just bury them in the backyard.

"Your uncle is going to be pissed," he adds.

I don't need to be told that. I know it. I live it.

"I'm giving you a shot at Page, and you're still flapping your lips."

His chuckle follows me back to my car. Fuck him. He'll help, but he'll do it in his own time. And maybe he's right: I should clean up the video. It spread faster than I anticipated, and Savannah's phone was just the catalyst.

She didn't record it.

I dial a number I memorized a long time ago.

"Yes?"

"Do you have a death wish?" I bark.

They swallow.

"Get rid of it."

"What?"

"Get rid of the fucking video—get it off every phone, every server, or so help me God, I will ruin your life."

Silence.

Then, "You didn't like the angle?"

I growl.

"Fine. Consider it done."

Margo isn't with Savannah. She knows that girl would do anything to get back in my good graces—including tell me if Margo showed up. Since I have no messages from Dunley, that leaves one option.

My little lamb thought she would outsmart me. But what she doesn't know is that I've been hemming her in since before she came back to Rose Hill. Trimming away at the number of people she can turn to, making it so eventually, she'll only have me.

I crack my neck. There's only one place—okay, two, if Theo ends up finding her at Amelie's—that Margo could be.

Next stop: Ian Fletcher's house.

Chapter 5
Unknown

"I don't understand your attachment."

I sigh.

No one does.

I've tried to explain it before. I've written it out, then torn the pages and burned them. There's a danger in admittance. People think confessing wipes away sin. Speak it out loud, absolve yourself with penance, move on. But confessing is a trap.

I'm done explaining myself.

The little figure sits heavy on my palm. On the screen, the video feed lags by a few seconds. I jostle it, count to three, and watch the image of me jerk and tremble.

This will work well.

I examine it closer, but even to my eye, the camera is hidden.

"Satisfied?"

I nod once.

"Where are they?"

"Strung across Rose Hill," I answer. "Little fires everywhere."

Just the way it should be.

Chapter 6
Margo

Ian's room is kind of what I would've expected. The walls are gray-blue; his bedding matches in darker tones. There's a hockey stick lying across his desk, a roll of white tape beside it, and a helmet on top of a few textbooks. His bag—thankfully closed, because I'm pretty sure hockey boys' pads smell awful—sits in a corner. The rest of his room is, for the most part, spotless. Closed black closet doors, plush carpet instead of hardwood.

I drop my bag and sit on the edge of his bed. Music kicks on downstairs, loud enough to vibrate the floorboards. People are already arriving, and I couldn't decide whether to remain where I was or hide in Ian's room, like he originally offered.

After only a few moments' debate, in which he showed me the sign he hangs on his door, I followed him down the hall and allowed him to close me in.

I slide to the floor and dig through the bag, pulling out my phone. I've avoided it, but now I turn it on. I'm not expecting much. Maybe a courtesy text from the Bryans, or one from Ms. McCaw informing me of what I already know?

I've tried for years to avoid loneliness. To push away everyone and everything in an effort to fortify myself. I changed homes frequently. At ten, I made attachments wherever I went. By twelve...

Past

Ms. McCaw was waiting for me when I got back to the DiMario house. The bus dropped me off at the end of the street, and sometimes they waited for me in their car. If Mr. DiMario wasn't drunk, that is, and if the weather was bad. Their excuse was that they didn't want a rain-soaked child dripping water across their floors. If he was drunk, then I walked to their house and tried to slip in undetected. Rain or snow or otherwise.

Anger. So much anger in one man.

She stood on the porch, typing on her phone. She seemed sad. Her lips were pinched, and her eyebrows pulled down in the middle.

"Hi, Margo," she greeted me. "Let's go, honey. Your stuff is in the car."

In a trash bag, no doubt.

"Where am I going?"

She just shook her head. "A respite home."

Respite. Temporary. A night, a week.

I was getting tired of this. Already. It had been two years—Dad was no closer to being free, Mom was gone. She had already been declared unfit anyway. But the fact that she didn't come back?

"What'd I do this time?"

"The family said you were stealing." She showed me a watch that belonged to Mr. DiMario. "I found this in your room."

My heart pounded. He wouldn't have called Social Services—he would've beat me silly. I'd been with the DiMarios for three weeks, but it was enough to instill fear. He hadn't touched me yet, but the threat was ever-present.

"I didn't. I don't even like stupid old watches."

She rubbed her eyes. "What am I supposed to do here, Margo? It's grounds for removal."

It was better this way. Mrs. DiMario stroked my hair until I fell sleep, but I was better off without them. Stronger without them.

I straightened my shoulders. I went to the trunk and waited for her to pop it. As soon as she did, I rummaged through the black plastic bag. Everything was there and accounted for—except one thing.

"Where's the bracelet?"

She shook her head. "What?"

I ran back inside, down the hall to my old room. It was no larger than a closet with a twin bed on a low frame and a dresser against the wall. Everything was stripped, even the sheets. I jerked around, falling to my knees.

"What are you looking for?" she asked.

"The bracelet," I said. I was frantic. Blue and gold. Blue and gold.

It had to be here somewhere. I should've never taken the stupid thing off, but it frayed. I was scared it would snap if I wore it.

Someone at school might see it and yank, and then he'd be gone forever.

I was halfway under the bed when she grabbed me and hauled me out.

"Stop," she said.

My attention was glued to the floor.

"There wasn't a bracelet in here."

Tears filled my eyes. "I put it—"

"I'm sorry, Margo, but..." She glanced around, throwing up her hands. "I don't know. We have to get you to the respite house."

She dragged me out. I barely registered where we were going through the tears, but then I was in the car, hugging my belongings to my chest.

I couldn't put into words what that bracelet meant to me. It was the only thing tethering me to what felt like a life drifting farther and farther away.

My time with the DiMarios? Easily erased.

How did they manage to do it so efficiently? It's evil the way kids like me could be wiped off the map. Didn't like her attitude? *Boom*, gone.

Like I never even existed in the first place.

Present

It's impossible to do anything except count cracks in the ceiling. The music is full blast, and the sounds of a million people layer on top of it. I tried scrolling Instagram, checking emails, listening to my own music...

Nothing drowns out the noise.

I can't do this. I can't just hide upstairs, waiting for it to end. I can only imagine the students downstairs. Classmates. And I wouldn't put it past Ian to tell them I was up here, if only so word gets back to Caleb.

Caleb.

I stand and check my reflection. I had taken off my makeup sometime last night, so my complexion is clear. It is a little weird, not having the armor that mascara and eyeliner affords me.

The walls are closing in on me. My restlessness is growing, until I can't stay in here a moment longer.

The odds of Caleb being here are slim... right?

I pull on a hoodie from Ian's closet—*the least I deserve*—and cover my head. There's not much I can do about my face, except let my hair half conceal it. Once my boots are on, I slip my phone into the hoodie pocket and crack the door.

The music is even louder in the hallway.

Remembering Ian's warning, I close his door behind me and try to act inconspicuous. There's a line for the bathroom, and people lingering in the hall, but no one throws me a second glance.

Maybe I *am* incognito—I make it all the way downstairs and to the back door without notice. There's no sign of anyone I'm friendly with anyway. No Riley, no Jacq. Eli or Liam would surely call me out, same with Amelie or Savannah.

And yet, I slip through unscathed. I open the door and step out onto the porch, inhaling a deep breath. The cold air is invigorating. Better than the warmth inside.

"Margo." Caleb leans on the house. He's in the shadows, but I'd recognize him anywhere.

Of course he's here.

Not only that—of course he's *outside*. Right where I've come for an ounce of relief.

I wonder if that's how he feels when he looks at me, too, or if every tender moment has been a fabrication. Is loathing all that exists between us?

"I'm trying to convince myself not to carry you out of here." His words are dark.

I go to the railing. I don't care to look at him. His words to my foster parents, how he *blamed* me for their daughter's death, echoes in my ears. So, no, I won't look at him. I can barely stand to hear his voice.

"How's that going?" I put my forearms on the painted wood, leaning my weight on it. It smells like snow. Still a bit early in the year, but it could happen.

Anything could happen.

"I'm not carting you over my shoulder, right?" His footsteps alert me to his approach. "Not yet anyway."

I shiver. My heart shouldn't be beating out of my chest like this. He's just a boy. He's just *Caleb*. But maybe that's exactly why. No matter what he does to me, I'll still feel something for him.

He leans on the railing beside me, so close his arm presses to mine.

For a split second, I imagine hurting him. Punching him in the face or kneeing him in the groin. Anything to make him mirror the agony I feel on the inside. There's broken glass inside me, pushing its way out.

"Margo," he repeats. He faces me. His hand comes up, sliding around my neck and into my hair.

It's too gentle.

"You just—" I shove him away from me.

His face doesn't show any reaction, like he's numb to this. God, I hate him. I follow him, hitting his chest. I can't stop, and he's not doing anything to make me.

—fists against the door—

I blink. What was that?

In one smooth motion, Caleb grabs my wrists and maneuvers us so my back is against the railing.

I'm not a violent person, but he just makes me so *angry—*

"Come back," he says in my ear.

I flinch. "Let go."

"So you can hit me again? Unlikely."

"Weren't we happy?" I meet his gaze. I'm not talking about our childhood—I mean yesterday.

His fingers tighten on my wrists, which he keeps between us. He narrows his eyes.

"Happiness is an illusion, little lamb."

I almost wish we were drawing attention, just to have an excuse to break free of him. As it is, my body is ignoring all the warning signs.

It's been less than a day. I miss him and I hate him. The ache in me is bone-deep. This hurts worse than Ian kicking me and biting me, or Amelie's snide words, or Savannah using the cheerleaders to make my life hell.

This is so much worse.

"It doesn't matter," he adds.

I gape at him. "How? In what world does *happiness* not matter?"

"You belong to me just as I belong to you." He says it like it's a fact. Simple, easy, absolute.

It's not.

We're live in all the shades of gray between.

"First to give in loses," I whisper. "I guess this is my big punishment. I fall for you, you ruin my life."

None of this belonging shit. He's ruined everything.

I can't go home. I don't even *have* a home.

His finger strokes over my bracelet, drawing my attention back to it. He still wears his.

Another mind fuck? What does it *mean*? I know what it represented to a young Margo Wolfe. The innocent version of me, who loved without restriction. Who didn't understand that bad things could happen to good people.

"Stop," I whisper.

I yank at my wrists, but he holds tight. The little metal cage around the woven threads on the bracelet, meant to protect it, now seems more like a threat.

"You're getting it now," he replies. "You can run, but there's nowhere you can go I won't follow."

Maybe I should go back to the Bryans and get it over with. Let my social worker take me out of this godforsaken town once and for all. Time has been ticking while I've been falling for Caleb Asher. I've got three months left until I turn eighteen, and then I truly will be unmoored.

"Even then, I'd find you. I'll never let you go. You know that, don't you?" He meets my gaze. "And you'll never let go of me either."

The metal around my wrist is warm, digging in under his finger. And beneath the metal, the threads that wove us together when we were kids. Dressed up like a bride and groom, tying on the bracelets, a kiss to seal the deal.

Look how far we've fallen.

"Stop." I pull my arms down, trying to get away from him.

He releases me.

For a split second, I'm free, and then he's back in my space, holding me captive by more than my wrists. His hips press into mine, and he leans his elbows on the railing on either side of my head. I have my hands, but he has my body. He leans in, bending me backward over it.

"No," he says.

Simple. Effective. I'm pretty sure I hate the word—and him.

"You're so hell-bent on destroying my life. Why not just drive the knife in deeper?"

He grins. He's insane—I know it. He surely is aware.

"You ran to Ian Fletcher." His gaze drops to my chest. "You're wearing his sweatshirt. How am I supposed to react?"

"I hate you."

His smile widens. "Right back atcha, baby."

There's a gleam in Caleb's eyes that scares me. He's out of his mind, and I'm only just now seeing it. Witnessing his demons take control. I shove at his arm and slip past him.

Caleb catches up to me in the living room. He grasps my arm, spinning me around, and puts me up against the wall. It doesn't hurt, but it has my attention. His palm covers my throat.

The party falls silent. Even the music cuts out.

Caleb doesn't tear his eyes away from me—and I can't look away from him either.

"What are you doing?" My voice is breathless. I don't mean it to be. I want to come off strong, even though my body is thrumming with electricity.

One day isn't enough to turn off all the emotions I feel toward him. And while I hate him, I think...

Nope. Not going there.

I wrap my hands around his wrist. I can't tell if I'm holding his hand to my throat or trying to get him to remove it.

"Party's over. Leave," he demands. He isn't talking to me. He's talking to... everyone else. He's ending the party. Trying anyway.

No one moves.

"Now!" he roars. He so rarely has to raise his voice.

Several people flinch, and it breaks the spell. It's a mass exodus, everyone just... stops what they're doing and rushes away.

He really is royalty.

His thumb brushes along the underside of my jaw. Small movements that he might not even be aware of. His touch brings out goosebumps.

I close my eyes until everyone is gone, and we're entombed in silence. He's everywhere. In my past, my present. His scent in my nose. His voice in my ear. His hand at my throat, capturing every beat of my heart.

"You will break for me, little lamb," he whispers in my ear. "This is just the beginning."

I shudder. "Why?"

"You and I..."

I open my eyes. His gaze sears into me.

And his thumb still traces a pattern, back and forth on my jaw.

Games and more games. My head hurts. My lungs ache.

"You're mine, Margo. Forever. And you'll break for me —don't think that you won't."

This is just the beginning.

"I won't," I swear.

He leans down to kiss me. I press my lips together and turn my head to the side, exhaling through my nose when his lips land on my cheek. But he doesn't stop. His lips travel over my cheekbones, touching my eyelid, then my forehead.

And his hand tightens on my throat. White spots explode in front of my eyes.

A soft whimper escapes me.

"Kiss me."

I keep my head turned away.

"You bastard," I choke out. Fear winds through my chest. It'll make me do anything—including give in to Caleb. And that's just... *not an option.*

"What do I have to do to prove that you're mine?" he asks.

He tugs my pants down in one swift motion. He spreads my legs with his knee, and then he thrusts his finger into me.

I cry out, but the sound is strangled. *I'm* strangled. I push him, but he doesn't budge. It'd be easier to move a boulder.

"Wet." The word is an admonishment. "Kiss me, Margo, and I'll leave you alone. For the night anyway."

Tears run down my face. I hate that I want him to keep touching me. That my hips move forward the slightest bit when his nail scrapes my clit. His fingers plunge back into me, stroking a spot deep inside me.

He kisses my cheek, his tongue darting out and catching my misery.

"You fucking love this," he says. "Don't pretend otherwise. Don't pretend that you don't wish it was my dick inside you. Maybe next time, I won't send them away. They'll get a live show—"

I grab his face and pull him to me. Our lips are magnets.

Better make it a good one.

I taste my own tears as I part our lips, sliding my tongue along his. He takes over, slamming me back. My head thumps against the wall. His teeth tear at my lower lip.

He's still toying with my clit, alternating between rubbing and pinching.

That, the kiss, his hand at my throat...

An orgasm comes out of nowhere.

I groan into his mouth, and he takes it all. The orgasm, my noises, the kiss. My anger. My frustration.

His hand loosens on my throat, slipping down. His palm stops on my chest, over my heart.

"Well?" I manage.

His blue eyes haunt me. "It's a start."

He backs away, his gaze lingering on my face. It seems like he's *disappointed*. I'm so glad there's a wall at my back, because my legs would've given out otherwise.

He leaves. It isn't what I was expecting, although it is what he promised.

Hate him, Margo, I tell myself.

I pull up my pants slowly. My muscles ache. Hair in place, hoodie straightened. Piece by piece, I reassemble myself. Caleb's a hurricane force, but I'm supposed to withstand him and everything he brings.

I've got to be stronger.

I walk into the kitchen and almost jump out of my skin.

"That was quite the performance," Ian says, lifting his cup. He sways a bit. "I can see why he's into you. The noises—"

"You were *listening*? Did you see—?"

He snorts and waves. "God, no. Asher would've probably murdered me. Although I'm sure he realized I was there... I dropped a bottle." He points to a shattered beer bottle on the floor in front of the fridge.

"I didn't—"

"You were a little preoccupied." He winks. "And wearing my hoodie, too. See?"

I roll my eyes. "See what?"

He raises the cup to his lips, then smirks at me. "You're not the docile lamb everyone thinks you are. You're devious."

"Ugh." I shake my head. "You said whatever I felt was a manipulation. You were right."

"Was I?"

He's drunk. He wobbles, then saunters toward me. "Best run off to your room before I do something I shouldn't."

My stomach flips. He *would* do something. Kick me, kiss me. I don't want to know. I back into the counter, knocking over cups with my elbow. I feel my way to the door without turning my back to him. I glare while he laughs.

Once I'm out of the kitchen, I bolt.

He doesn't chase me, but I run like he is. I yank open the door to his bedroom with shaky fingers and grab my bag, pivoting and heading back into the pink bedroom. I shove the dresser in front of the door and exhale sharply.

He shouldn't be able to get in. No one should.

I survey my handiwork, then flop back on the bed.

I've had a night.

My emotions are all over the place.

Pushing everything down, I crawl farther up the bed and curl into a ball. Sleep will cure everything. *I hope.*

Chapter 7
Caleb

I let Margo have the night. I'm not an idiot—I know what today cost her.

But the important thing is that we're on the same page. Neither of us are going anywhere. She needs to know how it feels to be systematically crushed.

And then we'll see how well she puts herself back together.

"I was going to call you." Theo leans against his car, and he straightens as I walk up the driveway. "But I figured you might be busy."

I stifle a laugh. "You find Amelie?"

He follows me into Eli's house. "She wasn't home."

I grunt.

"You found Margo."

"Indeed, I did." I flick the lights on. I leave my shoes at the door and lead the way to the basement. "Why are you here?"

He shrugs. "Figured you might do something stupid."

"Like?"

"Kill Ian."

I chuckle. "I thought about it."

"Everyone's talking about how you kicked them out of Ian's house," he says, throwing himself down on my couch.

Margo and I sat there not too long ago. She was the last person down here besides me.

I shake my head. "We needed privacy."

"That usually includes a room, you know? A locked door."

"She's turning into a ghost," I say to my dresser. I yank out a clean t-shirt. "She needed reviving."

"Is that what you were doing?" He scowls.

"I don't think she even noticed it was a costume party." I get changed, then flop down next to Theo. I stare at the television, which is currently off. "Video games?"

He shrugs. "Sure."

I flick it on and hand him a controller. It isn't the most intelligent thing for us to be doing. In fact, it kind of feels like a mind-suck after a while. I enjoy the empty feeling it gives me, so I let our playing time stretch from a few minutes into almost an hour.

I finally drop it and check the time. It's past midnight.

"Do you ever sleep?" I ask Theo.

"Not really."

I grunt. "Well, I do."

He puts aside his controller and stands. "I can take a hint, Asher."

He slaps my shoulder on his way out, and then...

Silence.

I lock myself in the bathroom, scowling at my reflection. I turn on the shower and wait for the steam to fog up the mirror. It only takes a minute, then I shed my clothes.

I hate looking at myself. My reflection. All I see is the scared little boy who Margo turned me into. Old rage works up my throat. I pound my fist on the counter. There are hickeys on my chest from last night. The memory of her lips on my skin is almost enough to erase seven years of trauma... but not quite.

I used to smash mirrors. My hands are covered in faint white scars, barely visible, from my time as an angry child. My mother once walked in on me punching the shit out of a mirror in the bathroom. There was blood everywhere. She dragged me to the emergency room, where a doctor picked glass out of my knuckles for thirty minutes.

That was a hard lesson to learn.

Once I'm under the hot water, I relax. It's almost hard to breathe with the amount of steam in the shower, and it reminds me of the way Margo's pretty lips parted when I squeezed her throat. My dick gets hard at the thought of her.

I should've fucked her against the wall in Ian's living room, even if the prick was eavesdropping around the corner. *Especially* because he was eavesdropping. I stroke myself, remembering the way she reacted to me tonight.

Afraid.

Turned on.

Fiery.

The way her pussy clenched around my fingers when she came.

Fuck.

I pump faster, desperate to relieve my growing tension. It's the memory of her anger that does it. The way she fought. I groan and come, spilling on the tiles. Sparks zap through me.

This wasn't supposed to be this way. I wasn't supposed to let Margo get to me—*again*. But she has. I've let myself hate her for years, and it's easy. What isn't easy is admitting that every tear down her pretty face tightens my chest.

Why does her crying affect me so much?

I finish washing and get out, ignoring the mirror. Theo was a good distraction, but all I want to do is crawl into Margo's bed. I'm torn between making her pay and protecting her from the shitstorm that's brewing.

I could throw her out into the cold. It's already in motion.

Dad used to relate Newton's laws to human behavior. An object in motion will remain in motion unless acted upon by an outside force. His favorite was: Every force in nature has an equal and opposite force.

He meant to balance us out. Every decision carried weight. It was harder to make a change once a course of action had been decided on. He would know best of all. Selling his company, the shit he pulled with Margo's family...

My trajectory has been set toward Margo since we were children.

It's too late to stop.

But... she might just be my opposite—and equal—force. If she can find her spine.

I shake my head, water droplets flying. It's going to be a sleepless night. The rattle of restlessness will keep me awake for hours. It leaves me with two options: fight to keep my eyes closed or burn off energy so I eventually crash.

Option two usually works best.

I lace on running shoes and yank on a sweatshirt. Eli's parents are on the couch in the living room, the television screen flickering blueish light over their faces. They don't seem to notice me slip past them, out the front door.

As soon as I hit the sidewalk, I run.

There are a million ways to exhaust the body.

A million ways to burn energy.

Running isn't my favorite—I think my first choice is a tie between sex and skating—but it works just fine. Well, I think it does, until I find myself standing outside the Bryans' house.

All the windows are dark. I walk across the lawn and tip my head back, watching Margo's window. She's at Ian's house, hiding like a coward.

I scale the trellis with practiced movements. I never told her that Liam's family used to live in this house, and he used to sneak out often.

Her window is unlocked. I slide it open with one hand, then lift myself in. My entrance is nearly silent. I straighten and glance around the dark room. Her bed is made. Her uniform is crumpled toward the foot of the bed, a pair of running shoes just below it. She took her boots and high heels with her.

I lie down on the bed, fluffing the pillow under my head. It smells like her shampoo.

She isn't a girl who wears a lot of perfume. Her scent comes from her skin and her soaps, and I think I like that best. Amelie and Savannah—and any other girl who got close enough for me to notice them—coated themselves in expensive shit.

Not Margo.

She forgets that I knew her as a child, too. Memory isn't a one-way thing.

I catch her looking at me with regret. Maybe longing. And I know it's because she wishes she could untangle the mess she made. The knots bind us so tightly together, it's *killing* us.

Through the walls, one of her foster parents is snoring.

I shift around on the bed, leaving my mark. I have no doubt she'll notice it when she returns. She's tuned in to me. And make no mistake: she is going to return. The Bryans will find her and bring her back, even if it tortures them.

They're honorable like that.

Why couldn't Margo have been placed with someone else? A family less forgiving?

I'd call it fate that Margo was put with the Bryans, but unfortunately for them, fate operates by a different name: Lydia Asher.

My mother.

I pick myself up off Margo's bed. I still have a pair of her panties in my dresser. The pair I ripped off her. But I cast a glance around the room and I can't help but to think that this place doesn't feel like her home. She's inhabited the closet and the bed, a few drawers in the dresser. Beyond that... nothing. No pictures or posters on the wall. The same fucking bedspread that was probably there the day she arrived...

It's understandable why she doesn't call it her home.

And after what I did, it'll feel even less like it.

I've been spinning off-kilter for years. It's justifiable to want the same for her.

How does it feel, Margo?

I run my finger over the top of the dresser, and then I step into the hallway. There's more risk out here. Robert or Lenora could come out any minute, half-awake and stumbling to the kitchen for a glass of water.

It's almost pitch-black in here, except for the moonlight filtering through the window at the end of the hall. I lean close to one of the frames on the wall.

Robert, Lenora, Isabella. One happy family—on the surface. Of course, this photo was before Isabella got addicted to drugs and derailed her entire life. Theirs aren't the only ones destroyed by Amber Wolfe.

The list goes on and on...

I lift the photo off the wall and unclip the back. I intend to take the picture—there are so many on this wall, it'll take them weeks to notice it gone—but there's a folded piece of paper in the back of the frame.

Intriguing.

I take it and put it in my pocket. I leave the photo. No need to raise undue suspicion. Carefully, I place it back on the wall and cross back to Margo's room. I slip out of her window, closing it behind me, and climb back down to the ground.

Anticipation licks at my skin.

But no: first, the punishment.

I shouldn't have come to the Bryans' house in the first place.

Scrub out the weakness, son.

So I do. I'll run until I puke, and then I'll read the note burning a hole in my pocket. And maybe then, I'll be able to sleep.

Chapter 8
Margo

It's nice to wake up alone. No one staring at me, or glaring. No pressure to go to school—one, because it's Sunday, and two, because I'm definitely not going back with the video floating around.

I can't stay at Ian's house forever, but it sure is nice to stretch out and bask in the sunlight coming in through the window. I arch my back and do just that—stretch out. Until my hand hits something—some*one*.

I yelp, scooting to the edge of the bed and rolling over.

I expect Ian. Honestly, I do. Even with the dresser in front of the door, he seems like the type to figure out a way around it. But it takes me a few seconds of blinking like a madwoman for my brain to engage with what I'm seeing.

Because it's definitely not Ian Fletcher.

Amelie leans against the headboard. "God, you sleep like the dead."

"What are you doing?"

That's it. I shove the blankets back and stumble to my feet. A surefire show of confidence in front of the school's queen bee. I grab a sweatshirt and tug it on, my face heating.

I hate embarrassment. And her catching me *sleeping* seems like the worst offense possible.

"I came to see if you were okay." She picks at her nails. "After your little show last night."

Oh, jeez.

Wait. She's still in a sparkly dress, leaving bits of glitter all over the comforter. And while her makeup and hair seem perfectly done, it doesn't mean...

"Did you sleep here?"

Besides being in last night's dress, she's picture-perfect. It's barely eight o'clock in the morning. I run my hand through my hair. My fingers get caught on invisible knots, and she watches me work to free the strands.

"You've got a bit of drool." She touches a painted nail to the corner of her lip.

I swipe at it. I'm going to burst into flames at any second, I just know it.

And I guess I did sleep like the dead.

"Ian and I aren't really a thing," she adds. "So don't get your panties in a twist over it. I wasn't... Didn't feel like going home. His bed is a nice place to land."

That's a mental picture I don't need.

"Anyway, you should've put something heavier in front of the door."

Her gaze goes to the dresser, which has been forcibly moved to the center of the room. How the hell did I miss that sound?

"The fact that the Fletchers put all their furniture on sliders to protect their precious floors doesn't help."

Ah.

Well, I did have an easy time shoving it in front of the door. I shouldn't be shocked that someone else had an easy time removing it.

It's a little nerve-racking to have Amelie in my space. I know it isn't *mine*, but... Still.

"Are you going to tell the Bryans I'm here?"

"No, I'm pretty sure Caleb will take care of that."

She stands, picking up her purse from next to the bed.

"Then why are you here?"

It's like she's been waiting for me to ask, because her shoulders drop.

She exhales. "Caleb wronged both of us."

I squint.

"And you're just going to let him control you like that?"

"No." I cross my arms.

"Exactly." She taps her fingernail on the dresser. "A united front, you know?"

"I thought you hated me." *And this could be a colossal trap.* "Besides, I don't trust you."

Be a wolf, Margo.

"You don't have to trust me," she says. "What matters is that Caleb doesn't win."

I slowly nod. Even if I don't like her, or trust her, she's right. He's been playing both of us to certain degrees. Why he chose to use her against me—and vice versa—I'll never know. But right here, right now?

We could change the game.

"What are you proposing?"

Amelie goes to the window. "Your family is here."

I flinch. "Foster family."

"Right," she whispers. "Whatever."

Not whatever. There's a massive difference.

I join her at the window, and we watch the familiar car pull into Ian's driveway. Ms. McCaw's car isn't ahead or behind them. Most fosters wouldn't come do the dirty work

—they'd let the case worker clean up the mess. Even if the Bryans wanted to watch the show...

They get out of the car.

It's just them.

"I doubt they're going to rehome you." She pats my shoulder.

"You'd be surprised."

"You need to trust people more," she says. "Seriously."

Yeah, right. The more I trust, the more it bites me in the ass.

The sound of a doorbell echoes through the downstairs, traveling through the walls. I flinch again, stepping away from the window.

This is it.

Ian's cheerful voice floats up toward us, but I can't make out what he's saying.

Amelie grabs my arm. "They're going to make you go back to school."

"Yeah."

"You'll have to see Caleb every day. You're in what, three classes together?"

I shrug. That's exactly right, but I don't want to tell her that. Or admit that I've counted. "Something like that."

"Meet me in the courtyard before lunch."

I shake her loose. "Isn't that place kind of obvious?"

She flips her hair back. "Isn't the library a little obvious of *you*? He knows you hide away there."

Fair.

I follow her into the hallway. She goes toward Ian's room, and I eye the stairs. Lenora's and Robert's voices are clearer now, but I can't pick up the anger. Not yet. I force myself to go closer, perching on a step halfway down. The staircase is broken into two sections, with a landing in between, and I'm hidden in my position.

"She was scared." Ian's voice floats up.

My hackles rise. Of course his parents wouldn't be the ones to answer the door—they're not even here.

"We appreciate the explanation," Robert says, "but we'd like to see her."

Someone sighs.

"Margo!" Ian's voice is shockingly loud. His head pops around the corner. He's not surprised at my closeness, and he smirks. "Listening in?"

"Shut up," I mumble.

I don't have a choice, now. They know I'm here—Ian admitted as much. Wonder how they found out?

I hoist myself up and pass him. The descent is the worst, with their gaze right on me, but I can't even look at them. I propel myself forward through sheer force of will and stop in front of my foster parents.

After a moment of silence, I glance up. They seem the worse for wear. But what plagues *me* is the guilt and shame.

"I'm sorry my mom killed your daughter." My voice is barely audible, even to my own ears.

They stare at me for a second before Lenora moves. She drags me into a hug, crushing me to her chest, and bursts into tears.

My arms hang at my sides.

She holds me like I might evaporate.

"We were so worried," she says in my ear. "Thank God you're okay. And you're here. And—"

"Let her breathe, Len," Robert interrupts.

She steps back but keeps her hands on my shoulders. She grips me with surety, not letting me retreat.

I didn't get a chance to hug her back. My expression

must be stupefied, because I was expecting them to tell me that I was leaving. Bags already packed.

Anger.

Hatred.

"Margo," Robert says. "Your mother's actions don't define you. And they certainly don't define us. We feel horrible that you overheard Caleb."

I feel horrible, too. Like my gut has gone through a blender.

"It doesn't change anything," Lenora says. Her hands push and pull my shoulders, so light I don't think she realizes she's doing it.

—head snapping back—

I cringe.

She releases me, eyes wide. "Honey—"

Nope. I shake my head hard. It doesn't change anything about *what*, though? As far as I'm concerned, Caleb's story changes everything.

"What does that mean for me?"

"We're taking you home," Robert says firmly. "No ifs, ands, or buts about it."

My eyes burn.

"I'm glad you worked things out," Ian says behind me. He sets my backpack down at my feet. "Can't say I'm sorry to see you go, though."

I take it, eyeing him. Did he call them? No one else would want me out of Ian's house more than he does... except Caleb. Did *Caleb* call them?

I frown, first at him, and then at my foster parents. "What did Ms. McCaw say?"

Robert winces, bracing the door open with his back. Lenora slips out first, and I follow.

"Well, we didn't tell her."

My jaw drops.

"We hoped we could find you before it became necessary," Lenora explains. "It's a bit unorthodox. And it could've backfired on all of us."

"But the consequences would've been worse," Robert adds. "You're already labeled as a runaway risk. I'm sorry, but it's true. If she knew we lost you..."

I cringe. I *am* a risk—because of Caleb. It's time I accepted that he's been the source of my life's upheaval for years. And, like Amelie suggested, I should do something about it.

But not right now.

Now, I buckle myself into the backseat and lean forward, still in disbelief that they didn't follow procedure and report me.

"You didn't tell her," I repeat. "She doesn't know."

Relief. Confusion. It's all white noise buzzing in my ears.

They saved me after everything.

"We didn't," Robert confirms.

"What now?" I shoot one last glance back toward Ian's house.

He wasn't that bad—better than I expected with nowhere left to go. Would I do it again? No. Was his behavior toxic, even if he wasn't actively hurting me? Yeah, a bit. And then there's Amelie...

"We're going home, and we're going to figure this out," Robert says. "But you're not going anywhere unless you want to. Do you?"

I blink. "Do I what?"

"Want to go to a different family?" He readjusts his grip on the steering wheel.

"No." I bite my lip. It's time to stop hiding behind fear and speak what I want into existence. "I want to stay."

Lenora sniffles. "Good."

We ride the rest of the way in silence. I'm exhausted from the past two days. There are too many emotions swirling around my head. The sudden switch from liking Caleb to *hate*—it's left me cold. And confused.

I shudder.

Back at the Bryans' house, I shoulder my bag and make my way to my room. It's kind of strange, returning here. Everything is exactly the same as the way I left it.

I lie down, and Caleb's scent surrounds me. Another tear slides down my cheek. I could sleep away the whole day. But after a few minutes of breathing deeply, I push myself up. I have to go to school with him tomorrow.

Where he'll undoubtedly try to act like nothing has changed between us.

I switch into fresh clothes and scrape my hair up into a bun. There's somewhere I need to go. There's something I need to remember.

It's clawing at the wall in my mind, desperately insistent to be acknowledged.

I find Robert in his office.

He looks up when I knock on the open door, a grin spreading. "Margo. I thought you might decide to rest today."

I frown. "I was actually hoping... I need to go out."

His eyebrow jumps, then settles. "Where?"

"Caleb's house."

He sighs. "Why?"

"There's..." I spin the bracelet on my wrist. "There's just something that's been bugging me about my old home. And I was hoping to take one more peek..."

He stands. "Okay."

He slips past me, down the hall.

"What are you doing?" I call.

"Driving you," he answers.

My mouth drops open, and I chase after him. "You don't have to. I can walk—"

"It's no trouble." He holds up the keys, winking at me. "We can stop and get a pastry on the way back."

I nod slowly. The car ride is quick, and then we're there. In the same driveway, staring up at Caleb's empty house.

"No one lives here," I tell him.

"I know." He glances at me. "We recognized your last name when Angela was searching for a home for you. Most of the foster families in the town were aware of what had happened between the Wolfes and the Ashers."

"I don't really remember it."

His smile is sad. "Trauma affects children differently. Some lash out. Some get quiet. We took a class on dealing with loss—"

"I didn't lose anyone." I cross my arms over my chest. "They're both still out there."

He twists toward me. "If you want to see your dad, Margo, we can arrange that—"

"I don't."

Mom left. Dad was taken away.

They're still alive. And if I hadn't done whatever it is Caleb thinks I did—

I open the car door. The answers I want are in that house.

"I'll be back," I tell him.

Down the side driveway, around the main garage, and suddenly the Ashers' guest house is in front of me. I should stop thinking of it as home, even though it's the only one I really knew. That apartment in the city before we came here is just flashes. We were *here* for most of my childhood —until I was taken away.

The door is locked, but we used to keep a spare key in the plant box under the window around the corner. I'm sure Caleb was the one to lock it. He's the only one who would want to keep me out.

I find the key and brush off the crusted dirt. It's dull, with rust spots, but it still works. The door opens under my hand. Absently, I pocket the key.

It's like walking into the past—but not the past that I want to remember. Not the disrupted, angry place that I've forgotten. No, it's like...

Sunshine.

Past

"Margo!"

I jerked upright. The sun had felt so good beating down on my face that I closed my eyes. It was just for a minute.

Mom stands in front of me. "What are you doing on the floor?"

I shrugged.

Sundays were a big day for her, which meant her white chef's coat was pristine. She meal-prepped lunches for the Ashers to take to work for the next week, and then she came home and do the same for us. After, she'd return to their kitchen and make a big Sunday roast for them.

Now she smoothed the coat down. Nervous habit or calming gesture, I hadn't quite figured it out. But it usually carried some amount of tension in her.

I stand carefully.

"Lydia wanted to know if you would like to go to the park with them."

I perked up. I wasn't allowed to call Mrs. Asher by her first name, but Mom was. I guessed it was an adult thing. Caleb called my mom Amber.

So maybe it was a *me* thing. They never bothered to explain that.

"When?"

"Now." She laughed. She came over and held out her hands, lifting me to my feet. "If you want. I made sandwiches for a picnic."

"Are you going?"

She shook her head. "No, I have some things to do around the house."

I bit my lip.

"Your dad will be home later," she said. "He just got caught up at the office."

On a Sunday.

"Okay," I said.

She brushed her hand over my clothes, straightening my shirt and smoothing my hair. I sometimes liked the way she made sure everything was in place, but other times it scratched at my skin. Like now, when she was only doing it because I'd be going with Mrs. Asher and Caleb.

"Perfect," she finally said, releasing me.

I smiled.

Caleb and his mom were in the kitchen when we walked in. He sat at the breakfast bar, dutifully finishing breakfast. It looked like he got scrambled eggs, roasted potatoes, sausage. The smell of it fills my nose.

I ate hours ago, pouring myself a bowl of cereal after I

woke and discovered the house empty. Now, my stomach growled.

Mom tapped the back of my head like it was *my* fault my stomach was being loud.

"Good morning, Margo," Mrs. Asher greeted me.

I smiled at her. "Hi."

Caleb twisted around. "I lost a tooth."

I climbed up on the stool next to him. He gave me a wide smile, showing a gap in his teeth. While he was proud, my stomach turned. I didn't hide my grimace. I hated plucking out loose teeth. The last one that wiggled, Caleb reached in my mouth and snatched it out before I could stop him.

He wouldn't give it back for the tooth fairy either.

My mom kissed me on the head. "Have fun. I'll see you later."

We watched her go back the way she came.

"All right." Mrs. Asher clapped. "Ready?"

Caleb pushed away his place, and we followed her into the garage.

She buckled us into our seats in the car. We were old enough to do it ourselves—that's what Caleb told her anyway, but she just smiled.

"You're growing up before my eyes." She kissed him on the forehead.

Something in my chest tightened and loosened at the same time.

Mom liked me. But she didn't like me *that* much.

And Dad...

"Are you okay, Margo?" Mrs. Asher asked.

Mom would kill me if I told the Ashers anything, so I nodded.

We got to the park, and Caleb's mom laid out a blanket. It was warm and sunny, and Caleb took off toward some of his friends. I sprawled out next to Lydia and closed my eyes again. The sun heated my body.

In the distance, Caleb and his friends were laughing.

Laughing.

Screaming.

Blank.

No, I need to remember.

Caleb and his friends were playing.

I sat up, confused. Alone.

Blank.

I screamed.

Present

I open my eyes, looking around slowly. I'm in my old bedroom, curled into a ball on the floor. How I got here is a mystery. One minute I was walking into the house, the next... a memory.

But it isn't as sharp as I need it to be.

It isn't as clear.

I stand and go to the dresser, acting on a suspicion. It's a shock more than anything to see a trail of disturbed dust.

Caleb and I were in here before, and then he shows up with the bracelet at the ball?

I had lost it. It was one of the times I was moved without warning... All that time, I thought a foster sibling had taken it, or the parents tossed it.

He stole it.

He brought it back here, set it on my dresser in a house that hasn't been touched in seven years.

Who's pretending now?

Chapter 9
Margo

I expected, on my return to school Monday morning, to be bombarded with ugly stares and horrible comments whispered under their breath. Teenage bullying at its finest.

Nothing happens.

No one does a fucking thing.

"Is it me, or are we blending in more than usual?" Riley asks me.

"Um..." I shrug helplessly. I spot Ian down the hall, talking to Amelie and another cheerleader, but I'm not about to open that can of worms by asking either of them. I'd have to assume the video is gone, a fact that Riley confirms by trying to search for it. But not only that, all residual conversation *about* it, which would normally keep such a thing floating in gossip circles for at least a few days, are nonexistent.

"Let's hope it keeps up," Riley says. "See you at lunch."

Homeroom is quick, and then I hurry to first period. Not that I'm *in* a hurry to get there, I just don't want to be caught lingering in the halls, alone, for the other shoe to drop.

I slip through the clusters of students like a ghost, and it leaves my skin prickling with anticipation.

In the first period class, history, my gaze lands on Caleb. He leans against my usual desk, and he's already spotted me. His expression is heated, and a smirk curls at his lips.

He's proud of himself. It leaves me rattled. With conviction, I know he did this. I'd bet money that he made the video disappear. Still, how he erased it from everyone's eyeballs is a whole other issue.

How did he persuade an entire student body to forget?

"Good morning, little lamb."

My spine is ramrod straight.

Without acknowledging him, I take a different seat. Ian's, in fact.

Savannah glances at me and opens her mouth, then seems to change her mind. A second later, someone leans over me.

"I don't much like being ignored," Caleb says.

"I don't much like being made a fool."

"They took you back." He puts his elbows on the desk.

Our faces are inches apart—but I'm not going to back down from this challenge. My gaze goes from his eyes to his lips and back again.

I've called him many things in my head.

Demon.

Monster.

Bully.

The most accurate? *Devil.*

Every word out of his mouth is a damn lie. I have to hold on to that and remind myself when he once again flips a switch and tries to soothe away the hurt.

"I'm not doing this with you," I say carefully.

He smirks. "I think you will."

"We're over, Caleb." I flash him my bare wrist.

Yesterday, before I left my childhood home, I removed it and set it back on the dresser, right where he had originally returned it to after stealing it.

I kept the key. It seemed more valuable than not, and it sits at the bottom of my bag. Better safe than sorry. And who would think twice about a rusted old key?

He grabs my wrist, his lips pressing into a thin line. He's still wearing his. It doesn't appear feminine on him, though. Quite the opposite.

Who knew?

I let him push my sleeve up. Maybe he thinks it's a trick.

Nothing but skin, baby.

He growls under his breath. It could be an accidental slip because I got to him. Surprised him for once. Or it could be part of the game. Another lie.

This just in: we're playing *my* game now.

I smile. "As you can see, we're done here."

He straightens, fingers slipping off my skin. "We'll see."

He returns to his seat, and I exhale. One encounter down... just a million more to go. But I can't help the smile that creeps across my face.

Margo: 1

Caleb: 0

The bell rings, and I stand. Savannah shuffles along behind me, muttering. Her attitude—feigned interest and then an abrupt change—piques my interest. I slow down in the hallway, waiting for her to pass me. Her class is a few down from my next one.

She hesitates next to me. "You're going to try and take down the royalty?"

I raise an eyebrow.

"What's that look for?"

"Royalty, as in all of them? Why on earth would I do that?" A fight with Caleb is going to be hard enough as it is. I don't need his three friends involved.

She makes a face. "Amelie mentioned something."

"They don't all need bringing down." I don't know what Amelie said. Again, my mind goes to the worst possible place: *Trap*.

This school is filled with vipers. It's like I'm asking to be bitten by just existing here.

"Gotta go." I duck into my classroom, leaving her standing outside.

It's quiet. Thankfully. I make it through the rest of my morning classes in peace, only once passing Riley in the hall and giving her a nervous smile. Fifth period, right before lunch, I take a seat as Ms. Devereux starts her lecture on a story we read over the weekend.

My gaze moves from her to her desk in the corner. She's got a picture of her son on it. He's young—probably only seven or eight—and is dwarfed in hockey gear. I spotted it the other day, back when I appreciated that Caleb plays hockey, and she's mentioned him in passing. That she has to get home to her family, or when she'd miss a day because of a hockey tournament or doctor's appointment.

Whatever the reason, it's clear she loves him.

I learned from Riley that my teacher's husband is moving up in the political arena. He's currently holding down the position of lieutenant governor for the state of New York. It's a little intimidating, knowing Ms. Devereux's husband is in politics.

Now, I just hope Greyson doesn't end up anything like Caleb Asher.

I jerk my attention away from her desk. I shouldn't be thinking about her family. It feels a bit like a boundary I'm crossing, even in my head. It just seems nice, is all, to know she cares *so* much for her son.

Eventually, the bell rings.

And I need to meet Amelie.

For a moment, I consider tracking down Riley and asking her to come with me. But I don't want to risk upsetting the delicate truce Amelie and I seem to have struck.

And just because I'm doing something scary doesn't mean I can't do it alone.

Swallowing my nerves, I head toward the courtyard. Some students eat lunch out here in nicer weather, but the chill of November has driven everyone inside.

Amelie sits on one of the benches, her pleated skirt fanned out around her. Her toned, tan legs extend out from under it. Her ankles are crossed, her posture straight. Everything about her is picture-perfect. Curled, long blonde hair, subtle makeup, the way her shirt fits to her torso.

I swallow down my creeping jealousy. That's not what this is about, right?

It's about getting back at Caleb.

"About time." She checks her phone, then raises an eyebrow at me.

"I was debating whether or not to come."

"You made the right decision," she says. "I heard you snubbed Caleb this morning. Everyone is whispering about it."

Unlike the video?

She flips her hair back. "Caleb's been meddling in your life forever."

"I know." I sit beside her. "That isn't news."

She scowls. "What do you remember?"

"Of what?"

"When you up and left. We were ten. What do you remember?"

I shake my head. "First of all, I did not up and leave. I was taken away."

—head snapping back—

I press my fingers to my temples. "I don't want to discuss this."

"The boys in this school," she mutters. "They're out to get us."

"What are you talking about?" Is she referring to someone else along with Caleb?

"Caleb played us all, don't you get it? He *seduced* us—"

I drop my hands and glare at her. This isn't going how I thought it would. No, actually, it *is* going how I thought it would. I'd just hoped for something different.

"He didn't seduce me."

Okay, well, he laid out a sticky web, and like an idiot, I fell right into it.

"And anyway, it didn't work, because he and I are done. And you know what? I think this conversation is done, too."

She's prying and invading, and why didn't I see this side of her before?

I move toward the door.

"He charmed the pants off of me and Savannah," she says quietly.

I stop in my tracks.

"You knew that, right? Him sleeping with her, then dating me? Well, if you can even call it *dating*—"

I spin around. "I don't want to hear about how you fucked Caleb! God, Amelie. Really?"

She has tears in her eyes, but I'm so over it.

"Why do you think he did it?" She waves her hand. "He

knew I was in a vulnerable position, but he just couldn't resist one day holding it over your head. Because he knew you'd come back. And you're letting him steamroll you, Margo. Don't be an idiot like me."

"What vulnerable position?"

She stares at me, blinking away the tears. Somehow, they don't fall, they just... I don't know, get reabsorbed back into her eyes? It's magic that doesn't mess up her makeup.

"My family is in some thorough negotiations, is all."

Negotiations? Could she be any more vague?

"I'm going to lunch," I tell her.

Obviously, we all grew up differently. I bounced around homes. She bounced around countries. She was studying abroad in *Paris* when I got back to Rose Hill. Her family has a second house in the south of France.

What negotiations could her family be going through that affect her so drastically?

The answer doesn't reveal itself, and I shake my head on my way to the door.

"Ask yourself this, Margo," she calls. "How did Caleb find you in the woods?"

I know how he found me. Unknown sent me the proof —a picture of Ian dragging me across the field.

This is the only time I help you. They said that.

Unknown messaged Caleb. I think I knew that, in the back of my head. They sent me the photo, but then they sent it to him, too.

"Savannah told him where to find you," Amelie says.

Wait.

What?

"She texted me about you two, but I told her I didn't give a shit. So she messaged..." Her voice distorts.

Or maybe that's the ringing in my ears.

I nod, holding my expression blank, until she leaves. She doesn't head into the building—she goes toward the parking lot. All I can focus on is my heartbeat thundering.

Savannah is Unknown?

My chest tightens, and my breathing turns ragged.

This is probably a panic attack. I recognize that, but it doesn't help me when I'm hyperventilating. I press my palm to my chest, my gaze locked on the ground.

"Margo?"

Gravel bites into my knees.

"Up you go." Robert lifts me to my feet and guides me to a bench. "Follow my breathing."

He exaggerates his inhales and exhales, repeating them patiently until I copy him. Until my heart rate finally comes under control and the bands around my chest loosen.

"What happened?"

"I... I just got overwhelmed." I bury my face in my hands. "I'm so sorry."

"Come with me," he says. "I just have to meet with a student and then I'll take you home. Okay? This weekend was a lot."

Tears escape my closed eyes. I drop my hands and fumble for a tissue in my bag.

"Oh, honey, don't cry." He rubs my back in circles.

"I shouldn't have run away." It made everything worse.

All of my fight is gone. I used it on Caleb and Amelie, and I don't want to take it out on Robert. I follow a half step behind him all the way to his classroom and sit at a desk in the back while he chats with another student. A sophomore, I think. She throws nervous glances in my direction.

I doodle profiles of boys with black holes for eyes.

"Ready?" Robert asks.

I jerk, crumpling the page. I'm not a fool—I just can't stop drawing Caleb. And if Robert sees, he'd know, too. I toss it in the trash on the way out. There's still the portrait to complete. More of Caleb to see, to delve into. Would I fail if I gave him the devil's red eyes and horns peeking out of his hair?

In the car, Robert glances over at me. "I hope you don't take this the wrong way, Margo, but lately you seem lost. Don't get me wrong—it's perfectly okay to feel lost at seventeen. It's Len's job, and my job, to help you navigate to where you want to go. But this might be more than that because of your history. Am I onto something here?"

I bite my lip.

Am I lost?

"It can take time and soul searching," he adds. "And reconnecting with your past, like visiting your childhood home. If you want to talk to anyone—"

"A therapist?"

I've talked to too many state-mandated psychologists for my liking. There was nothing wrong with them, except their soul-sucking nature and endless questions.

"Or your dad," he says quietly.

I freeze.

"He's only twenty-five minutes away. And we'd be happy to take you if you—"

"I'm not ready for that." I look out the window and decide to admit one thing. One ugly feeling. "I tried to visit him when I was twelve. Ms. McCaw said I was on the approved list. But we got there, and he had revoked it. The guard passed along that he said it was no place for..." My throat closes, and it takes a few swallows to get the rest of the words out. I lamely finish, "A child. And technically, I'm still one."

"You've grown up a lot since you last tried." He sighs. "I can reach out to Angela, see if we can arrange something—"

"Please. Not today."

He pulls up to the curb in front of his house. "Len will be home early today, okay? You won't be alone for long."

"I think I'm just going to catch up on homework and be antisocial for a while."

"Perfectly acceptable."

Chapter 10
Caleb

Amelie smirks at me from her table at lunch. She came in late, her gaze finding me and lingering. Riley is at our table, down at the end with Eli and Liam. Liam is doing the work of entertaining both of them, while Theo sits across from me in silence.

They all know I'm in no mood to be nice.

My bad mood isn't infectious, but it sure does stink. That's what Theo told me approximately ten minutes ago while I waited for Margo to return to sanity. And by sanity, I mean to stop this fucking avoidance bullshit.

Riley is here, which leaves me clueless to Margo's whereabouts. Riley's phone chimes, and my head automatically turns.

She glances from Eli to me, then frowns.

"What is it?" I snap.

She flinches.

I snatch her phone away.

Margo: Robert took me home.

I growl under my breath and slide her phone back.

"Dude," Eli says. "Not cool."

"What's not fucking cool is this cat-and-mouse game Margo's playing." I stand, my attention tripping over Amelie again. Her lips are curled in a shit-eating grin—which means she's probably up to something.

I head toward her.

She stands and meets me halfway, running her finger down my chest.

I grab her wrist, squeezing hard enough to send a message. *Don't fucking touch me.*

"You like using girls?" There's a slight shake to her voice. "I told her where the text came from."

The text... the only text of consequence would be the one Savannah sent me about Ian and her. And even then, it came far too late for me to protect her.

I should've told Margo that, but I decided to keep it to myself. I keep a lot of things close to the vest—sue me.

Whatever Sav wanted to imply by telling me Margo and Ian were absconding to the woods, her message wasn't received. Ian and Margo aren't having some affair—I never would've assumed that. And he *hurt* her. I'm inclined to break his jaw just thinking about it, but hockey is on the line.

Still, I drop Amelie's arm like burning coal. "Are you trying to make your life miserable?"

Savannah isn't at the cheerleaders' table. While her supposed best friend throws her under the bus, she's nowhere to be found.

Interesting.

"I had to," Amelie argues. "She's finally standing up to you—"

"You know nothing," I growl.

Margo standing up to me—my blood runs hot. Hotter anyway. I couldn't have possibly predicted that I would *like* her fire. But damn it, I do. She ignores me? It's only going to make me hold on to her harder. She fights me? I'll fight back dirtier.

I brush past Amelie, more than done with this conversation.

"Where are you going?" she calls after me.

She and I both know the text about Margo and Ian didn't originate with Savannah. Whatever games they're playing, I can do better.

And so can Margo.

I'm halfway down the hall when Coach Marzden steps out. He takes one look at me and scowls.

"Asher. Come with me."

I gnash my teeth. Worst fucking timing. But I follow him to his office, especially if it means I'll get back on the ice sooner.

He's allowed me—no, required me—to attend practices. I'm the captain. I have an example to set. But games, I'm not allowed anywhere near the rink. Not until my suspension is up.

"Sit." Coach takes hockey seriously. His whole career rides on it. If one of us screws up, we're out. It's how it's always been. He sits across from me, leaning his elbows on the desk. It's covered in papers, but he doesn't seem to care. The whole office is organized chaos.

"You're slipping," he tells me.

I stare at him, unsure of how to answer. On one hand, I've already slipped pretty far. On the other, I've made sure to stay out of trouble since my fight with Ian.

"Margo Wolfe," he says.

I stiffen. "What about her?"

"Is she going to fuck with your head? You've never gotten into a fight with your teammate before, and I know how tensions can soar around a pretty girl. Teenagers are brutal, but you're not *just* a teenager. You're the captain."

School royalty.

That weight sits heavy on my shoulders at all times. I can't exist without being reminded of the eyes on me. Not just fellow students. Teachers. Parents. *Everyone.*

"You're not telling me anything new." I lean back. Fuck Coach and thinking this sport gives him free rein over my life. Over what I do with Margo. "Wolfe isn't a problem."

He raises an eyebrow. "Oh? So, you weren't about to skip class. Maybe go see the girl who was just checked out of school by her foster father?"

He knows too much. But still—whose business is it if I want to leave?

"No one fucking cares, Coach."

He lunges across the desk and grabs my shirt collar, jerking me up. "Don't play that game with me."

I glance down at his fingers curled in the fabric at my throat.

We clash sometimes. He's one of the original hockey royalty—the original asshole who ruled Emery-Rose when he was a student. The team has long acknowledged that he has a temper to match his infamy.

This, however, is *nothing.*

"Fine," I grit out. "Wolfe and I are in a relationship. But she's not a problem."

"I need smooth sailing from you," Coach says. "From now until graduation. Impress the scouts, and it's your choice of schools, right?"

He releases me, and I slowly retake my seat. He does the same. I adjust my shirt while he watches.

"Where are you applying?"

I lift one shoulder. "Mom wants me to go for Harvard."

He snorts. "And?"

"And it's an option." I'm not set on it. *Boston*. It seems so far away.

"Deadlines are approaching," he says. "You toured schools over the summer, got an idea of some you'd go to if college hockey doesn't work out."

"Have you been talking to my mother?" My anger is waking up again. How dare she call my coach? "Is that what prompted this whole fucking thing?"

He rolls his eyes.

"Coach."

"Cool it, Caleb. I can see the smoke coming out of your ears."

"Because she—"

"Loves you?"

No.

Because she's worse than Uncle when it comes to twisting the world into her own masterpiece. No one else's opinions matter.

"What'd she say?"

"She wants you to apply for Harvard," he says. "Early decision."

I cough.

"Fuck, no." That would lock me into it if I got in—and there's a high chance someone would donate in the Asher name, and suddenly I'd be hiking my ass up to Cambridge, Massachusetts.

"Make a list," he orders, standing. "I want to see where you're thinking of going, and I'll do my best to get some recruits to your games. Once you're back on the roster, of course."

I stand, too. I know a dismissal when I hear one.

I don't wait for him to roll out the red carpet and usher

me out. He closes the door behind me, and I duck into the locker room down the hall. There's a door in the back, much like the girls'. I unhook the alarm and shove the door open.

So fucking done.

Of course my mother wants to micromanage where I go to school. It's not just hockey that's a concern. In fact, they'd be thrilled if I *didn't* play hockey. They think I should focus on business classes. Double major in two fancy degrees, then go on to get my master's in business.

All of it to prepare me to take over the family business, but even that wouldn't happen until years of working under my uncle.

It's stupid.

I can't speak out against it, though. Not to anyone except my coach and friends... and maybe, eventually, Margo.

I get in my car and speed back to my house. Not Eli's, because his parents would absolutely question me being home too early. *Mine.* I go through the house, ignoring the drab, dust-coated interior, and unlock the glass door that leads to the patio. There's a path down to the guest house, which was built a moderate distance away from the main house.

Goosebumps rise on my skin the closer I get. I unlock the door to Margo's old home and turn on a light. We rarely came in here as kids. I think her mom preferred the luxury of the main house—or the solitude after we were gone. Either way, most of my memories of Margo are either at school, in the backyard, or in my house.

Before Margo returned, I hadn't been in here in years.

Now, I examine it with a new light.

Her parents' room is a wreck. I crack that door, taking in

the broken furniture, the scattered clothes and glass, bits of wood. The air is stale and a little sour.

This place doesn't affect me like it does Margo. But then again, I don't have visceral memories. My imagery comes from stories Keith Wolfe spun on the stand while he begged for a not guilty verdict. The trial ended abruptly, after two weeks, with a plea agreement between parties.

It's not what he deserved—but the prison time made the deal worth it. Especially when my uncle told me he could've gotten off completely free.

Margo's father's lies encompassed all of us. Me, my parents, Margo, her mother.

She doesn't know—but she might begin to unravel it. She's digging. Trying to remember.

I go into Margo's old room. It feels like it's been frozen in time. Unlike her parents' room, which a tornado went through and then was abandoned, a ten-year-old Margo could've raced in behind me and I wouldn't question it.

I close the door and touch the scratches in the painted wood. Long gouges, about waist-high on me. A thousand of them.

What would make a ten-year-old *that* desperate to get out?

Old blood has dried to a dark brown. Broken nails... a cut? I don't ever remember her being injured like that, so when did this happen?

On the dresser is what I came for: the bracelet Margo refuses to wear. I palm it, holding it tightly for a moment before sliding it into my pocket. Half of me wants to march back to her room and superglue the latch—then she really would be stuck with it.

It's not a bad idea.

I did what I wanted to do: I broke her. Getting caught

wasn't part of the plan, and neither was her memory issue. I expected her to know exactly what her parents did. I expected meekness, and instead was met with fire.

It's thrown a dazzling wrench into my plan.

We belong together.

I lost her once. I'll be damned if I'll lose her again.

Chapter 11
Margo

Caleb's hand coasts up my arm.

Goosebumps break out, but I keep my eyes closed. I knew he would figure out how to get into my bedroom, even with the window locked. And now here he is.

His thumb caresses the hollow point at the base of my throat. I swallow as his fingers wind around it. He squeezes softly, and my eyes fly open.

"Shh." His lips touch my ear, anticipating my balking. "Don't say a goddamn word."

My heart picks up speed. *Thump, thump, thump.* It's so loud, it practically fills the room. I stare at him. There's just enough light to see his face, but not his eyes. I can't see the set of his jaw. All I have to go on is his dark tone.

"Here's what's going to happen," he continues. "You're not going to move. You're not going to make a sound."

His thumb brushes over my lips.

"If you make any noise, they're going to know."

I glance at my bedroom door. It's wide open, a dim light spilling in from a night-light in the hall.

Fuck.

Any little sound is amplified at night. Which explains why he was whispering. Why he stopped me from speaking.

He releases my throat and drags the blankets down my body. He stands with the window at his back, a scary, silent silhouette. Once the blankets are gone, he goes for my pajama shorts. His fingers inch under the waistband, and he tugs the fabric down slowly. So slowly. I lift my hips, helping him along before I think better of it.

Because I'd be lying if his dangerous side didn't turn me on.

I bite my lip. His threats are serious. And at the same time... I want him to make good on it.

His hands go to my shirt, and I automatically grip his wrists. I tug him down over me, spreading my legs. It's simple, he and I. He fits there neatly. His jeans scratch at my inner thighs, and if I didn't have a death grip on his wrists, I'd reach down and feel.

If only I was so bold.

He shifts, grinding against me. His erection presses through his jeans, and he hits just the right spot. My eyelids flutter. He does it again, while his hands rotate. Suddenly, somehow, he's the one who's holding *my* wrists over my head.

"Hmm." His head drops, and he bites at my breast through my shirt.

I whimper.

He continues to rock his hips into mine, scratching that *itch*, until shivers burst through me. Hell, I'm going to come like this. Come and then go straight to Hell for caving so easily.

He switches breasts. My nipples are stiff under my

sleep shirt, and his teeth and lips leave wet spots behind. He groans, his movements getting harder. I bring my knees up. A blush heats my cheeks when my hips rise to meet him.

I should not be enjoying this.

I bite my lower lip. I can't make a sound—not when he keeps rubbing exactly where I need him to. The friction of his jeans sliding along my core, hitting my clit, is too much.

My back arches, pushing my breasts into his face. He nips at my skin through my shirt. One hand moves down my arm and covers my mouth.

I gasp into his palm. The sensation crawls through me, fluttering and divine.

Unexpected, too.

When he lifts himself, he takes my wrists with me. He uses them to sit me up. Kneeling between my legs, he unbuttons his jeans and strokes his dick. In fast, jerky movements, he gets himself off.

I jump when his cock twitches and pulses, the only little warning for his impending climax.

Ropes of cum shoot across my belly and the apex of my legs. It coats my inner thighs. It's warmer than I expected, but I can't stop staring at his dick. He uses my forgotten panties to wipe himself clean, then tucks himself back in his pants.

He reaches out and picks up a lock of my hair. The gentleness of it freezes me in place.

"It's always been us," he says softly.

"It hasn't. It *used* to be us. Now there's nothing."

"Prove it," he demands. "Prove there's nothing there. That you feel nothing."

"Why does everything need to be proven? Why can't you just accept—"

He kisses me. I slam my mouth closed. I just let him

hump me into an orgasm—I'm surely not going to give in to this. His tongue slides across the seam of my lips, and I just press them tighter together. Not one to give up without a fight, he winds his hand through my hair, holding my head still, and he tries to get a reaction out of me.

He makes a noise in the back of his throat.

I give him *nothing*. I just gave him everything, and I am so, so tired.

"You're killing me," he whispers.

I meet his stare. We're still kissing-close. Our noses brush.

You killed me first.

He releases me.

"I want you to hurt." My chest aches, and I'd love nothing more than for him to know what I'm going through. "I want you to feel it."

"You want an apology?" he asks, shifting to the side and pressing his lips to my cheek. "You want me to say I'm sorry and beg for forgiveness?"

I will not bend.

Maybe he can sense the *yes* forming on my tongue.

"It won't happen, baby. We're meant to be broken." He takes hold of my chin, tipping my head back until I meet his gaze.

I hadn't realized I looked away.

"You and I can't do happy or perfect or *neat* like you think you're going to get." His grip tightens. "Maybe you'll see that eventually."

"Get out," I breathe.

He drops his hand and stands. "Dream of me."

"I won't."

I don't believe myself.

"We're inevitable," he says. "You'll see."

He makes it to my doorway before he pauses. He holds something up, but I can't make it out in the darkness.

"I know you don't remember, but if you want to... You know where I'll be." He tosses it onto my dresser. The object hits with a *clunk* of metal. The sound is loud enough to travel. He watches me a moment longer, then disappears into the hallway.

No window exits for him, I guess.

My breath catches in my chest. I almost expect the stairs to creak, the front door to slam—something to alert the Bryans of his presence. But he's a ghost. Here one minute, gone the next.

Tears burn the backs of my eyes, and I touch my chest. The two wet spots left by his saliva. My breasts ache, even when I scrape my nail over my nipple. It sends little zaps straight down to my pussy.

I can't do this.

I flop backward, mindful of the object taunting me from my dresser.

My hand has a mind of its own. It goes through the mess he left on the lower half of my shirt, my exposed abdomen, between my legs. It eases the path my fingers take, slipping along my clit.

Working myself up again.

One hand over my mouth, the other thrumming between my legs, I tip myself over the edge again, with the memory of Caleb's mouth on my breast burning in my mind.

I breathe slowly, my muscles trembling, and finally get up from the bed. I close my door and flick the light on. If there's one thing that must be true, it's how Caleb Asher knows *exactly* how to get in my head.

My bracelet sits on the dresser.

He knew where to find it.

He went there for it.

I run my finger over the web of metal, shaking my head. I can't do this right now. I can't forgive him.

I leave it where it is and crawl back into bed. I don't have the energy to try to deal with Caleb's mental games. After everything that's happened today, my mind hasn't stopped spinning.

My conversation with Amelie about Caleb's meddling... she thinks I shouldn't let him get away with it. Well, I won't.

And then the more devastating piece of news: Savannah texted him the picture.

My eyes pop open again. I can't believe that I forgot about it. *Savannah is Unknown.*

I should've suspected her sooner.

I sit up and grab my phone, scrolling through past messages with Unknown. I linger on the picture of Ian and me. Is it true? Does Savannah have that big of a vendetta against me that she'd try to ruin my life—and threaten me to stay away from Caleb?

She was at the party where the video was taken. And while she had some noticeable absences from school, I'm pretty sure she *was* there the day Ian dragged me into the woods.

It makes sense, too. She didn't like that I came back and never hid the fact. She could've driven by and seen me arriving at the Bryans' house.

How she got my number would be another question, though.

And how she's kept up the façade in school.

But has she? She's never hidden the fact that she doesn't like me.

I put my phone on the nightstand, flopping back.

The suspects include: Amelie, Savannah, and Ian.

Yes, Ian, even though he was the one *in* the picture. He could've paid someone to take it and send it to Caleb. He could've paid Savannah.

Caleb should be included, too. His whole friend group is on my suspect list. Any of them could want me to stay away from him for his own sake. For his sanity.

It's because of me that he's been suspended from hockey.

It could be no one on my list.

This endeavor seems hopeless. My only solution would be to get Unknown to give me some bit of information I can use to tie back to them. Or catch them in the act...?

What act? *Texting?*

Everyone my age has a cell phone. And nowadays, it's easy to block your number, make it private, or even get a number through a texting app.

I toss and turn in bed, my sleep tinged with worry. Every so often, my thoughts circle back to the bracelet on the dresser, and Caleb's...

You're killing me.

He's confusing and complicated.

Eventually, I fall asleep. I dream of Caleb and my mother.

They're arguing in his house, just beside the screen door. I can see them from where I'm crouched. Caleb has gray streaks in his hair. He's older—maybe older than both my parents. My mom is red in the face. Their hands wave. Their lips move, but I hear nothing. Spit flies from Caleb's mouth, and I instinctively hunch lower. Their anger scares me. I'm frozen in my hiding place.

I wish I could hear what they're saying.

She throws a glass. Not at him, but at the wall. It shatters. I hear *that*.

I scream, and both of them whirl toward me. Angry faces, brows lowered and mouths agape.

Someone yanks me backward. I fall and go straight through the floor.

I fall and fall and fall.

Caleb catches me. His arm across my back, the other under my knees. He doesn't seem surprised to find me here, but I can only stare at him. His face is young—fourteen instead of seventeen. A bit of acne, a slight padding to his face.

"Be more careful, Margo."

"You were just fighting with my mom." I look around. There's nothing but high grass around us. "Where are we?"

"We used to come here." He mirrors my actions, head swinging back and forth. "Don't you like it?"

Don't you like it?

"I don't..." I don't recognize this place. It's just grass and bright-blue sky, the sun so hot on my skin. "Why were you fighting with Mom?"

His face hardens. "I wasn't."

He drops me.

The grass reaches for me, brushing my exposed skin. I fall through the ground again, straight into darkness. Straight into my bedroom. I land on the bed with a bounce, and it takes me a long moment to collect my breath.

It's not the one at the Bryans'. It's in the Ashers' guest house.

I lunge for the door, but it's locked. Everything is blurry. Big fat tears fall down my face, and I pound on the door. Panic constricts my chest, choking me. It heightens my terror.

Why am I scared?

I'm trapped.

There are no monsters in this room, but I can't fight the urge to *run*. I scratch at the door. Pain pricks my fingers, my nails crack, but I still can't stop.

"Let me out!" I scream. "Let me out let me out let me—"

It flies inward. It hits me, and I tumble.

"Dad?" I moan, rolling onto my side. "Dad, Mom—"

It's not Dad. Why did I think it would be Dad?

Mom looms over me. She straddles me, pressing my shoulders into the floor. Her face is a mask of fury.

"Wake up, Margo."

I open my eyes, and I'm in my bed at the Bryans' house. My heart is going a thousand miles a minute, and I take a shaky breath.

It felt real. Too real. And for once, I remember every second of the dream.

I fumble for the lamp's switch, needing to extinguish the shadows. As if that would banish the shadows lingering in my mind, too. The sudden light blinds me. I raise my hand to block it and stop suddenly.

There are long scratches on the tops of my forearms... and blood under my fingernails.

So while I was trying to get out in the dream, I was really just hurting myself.

My stomach cramps. This wasn't a normal dream. It can't be.

There are pieces of my past trying to come out.

Chapter 12
Caleb

My uncle slides a pawn across the board between us. He raises an eyebrow at me, perhaps daring me to say something.

This is his time to lecture—I know that. It's why I keep my mouth shut.

He's dressed for work, and I'm in my school uniform. With our schedules, six o'clock in the morning was the only time convenient for my uncle. The text summons came in last night.

But it's fine, because the early hour means there's a time limit on how long this can go on.

After an appropriate pause, I move my knight. He likes me to analyze the board. Not doing so would only invoke his ire. So I usually end up counting to twenty in my head before each move, although it doesn't do any good.

I've never won against him.

He pushes another pawn forward. This is just the beginning of the game, where positioning is important. There will be time for attacks later. First comes structure.

Everything is wrapped in theory I only vaguely remember.

We play in silence for another five minutes, until he takes one of my pawns.

"Your coach informed me of your suspension." He firmly sets my black piece down beside the board. "You've already missed two games."

And another two on Friday and Saturday. We're playing a doubleheader, hosting an away team here for the weekend.

"Yes," I agree. There's no denying it.

"For fighting," he condemns.

I hesitate, then nod.

"And practices?"

I clear my throat. "I'm still attending practices."

"We wouldn't want you to get sloppy. Out of shape."

I slide my rook across the back row and castle. Essentially, allowing it to jump over my king, trading places with it, to better protect it.

My uncle scoffs. "Lazy."

I stiffen.

He glances up. Someone must be behind me, in the doorway, because he motions for them to enter.

Tobias Hutchins comes in and pauses at our table. He's Keith Wolfe's lawyer. Is. Was. I don't know. I have no idea if he still holds the position while his client—or former client—rots in prison.

He looks first to my uncle, then me, and then the board.

The tension in my shoulders seems to double. There's no reason for him to be here—not now. But he has a briefcase in one hand, and there's a faint sheen of sweat across his brow.

"Speak," Uncle demands.

Hutchins barely refrains from flinching. He reveals just the barest twitch of muscle before he locks it down. "There has been a visitation request."

"By?"

"Ms. Amber Wolfe."

I glance sharply at Hutchins.

Uncle's gaze flicks to me. "Amber Wolfe, hmm?"

I get a sinking feeling in my stomach.

"Yes, sir," the lawyer echoes.

"Put an end to that." Uncle moves another piece. "Checkmate, Caleb. Pay more attention, next time. Act like you're trying."

I bite the inside of my cheek to keep from swearing.

"Anything else?" Uncle asks the lawyer.

"No, sir." He pivots and leaves quickly.

I understand such a notion. As soon as the heavy wooden doors shut behind him, my uncle levels me with a glare.

"As I said before: sloppy."

"I—"

"Careless," he continues.

He swipes his arm across the table. The chessboard and pieces go flying. He lunges forward and grabs my throat. He yanks me up, half over the now-empty table, and stares into my eyes.

What he sees is anyone's guess.

He releases my throat and trades it for a punch to my stomach. The air leaves me in a rush, and I nearly double over.

"What good is your education if I can beat you in *sixteen moves*?" He hits me again. Knuckles striking into my ribcage. It's all below the collar to keep up appearances.

I'll have to get in a fight during practice, or with Liam, to cover for this.

My mind ticks ahead, calculating, while my uncle exorcizes his demons on my skin.

It's always been this way.

"You will not embarrass me," my uncle whispers, leaning over me.

The quieter he gets, the more dangerous.

Isn't that something I've always learned?

"Deal with Amber Wolfe. I don't fucking care what you have to do—this is your mess."

He throws me towards the floor. If I fight, he'll come at me five times harder. It was always like this. He made sure I knew he could break me from a young age. And now it's cemented there, so his anger deflates me. I hit the floor on my side. The impact rattles my bones, but I manage to protect my head. Not that he'd go for it—but slamming my temple on the floor would add up to sheer stupidity in his mind.

Not a fault of his.

"Despicable," Uncle curses. "Do *not* be late to school. Do you hear me? I will not have yet another stain on this family name by your lack of self-discipline."

He waits.

"Yes, Uncle," I finally reply.

"Good. Clean up this mess while you're at it."

He steps over me. I stay where I am until the door shuts with a soft *snick* behind him.

Every instinct is screaming at me to get out of the house. But it's a case of willpower to slowly gather the chessboard and pieces. I reset the board slowly. My ribs ache—more so when I press my palm to my side. My abdomen is sore, too.

It's not as bad as it could've been.

Not as bad as it's previously been.

I straighten my clothes and force my shoulders back. When I exit the study, I come face-to-face with my mother.

It's been a while since I last saw her. Her hands flutter around my arms without touching. Seems she's at war about whether to drag me into a hug or just stare at me.

"How bad?" she whispers.

I shake my head once. No doubt she overheard. Houses as big as this one, sometimes it's impossible to know if you're in it alone or if someone is right around the corner. Or if the air duct vent in the corner routes to the room above, allowing voices to travel with clarity...

"Let me take care of Amber," she says. "You've got enough on your plate."

I do, indeed.

When I leave, I don't go straight to school. I go to Margo's house.

Riley is already parked on the curb. She got her license as soon as she could. She's one of the only juniors who drives to school—a privilege usually reserved for seniors. But right now, she's getting in the way.

I hop out of my Audi and go to her car. I tap on the window, and she shrieks.

I smirk.

Her window goes down an inch. *An inch.* Guess someone's been filling her head with poisoned thoughts. I was never cruel to her. Never bullied her. In fact, I've been nice enough to not interfere with her acquaintance with Eli.

"I've got it," I tell her.

She scoffs. "On your life."

"Exactly. Now leave."

Her eyes gleam. "Because if I stay, you think she'll choose me over you?"

I lean down. "I'd hate for her to pick wrong and be punished for it."

"Punished," she echoes.

"Hmm." I smirk. "And we'd tie it right back to you."

She thinks that over, then finally nods.

I point to the second coffee cup in the holder. "Is that for her?"

Riley grits her teeth. The window comes down farther, and she hands it to me. "You're kind of an asshole, Asher."

"Right back atcha, Appleton."

She scowls. I step back, waving my free hand, and she pulls slowly away.

Just in time—a moment later, the front door of the Bryans' house opens, and out comes Margo Wolfe. She's in the process of putting her coat on, her bag slung over one shoulder. Her dark hair is loose, and she trots down the steps. Her makeup is more subtle today, less like a warrior headed into battle, more like...

A beautiful girl.

Don't get me wrong—she's gorgeous whether she's fresh-faced or layered with makeup armor.

When she sees me, she stops mid-stride.

"Good morning, baby." I meet her halfway, lifting her bag from her shoulder.

She lets me take it, although her expression is wary. She's stiffer than I was at my uncle's house, which should say something. I'm not about to beat her.

Even hoisting her bag up has my muscles pulling, and I barely manage to keep my expression stoic. My uncle's warnings ring in my ear with every step back to the car.

"Is that for me?" Her voice is breathy.

I glance down at the coffee in my hand, ignoring my

body's immediate reaction to her. I need that voice whispered in my ear when I'm deep inside her.

"Yes." I hand it over.

She smiles.

A true one.

I put my hand on the small of her back, ushering her around and into the passenger seat. Her bag joins mine behind me. My hockey bag is in the trunk, along with my stick and skates. I've got exactly zero expectation that I'll be doing anything except conditioning today... like the week prior.

Coach holds grudges.

I glance at Margo, considering. Would she tell me about her mom? If she heard from her? I'm not too sure Amber would reach out. There's some bad blood there, even if Margo is unaware. But it seems like Amber is in town, and now she wants to talk to her ex-husband?

I heave a sigh. My mother said she'll take care of it... I've got to trust her. But if she fails, then it's going to fall back on me.

Just focus on Margo.

"Did you sleep well, baby?"

Confession: I nearly came in my pants. It was all I could do to hold off until after she came, then release my tension by jerking myself off in front of her. Her gaze on me... I can't beat that rush.

Walking out of that room... I could've easily stayed there.

Her birthday is coming up soon. Eighteen ticks closer every fucking second, and I know it's weighing on her. That *snap* of a cord breaking, the foster system suddenly relinquishing its control over her...

What will she do?

Where will she go?

The answer is obvious. If the Bryans kick her out—and that is my intention to get them to that point, pressing on wounds just enough to make them uncomfortable with her staying—then she'll come to me.

All part of the process, of course.

"Why are you picking me up?" Margo asks.

I glance at her. "Because I wanted to see you."

"You saw me plenty last night."

"Hmm." I flick my blinker on a second before I touch the brake, swinging my car onto a side street. Then another, until we reach a pull off for the lake. "I think you want a repeat."

Her cheeks turn the prettiest shade of pink. And yet, while I was deviating from our course, she didn't so much as make a peep.

I scoot my seat back as far as it can go and slowly undo my pants. I push them down, along with my boxers, and keep my gaze on her face. Even though my cock, now standing at attention, begs to be touched.

"Sit on my lap," I order.

Is it a test?

Part of the game?

We're alone here, with nothing but the water ahead of us, an empty parking lot around, and trees beyond.

She unbuckles her seat belt.

"Take off your panties, first," I add.

Her lips part. I want to take a fistful of her hair and make her move faster, but the anticipation is working for me, too. I don't give a fuck if we're late, because I need Margo's sweet cunt squeezing my dick right now.

She lifts her hips and reaches under her skirt. Slowly,

the black silky fabric appears. She drags it down her pale thighs, over her knees, and removes them entirely.

I point to the gear stick. She loops it over it, then shifts onto her knees. She crawls over the center console and swings her leg over me, settling on my lap. Her skirt fans around her. My dick is right in front of her, pulsing between us.

Leaning my seat back, I grab her hips and tug her closer. She lifts, and I slide the head of my cock through her center. She's wet.

I knew she liked this shit.

From virgin to... experimenter?

"Hold your skirt out of the way," I murmur.

She lifts the front, giving me a view of her pussy. She leans back slightly, her knees widening, and lowers herself onto me.

I hiss out a breath. There's nothing better than this. Her eyelashes flutter, her head tipping back. The smooth, pale skin of her throat disappears into the collar of her white dress shirt.

She rises, then drops back down. The groan that breaks from between her teeth is too fucking much.

I touch her. Palm her breasts through her shirt and bra—*too much in the way.* I undo the buttons of her shirt, somehow refraining from popping them open, and tug the cups of her bra down. Her breasts are exposed, lifted by the underwire and flipped-down cups, and I lean into her.

My mouth lands on one perky, pink areola. Her nipples stiffen in the cool morning air. I press one hand to the small of her back, keeping her chest arched toward me. I kiss it. Lick. Suck her tender flesh into my mouth.

She rides me slowly, her movements too unsure to belie any experience.

"That's it," I murmur, dragging my mouth from her breast up the front of her chest. I nip at her collarbone, then her throat. I hope to leave marks on her that she won't notice until later, when our classmates are staring and pointing. "Just like that, baby."

She grips my shoulders.

Another car pulls into the lot, but she doesn't notice. Her eyes are closed.

They park a few spaces down, but there's no fucking mistaking what we're doing. The older man gets out and stares at us.

Well.

At the rocking car and the tinted windows. He can probably see our silhouettes.

I roll down the window and extend my hand, middle finger up.

Margo goes still.

Ah.

She's opened her eyes, her skin now coated in goosebumps, and the guy is staring at her. Well, us.

"Be a wolf," I whisper.

Her head whips forward, glaring at me. But carefully, her hand lifts, and it joins mine out the window.

Middle finger *up*.

I grin, and she mirrors it.

The guy—well, I don't know. I don't really give a shit. I roll the window back up and place my hands on her hips.

"Double time, baby. Otherwise the next visitor we'll have will be the cops."

Her eyes widen. I thrust my hips, pushing my cock deeper into her, and her severe expression melts away. She bounces, her breasts swaying, while I control how high she goes. I don't need her to slip out and start over, breaking our rhythm.

I move one hand between her legs, feeling where we're joined, then sliding back up to her clit. Her lips part when I touch her just the way she likes. My balls are ready to unload, and I lean forward and kiss her hard. Her tongue touches my lower lip, then pushes into my mouth.

Her hands, from where they clutched my shoulders, slide up into my hair.

Fuck, I can't get enough of this girl.

I didn't pick her up this morning expecting this.

I didn't have any expectations, really, except for moderating my guilt.

That's not going so well.

She's not being vulnerable with me. Sex, sure, but I don't think she's equating that to *intimacy*. After all, I fucked her and then screwed her over.

Breaking past her guards and climbing into her soul is my next step.

Body, mind, soul.

I want to be on her mind all the time.

I want her to feel me on her all the time.

My uncle would be furious with me for being so selfish —but that's exactly why I've got to have her. The rest of my life isn't mine.

Hell, as soon as he finds out my frame of mind, I'll be punished.

Her hands move from my hair down to my ribs, and I wince.

She stills. Everything in her freezes. "What was that?"

I lean back, but I don't stop rubbing her clit. I watch her, caught in my web, until the sensation beats out her concern.

She gasps, the orgasm rolling through her. Her muscles

clamp around my cock, and I groan through my teeth. I manually lift her and slam her down, only a few more times, and finally let go.

There's nothing better than coming inside her.

I've never fucked anyone without a condom before. It was drilled into me that pregnant girlfriends would not be tolerated. No heir to the Asher fortune would have a child out of wedlock and embarrass the entire family.

So, yeah. Condoms. Girls on birth control or plan B just in case.

I don't know if Margo's on birth control—and frankly, I don't give a shit.

All I know is I'm never putting on one of those things again if it's Margo I'm seating myself inside.

I pat her thigh, and she slowly climbs off of me. She throws herself back into her seat and reaches for her panties.

"Do you have any napkins?" Her hand goes to the glove box.

I stop her. "No."

"No?" she echoes.

"No. I expect you to walk into school with my cum between your legs." I stuff my cock back into my pants, zipping up. "Do you think your panties will contain it? Or will it slowly drip down your thighs during the day?"

Her face flushes.

I flip her skirt up. She spreads her legs, and I smile. It's already oozing out, smearing across the insides of her thighs and getting on the leather seat.

Excellent.

I toss the panties at her. "If you go to the bathroom, you have to tell me so we can fix it."

She eyes me. "Fix it?"

I smirk, suddenly set on this new version of the game. "Yeah. *Fix* it. Do you promise? Either that or I'll have someone follow you around school all day."

"Fine," she bites out.

Glorious.

All that, and she seems to have forgotten about my wince.

The last thing she needs to know about is my uncle.

Chapter 13
Margo

We narrowly avoid the police cruiser. Which is an odd thing to say, but Caleb motions behind us just as we're turning onto a different street, heading toward school. I spot the cop turning into the lakeside parking lot, and then we're out of sight.

We're only mildly late to school. Caleb and I get slips from the office and head into first period, and I try to ignore the hush that falls over the students.

Coming in late? Sure.

Coming in late *with Caleb*? Not good.

As soon as Mrs. Stonewater's back is turned, whispers break out. I hunch lower, way too aware of the wetness between my legs. I want to bolt to the nearest bathroom and scrub myself, but the damage is done. My panties won't magically dry either, unless I hold them under the weak blowers...

Wouldn't that be fun to explain if someone walked in?

Anyway.

We survive—rather, *I* survive—first period. Although as

soon as students from that class get released into the halls, it seems like the gossip mill once again churns.

Riley meets me at her locker before lunch, and I clutch her hands.

"Where were you this morning?" I ask.

She wrinkles her nose. "Caleb made a convincing argument."

"He took the coffee from you, didn't he?" I smack my forehead. Coffee that, in the end, I didn't get to drink.

My stomach rumbles, but I was planning on talking to Riley on the way to school. Now, my dream comes roaring back to the forefront of my mind.

"I had a weird dream," I tell her. "And I can't figure out what's real and what's my imagination."

"What was it about?"

"My mom and an older Caleb arguing, then Caleb and I were in a field, and then I was in my room..." I shake my head. "I feel like I'm misremembering."

That's how dreams work. Let them sit in your brain long enough, and the finer details slip away.

We pause at the doors to the library.

"What were they arguing about?" she asks.

"I couldn't hear."

"An older Caleb—like his dad?"

I flinch. Why didn't I think of that? "Oh my God."

She bounces on her heels. "Okay, okay, so your mom and Caleb's dad probably argued at some point. Maybe you overheard it or saw them and didn't really understand? Or maybe you did understand and it scared you."

I hesitate. She was *really* angry in the dream. Angry when she burst into my room, too.

"You're having memory issues surrounding why you left, right?" Riley presses.

I don't want to think about that.

"Caleb stopped by last night."

And I left the bracelet on the dresser. Didn't even think about grabbing it this morning, even though my wrist feels shockingly bare without it. He didn't mention anything about it in the car.

"He wanted me to forgive him," I add.

Riley snorts. "Don't."

"I'm not going to." Even if he knows exactly how to touch me.

"And what did Amelie want? I'm sorry I didn't go with you, I just... I don't trust that girl. You didn't agree to do anything with her, right?"

"Um, no." I make a face. "She was encouraging me to dump Caleb and tell her what I remember. And... you know those texts I showed you at the beginning of the school year?"

She tilts her head. "The creepy ones from the blocked number."

"Yeah. Well, they didn't stop."

"Margo Wolfe! You never said."

Heat crawls up my neck. "I didn't want to freak you out."

"Give it to me."

I wince, then open my phone to Unknown's conversation.

She scrolls through it, getting paler by the second. "Fucking hell, Margo. You kept this a secret?"

"I didn't want to drag you into it," I whisper. "I mean... I don't know who it is."

The overwhelming majority of messages in that thread are from Unknown—my rare replies don't seem to dissuade them.

"They were the ones who took the video? And leaked it."

I sigh.

"And they sent the picture of you and Ian..." She purses her lips. "Wait. So they were at school? Obviously it's a student."

"Or a teacher."

She pauses. Then, "They ask a lot of rhetorical fucking questions. We know anyone like that?"

I laugh. "I doubt it'd be that easy... but Amelie said the text came from Savannah."

Riley gasps. "Excuse me? I'm going to kill her."

"If we can believe anything Amelie says."

"True. She *is* a dirty backstabbing snake. Savannah just kind of shunned you to survive. You don't think it could be both of them, do you? Amelie's just planting the seed to throw suspicion off of herself. Plus, she was in Paris when you first started getting the texts."

I groan. "There are so many questions and virtually *no* answers."

"Agreed."

Riley opens the library door, but the librarian seems to have been waiting. She clings on to the door, stopping Riley from opening it farther.

"There's a staff meeting in here today," she whispers. "Go away."

I groan. Riley nods slowly, and we share a glance. I try to ignore my dread and follow her to the lunchroom.

"Bathroom break," I say, tugging her with me.

I can't wait any longer—and I kind of want to see if he's going to notice from his earlier stipulation. About... *you know*. Will he do anything about it? A thrill goes through me, and as soon as my hands are washed and dried, we continue into the packed cafeteria.

"We can just snag seats at one of the empty tables," Riley murmurs.

We both bring our lunches, so it's not like we need to wait in the huge line. I follow her down the main aisle. I ignore the table where Amelie reigns, and Savannah tries not to glower. Then there's the hockey table, centered against the windows.

It's too easy to find Caleb, sitting in the center like a king.

The king to Amelie's queen.

My stomach knots, and I think we might slip under the radar when he glances up.

His gaze lands on me, and he raises his eyebrows.

"Why is he looking at you like that?" Riley whispers.

"No idea," I mutter.

But, yeah, I totally know.

I follow Riley to a table in the far corner. It's probably reserved for losers and outcasts, but isn't that exactly what we are?

Yes. It doesn't work, because Caleb drops down into the chair next to mine almost before I can take my own seat.

"Margo," Caleb greets me. He reaches out and runs his hand down my arm, lifting my hand. He pushes my sleeve up to expose my bare wrist. His fingers are cold, but it's nothing compared to the fire in his expression.

Goosebumps break out along my arms and back.

Disappointment flashes across his face, then his perfect mask is back in place. How he slides it on so precisely reminds me of the masquerade ball. The cool gold against my skin.

"Come with me," he says.

"I'm hungry." I cross my arms.

He raises an eyebrow, but he motions for me to proceed.

With him... watching?

He puts his elbow on the table, propping his chin on his fist. In no hurry to move, then, I scowl and face forward. I take the sandwich and mini bag of chips out of the brown paper bag, followed by a Ziplock of baby carrots and cucumber, then a tiny tub of hummus.

My stomach growls.

Caleb reaches out and opens the bag of chips. Before I can scowl at him, he sets the open bag on the table, facing me.

It would be nice if I didn't know he was actually a demon.

I take a bite of my sandwich. Then another. While Caleb *and* Riley stare at me. Finally, she eats, too, which makes it a little less weird.

His gaze burns.

When everything is polished off, and I'm no longer starving to the point of stomach cramps, he takes my hand and drags me out of my chair. Down the hall, then another. Until we reach the locker rooms.

I dig my heels in. "I'm not going in there."

"Uh-huh." He's an unstoppable force.

And I end up in the locker room.

Not a huge surprise, Margo.

We pass the rows of showers on the left, but he doesn't stop at any of them. They're too exposed for what I think he has planned.

Wait a second...

"Why don't they have curtains?"

"Guys would rip them down to be funny. The school

finally stopped investing in them." He glances back at me. "I don't really want to talk about shower curtains."

Right.

I know what this is about, and butterflies flutter in my chest. At the last row of lockers on our right, he pushes me against them and drops to his knees.

One minute he's looking up at me, and the next...

His head is under my skirt.

He pulls my panties aside, sliding a finger inside me without warning. I buck my hips, the sensation a shock. And also... a bit of pleasure. He reaches up and puts a hand on my abdomen, forcing me harder against the lockers.

My breathing comes in short bursts.

He's barely touched me—just a single finger, and his breath on my thigh—and I'm going to combust.

Carefully, he drags my panties down and lifts my leg. He leaves them wrapped around one ankle, and my free one he hooks over his shoulder.

Fucking hell.

"We're at *school*," I hiss.

"Better be quiet, then," comes his reply.

It's followed by his tongue on my clit.

Oh, fuck. The words of protest die in my throat, and he works me right to the edge.

And then stops. My foot touches the floor again, and he reemerges. He licks his lips, grinning up at me.

"Oh, I'm sorry," he mocks. "Did you want me to keep going?"

I gape at him. My body is thrumming with energy, although the climax is quickly fading away. It leaves behind a buzzing ache in my clit.

He smirks and rises, slowly turning me around. He manually puts my hands on the lockers and drags my hips back, until I'm leaning my upper body's weight on the wall of metal. When he flips my skirt up, the cool air kisses my bare skin. I shiver and glance back.

His focus is solely on my ass and his fist stroking his cock.

The bell has *got* to be about to ring.

We're going to be so late.

He lines up and thrusts into me before I can voice it.

Ah, fuck.

The dirtiness of this—and the fact that anyone could walk in on us—only turns me on more. I'm kind of ashamed to realize that, but it is what it is. He fucks me so hard, I can't take my hands away from the wall or else risk going head-first into it.

His fingers dig into my hips, pulling me back to meet him.

His cock hits just the right spot in me, the friction and stretch and *angle*—

"I'm going to come," I finally say.

He slows. "No."

I stare back at him. He's moving at a turtle's pace now, seeming to wait for my twitching pussy to calm.

"You had to let me find out that my cum was gone from your sweet cunt on my own," he says, his expression dark. "So, no. I hope it aches all day for you, baby."

After a long moment, he resumes. And just as it builds up again, the sensation almost tipping me to pleasure, he stills.

He groans through his teeth as he comes, and I close my eyes. My skin is too hot, and the need between my legs is almost unbearable.

When he slips out, he kneels and picks up my leg,

sliding my panties over my shoe. Up my legs, under the skirt.

Once again keeping his cum against my sensitive core.

He turns me around and inspects my face, then nods to himself.

"See you later, baby."

Chapter 14
Caleb

"Incoming," Liam warns. He nods toward the benches.

He wouldn't warn me about Coach. When I turn around, I spot Amelie.

I clench my jaw. We're at hockey practice, waiting on Coach Marzden to appear, and Amelie trots down the steps to the bench. I skate toward her, anticipating that she's only here to say something stupid to me about Margo.

I feel Theo at my back. He's my only silent shadow—the other two are a bit more obvious about it.

"Fuck off," I tell Amelie when she gets to our level.

She scowls. "Excuse me?"

"You heard me." I raise my eyebrow. "Unless you'd like Theo to remove you from my sight?"

Our practice is going to start any minute.

Nothing Amelie can say will make a difference about Margo. The lost lamb is mine. I know it. My friends know it. The whole school fucking knows it, no matter what she or Amelie say. The only one who isn't convinced is Margo Wolfe.

And what a little wolf she's becoming.

Theo moves forward, his arm brushing mine. A show of force.

Amelie steps back, glaring at him. "Okay, okay. I'll see you later."

"No, you won't."

She scowls.

When she's finally out of sight, I glance over at Theo.

He's scowling, too. Glaring back down the aisle the way she came. "What the fuck does she want?"

I shrug.

Liam stops with a shower of snow over our skates. "She knows she can't have you, Theo, so she's trying to get in Caleb's pants instead."

Theo laughs, and I shove Liam. Asshole.

"All right," Coach calls, blowing his whistle. He skates onto the ice. "Get over here, you lazy gits."

As captain, it's my job to keep the team together. To set an example. But my mind keeps straying back to Margo.

"Asher!" Coach snaps.

I jerk. "Yes, sir?"

"You're not alone in doing sprints today."

I suppress my sigh—but everyone else doesn't. The groans are audible, and Coach just chuckles. For every complaint, another sprint will be tacked on. Or two.

We line up on the goal line, at the ready, and wait for the whistle.

When it goes off, we skate down and back. My ribs and stomach hurt, the exertion pulling at my bruised muscles, but I force it out of my mind.

Down and back.

Again.

Again.

Again.

My lungs are on fire by the time he pauses, but no one complains again.

"Not bad," Coach says. "Take two minutes, then we'll get started. Asher, Alistair, with me."

Theo and I trade a look, but we follow Coach to the bench. I grab a water bottle and squirt it through my cage into my mouth. Beside me, Theo does the same.

"I'm making Theo your alternate," Coach says without preamble.

I lower the bottle. "Why?"

"Because your head is up your ass," Coach answers. "I got a call from your uncle yesterday. He thinks you need a little incentive to pay more attention. Besides—you're still suspended, and the team needs a leader."

I grimace.

Theo shakes his head. "I don't want it."

"You take it or I'm picking Ian—and he won't be an alternate, he'll be *captain*. Period." His gaze switches to me. "Attitude adjustment, or I'll strip that 'C' off your chest faster than you can say sorry."

Fuck, he's serious.

Theo looks at me, then slowly nods. Yeah, it's a blow to my ego, but I can suck it up. I would rather have Theo in my corner any day over Ian fucking Fletcher.

"Back to your sprints, Asher," Coach says. "You're not out of the doghouse yet."

Naturally.

While the rest of the team works on passing and shooting drills, I skate back and forth until my legs want to fall off... and then when they don't, it's because I've completely lost feeling in them.

I make it back to the goal line for what feels like the seven millionth time, and Coach stops me.

"Coach?" I question. Sweat pours down my face, drenching my undershirt. I take my helmet off and slick my hair back.

Gross.

"Practice is over, Asher." He appraises me. "Tomorrow we'll be back to normal."

I glance around, only to discover the rink completely empty.

How did I miss that?

"Where's your list of schools?" he asks. "We discussed this the other day."

Fucking hell. I'm so tired I can barely think—and that's probably why he's chosen to bring it up now.

"Did my uncle call to ask about that, too?"

He glares at me. "I mean it, Caleb. Get your head out of your ass and think smart. Deadlines are approaching."

"That it?"

Sometimes I make him mad enough that I think he's going to take a swing at me. Now's one of those times. The flippant attitude... I mean, it doesn't matter where I want to go to school, does it? My uncle is going to put me wherever he thinks I need to go.

My mother apparently wants me to go to Harvard... but why the fuck would she want that, unless it's something my uncle spoon-fed her?

"Go on."

Most of the team is done and gone by the time I get into the locker room. To clarify—a different one than where I fucked Margo earlier. The arena is down the street from the school. A different building entirely.

A quick, hot shower warms my bones. But I can't shake

the feeling that pressure is creeping up on me. My uncle, my mom. They're prying.

Liam waits for me by my cubby. His gaze drops to my torso, and his eyes widen. Not much can surprise him, but... "Holy fucking shit. What the hell happened?"

I glance down at the bruises from my uncle.

"Nothing good."

He just looks at me, and I force myself to hold his gaze. My friends don't really *know*. I don't think I've ever openly admitted what my uncle does for sport. But they do know that as soon as Eli's parents offered me the room in their basement, I jumped at it.

And on the topic of my conversation with Coach, I'm not about to tell Liam about college. About the prestigious route my uncle and mother have laid out for me. Liam seems to think it's iffy he'll even make it that far, unless he gets a scholarship. Which is totally possible—he plays hockey well enough to play on the college level. A division one school would be lucky to have him.

Coach is all about the sport. No time for lust or mind games. No time for drinking, partying, girls.

No fighting.

"How's Marg—I mean, Amelie?" Liam snickers.

I shake my head. "I'm not touching Amelie. She's fucking delusional."

"You may not be touching her, but she sure as hell wants you to."

I roll my eyes, grabbing my bag. We walk out together. "That's the problem. She's got an issue with Theo and wants me to save her from it."

Liam shakes his head. "Not gonna comment on that."

"And you? No girls you're chasing?"

"Nope. I'm free as a bird!"

He's a lying bastard. All of us are. It's the glue that holds us together. That and undying loyalty. I might want to punch Liam's face in sometimes, but I'd kill for him. I know he'd do the same for me.

"You seem... off."

"Maybe I am." I shrug on my coat and follow him to the parking lot.

"You're not going to tell me?"

We get to my car. His is in the shop—it's always in the shop—so Theo and I have been taking turns giving him rides. He lives in the middle of nowhere, which isn't terrible. I don't mind the drive. It gives me time to think.

But I've been thinking too much, holding on to things I should really get off my chest. It's no wonder Liam's picked up on something no one else has.

"I found something," I tell him once we're on the road. "A note."

"A note," Liam repeats. "What did it say?"

"Just shut up and fucking listen, would you?"

I haven't told anyone this. I've scarcely been able to think about it, let alone bring it up in conversation. I learned early on that secrets only remain such if they're held with one person.

"After Margo went missing, I broke into her room at the Bryans' house. I was going to take a picture of the family because it piqued my curiosity, you know? After I told them that Margo's mom was responsible for giving their daughter drugs. But..."

"Isn't that what happened?" Liam eyes me. "You did tell them that, which is why Margo ran away from you."

"Amber didn't leave town like I told her to," I admit. "I was going to take the photo of the Bryans—including their daughter—and I was going to ask her if she recognized any of them."

"Fuck, man. That's a terrible idea."

"I threatened her to leave, but she hasn't. So she's here for something." I hate not knowing.

"Okay, so what did the note say?"

"It was actually kind of morbid." I frown. "The Bryans' kid was essentially apologizing for being a fuck up, said she hoped that when they took down the photo and eventually found it, that she had earned their forgiveness by then."

Liam whistles.

"Obviously it doesn't prove anything either way. Just a bit of weird foreshadowing."

We sit with that.

And then there's the fact that I took it with me, which...

"What about Margo?" Liam asks.

"Her mom might try to reach out," I allow. "But after what Margo did... I don't think that's why she wants to suddenly reconnect with Keith. I gave her cash, and she *still* didn't go."

"And you don't know where she is."

I grind my teeth. I haven't even had time to look for her again—and not only that, but my mother is on the job, too. My mother and Margo's... Uncle David knows Amber is here. The whole family knows, which means my leverage has vanished.

It's all just a clusterfuck that I need to keep Margo as far away from as possible. Which means sticking as close to her as I can, to steer her in the right direction.

Liam's driveway is long and winding. We finally get to his house on a hill, and I kill the engine.

"You'll find her," he says. "If you need to."

"Not without asking." And I'm definitely not asking

anyone who'll know. With the way Amelie is behaving, any gossip she overhears is out. Same with Ian fucking Fletcher.

He climbs out of the car. "Wanna chill?"

I shrug and get out, following him into the house. It's old. Their security system is the front door hinges that squeal, and little else. Liam's family used to be made of money like the rest of us, but that changed a few years ago. He's still at Emery-Rose because Coach helped him get a scholarship, and he's one of only a few students who received it.

It's hush-hush, though.

He casts a single glance down the hill to his neighbor's house, which stands still and silent, before entering his.

"That you, Liam?"

"Yeah, Mom," he calls. We kick off our shoes. "Caleb brought me home."

His mom rounds a corner and grins. She has flour on her cheek, and she wastes zero time pulling Liam in for a hug and kissing his cheek. She does the same to me, as if I were one of her boys. Liam swipes at the flour on her face, and she laughs.

"I was just making bread," she explains. "Are you staying for dinner, Caleb?"

With Eli's family out of town, I've been on my own. It hasn't been half bad, actually. But someone offering to cook for me...

"I'd love to," I say.

Mrs. Morrison is always quick with the smiles—something I find truly impressive after such a devastating financial loss. But their family was able to stay intact, so... maybe that's all that matters.

Or maybe it's all that matters *now*.

"Wonderful. Colby will be home soon."

Colby is Liam's younger brother. He goes to the public school, and the bus will deliver him.

I follow Liam up to his room. "How is she?"

He grunts and drops his bag on his desk. He motions for me to take the chair, and he flops onto his bed. "She's stressed as always. Colby just got his license, and our parents splurged and got him a car. I think they forgot about the insurance rate for new drivers. He's going to have to get a job if he wants to keep it, otherwise..."

"He'll get there." It might be a lie—I have no fucking idea how much car insurance costs.

Liam nods sharply. "What'd Theo say about the alternate captain thing?"

"Not much." I drop into his desk chair and kick out my legs. "He deserves it. I can't even play, although Coach hinted that I'll be rejoining regular practice again."

"Wow, the magnanimous Caleb Asher. Kind words, seeing as how you've held on to the captainship with a bloody grip since the beginning of junior year."

I roll my eyes. It's true, though. If it was anyone other than Theo, I would've been pissed.

And everyone would've known it.

My phone rings, pausing my retort. I flash the screen at Liam, and his eyebrows jump up.

"Didn't know your mom remembered your number." He hops up and leaves the room, closing the door behind him.

"Yes?" I lean back in the chair, and the front two legs lift off the floor.

"Caleb?" my mother asks. Like she's not sure.

"What can I do for you, Mother?"

She huffs. "What a greeting. Where are you?"

"A friend's house." I focus on the ceiling. Talking to her

is painful, like going to the dentist to have a cavity filled. She's out of touch with reality most of the time.

"But not the Black's? Eli's mother called to check in, said they were going to be in Chicago for another few days."

Silence.

"You didn't say they were out of town," she finishes.

"I didn't know you cared." My chair's front legs slam back down.

"We're having family dinner at David's tonight. Six o'clock."

I glance at my watch. It's almost five. "Thanks for the short notice. I already have dinner plans." They're at least a forty-five-minute drive from Eli's—longer from Liam's. Besides already telling Mrs. Morrison I'd be having dinner with them, I'd be late—even if I left now.

And that would be worse than not showing up at all.

"Caleb Asher," she starts.

"Sorry, Mother. If you want to get on my schedule, maybe you should book farther in advance."

I hang up and toss my phone across Liam's desk. There will be consequences for this. Not from Mother Dearest, of course. Uncle David will take it as a personal offense. And unfortunately, he has a bit more sway in my life than she does.

He should've mentioned it when I was at his stupid house this morning.

My phone immediately lights up with an incoming call from my uncle.

I leave it in the room and go downstairs, joining Liam and Colby at the table. They're playing cards while their mother bustles around the kitchen, and I try to ignore the swooping feeling in my gut.

They used to live in the Bryans' house until Liam's dad

got laid off. Suddenly, their whole family was put on a shoestring budget. No more fancy house in Rose Hill with an expensive mortgage, and no more private school for their son—until he got the scholarship, that is. Colby wasn't so lucky, even in that. He doesn't play hockey, so...

Still, this family has done the best they can. They converted their basement into a game room to keep the boys from going out and spending money, and they've always welcomed me, Eli, and Theo. The Morrisons are a blessing on lost boys like us.

Mr. Morrison got another job, although not one that pays well, and they stay afloat.

Somehow.

Barely.

"Your father is working late." Liam's mom places a pot of soup in the center of the table. "If you could pause the game, boys, we'll eat."

We each get our own oval loaf of bread to carve out, and then we dump the tomato bisque into the bread bowls. The love that went into this meal makes me uncomfortable. I eat with Eli's family most nights, but they have a chef who prepares most of the food.

This was... There's more flour on Liam's mom's cheek from the breadmaking. Not the loaves in front of us, but I suspect more dough for a future meal similar to this one.

Colby looks up and notices, his eyes softening. Liam worries about his brother, but as long as he's treating his mom okay...

I should know. It's the golden benchmark nowadays.

I'm lucky Margo doesn't know how I treat my mother—and hers.

Colby leans over and brushes the remnants of flour from her cheek.

She smiles, touching the back of his hand for a brief moment.

I shift in my seat. Affection is something that's been a little sparse in my life... except Margo. I don't think I've ever had anyone care as much as she does, even if she tries not to. Even if she pretends otherwise. Even if she's fucking *pissed* at me.

That's one thing I'll continue to be jealous about: Liam has a mom who gives a shit.

"The soup is delicious," I tell her.

"Thank you, dear. Old family recipe."

She asks Liam and Colby about school and sports. Colby goes on a rant about some offense one of his football teammates committed, while Liam snickers into his soup and his mother nods along sympathetically.

When he's finished, and Liam brushes off the subject, she turns her attention on me. I answer her questions the best I can—how I'm getting on and dealing with school and whatever. Every answer, I'm mindful of the bruises across my stomach and the bracelet on my wrist.

"Sorry about the interrogation." Liam says after dinner, back in his room. He picks up a roll of white tape—for his hockey sticks—and tosses it from one hand to the other.

"It's nice that someone cares," I mumble. "I gotta go."

My phone has three missed calls—one from my mother and two from Uncle David.

Once I'm in the car, I call him back.

"My house. Now."

I sigh. "I was invited to dinner by my friend's mom. I'd already accepted by the time Mother called to ask—"

"It's perfectly acceptable to tell them that your presence has been requested—"

"Request makes it sound like a choice," I interrupt. "If it

was an order, it should've been delivered as such from the outlet. Not sending Mom to ask nicely.

"Let me remind you who your legal guardian is until you're eighteen," he growls. "Do not make me—"

I hang up on him and finish the drive to Margo's house in silence. Riley's car is out front, but neither Lenora's nor Robert's cars are in the driveway.

If they don't try to teach Margo to drive soon, I'm going to have to take matters into my own hands. Not that I want to give her more independence, but... well, she should know how.

I park down the street, where hopefully my car will go unnoticed by Riley when she leaves, and slip across the front lawn. I scale the trellis up to the second floor. After the day I've had, every muscle is sore. But I keep going until I peek into her window. The light is off in her bedroom, but the window unlocked. Almost like she's expecting me.

I pull my leg through just as the front porch light flickers on and girls' voices drift toward me. Talk about good timing.

"See you tomorrow," Riley calls.

"Bye," Margo answers.

I sit on her bed and pick up the sleep shirt she left on her pillow. She might hate me, but I can't stay away.

I've tried—but life is so much more exciting with Margo around.

Chapter 15
Margo

Riley and I have been plotting. Not just about Caleb, but also about Savannah and Amelie. We're operating under the assumption that both of them are the mystery texter, but it could be a lot of people.

Either way, the idea of upsetting the hierarchy at Emery-Rose is too tempting.

It's not like either of *us* want to take over the queen bee position. We just want Amelie to suffer a little... and Sav, too.

"We can't go easy on them," I tell Riley. "Total annihilation."

"And how do you propose we do that?" Riley asks.

There are so many options. Rumors, public embarrassment, somehow turning them into social pariahs?

Imagine.

"What throne do the king and queen sit on?"

Something Amelie, Sav, and I had in common? We always knew how to push the buttons of every single person around us. It was a trait we first saw in Amelie in first grade, and later, it's what made me a bad foster kid. Because even after I was taken from my home, I didn't know how to stop that side of me.

After my third home, I learned.

"We go after them where it counts," I say. "Friends. Sports."

Riley groans. "You're talking... like... destroy them. And what are they going to do in return?"

"Are they going to do anything worse than what they've already done?"

She just looks at me, and it conveys her thoughts.

I grimace. "Okay, so any takedown can't directly involve us, unless we want to deal with their wrath. You make a good point."

"Maybe we should just... wait." She picks at a loose thread on her pants. "The worse we can be is rash."

My phone buzzes.

LENORA

Robert had to work late, so I'm picking up dinner. Will be home around eight! Sorry for the L8 dinner!

I snort at her shorthand.

ME

Okay, take your time.

Riley has to go home, so we say goodbye at the door. I close and lock it, then turn my attention to the kitchen. I put the empty glasses in the dishwasher and run a wet rag across the island. Leaving a space how I found it was always one way of staying out of trouble.

Lenora gets home, and I help her unpack the bags of Chinese food. My stomach cramps, suddenly reminding me that besides the chips Riley and I had when we got here after school, I've had nothing since lunch.

We dig in without Robert, and once finished, I retreat upstairs.

I grab my backpack on the way up. I close my door and eye my cracked window. A cold breeze blows inside.

"Caleb?"

I pause, glancing around the room. The closet is halfway open, and the rest of the room is silent and still. He doesn't emerge from any hiding place.

I cross the room and slam the window shut. If he's not going to make himself known, then I may as well do homework.

Robert gets home a while later and comes upstairs, knocking on my door. "Did Appleton leave?"

"Yeah, she had to get home for dinner."

He nods. "You need anything?"

"I'm good for now... and I need to catch up on this stuff."

"All right, back to work then." He taps the door, then closes me back in.

I look around the room, pulling my leg up to my chest. I wrap my arms around it and put my chin on my knee, closing my eyes for a minute. It isn't that I *want* to take Amelie's place. I just want her to realize how wrong she's been.

She needs to fall... and Caleb does, too.

He's been hoping to break me, and he took his best shot. But it just isn't happening.

I'm strong. Maybe not in the normal sense of the word... and maybe I do cave to his demands sometimes.

But he hasn't scared me off.

I'm not *broken*.

I close my books, turn off the light, and stretch out flat on the bed. It takes a long while for the energy to sap out of my muscles.

Sleep comes in small pieces, dragging me under and then waking me with a snap.

My mind swings from Isabella to Caleb, back and forth like a pendulum. I don't know why she's haunting my thoughts tonight, but I can't get the ghost out of my mind. I let her marinate in my head for a while: a girl I've never met, will never meet, and can't shake.

I wonder if she lived here. In this room.

Something taps my window.

I flinch, scrambling upright. I expect Caleb's face to be staring back at me. Instead, there's nothing except moonlight.

The tap comes again, harder, and I creep closer.

Three hours have passed. It's midnight.

And Caleb stands below my window. His arm winds back, and he tosses something toward me.

A little pebble hits the glass.

I jerk open the window, sticking my head out.

"Come for a midnight stroll with me," he says.

"Are you crazy?" I whisper-yell. "How?"

"You could sneak out the back door," he says. "Or climb down..."

I roll my eyes. "No."

He spreads his arms wide. "Come join me, Margo. Or I'll join *you*." The *again* is silent.

I swallow. One encounter at night is enough, thank you very much. Especially with Robert and Lenora just down the hall. They can probably hear our conversation.

"Five minutes." He sticks his hands in his pockets. He

wanders away, toward the street. His car is parked in front of a neighbor's house.

I grimace. He taught me how to do this, didn't he?

To do it or not.

Going back to bed—that would be the smart choice. Lock the window and the doors, hunker down. Avoid Caleb.

That would be letting him win, though. Past Margo would've let him come to her, just to prove that she didn't feel the magnetic fucking allure of Caleb Asher.

No. No more intimidation. No more being forced into doing things in fear of fucked-up consequences. I'm making the choice to see what he wants.

I pull my boots on, silently cursing my resolve. Going down to meet Caleb isn't giving in, right? His true victory would be if I *didn't*.

Him stealing into my room, pressing me into the mattress...

Stop thinking about it, I order myself.

I grab my jacket and creep down to the back door. It squeaks the faintest amount, but then I'm through, and it closes silently. Through the mudroom. Outside. No way am I going to climb down the trellis when I don't have to. If the door is locked when I get home, so be it.

A sensor light clicks on, illuminating the backyard, and I freeze. The light catches the first snow of the season falling around it.

They could think it's anything, I reason. A raccoon, an owl.

Not their foster daughter.

I edge along the house, keeping to the shadows, until I spot Caleb.

He smirks at me, lifting himself off the hood of his car.

"What do you want?" I demand.

His smirk widens. "Couldn't resist, huh?"

"I'd prefer you not be in my room," I answer. "Although am I right to think you were there earlier?"

"You were busy," he replies. "I got tired of waiting."

He doesn't look any the worse for wear, unfortunately. Full lips and eyes that pierce through me. He's handsome. Devastatingly so.

No doubt his looks help his devilish agenda.

"For what I have planned, your room wouldn't have sufficed."

I swallow. It sounds ominous, and I realize how stupid I am to have come out here.

He pulls his hand out of his pocket and tosses something to me. I catch it on reflex, then glance down at the keys in my hand.

"What is this?"

"Car keys," he says, like it's obvious.

I mean, it *is* obvious that they're his car keys. But why he would give them to me is anyone's guess. I'm tempted to chuck them into the bushes behind us. That'd serve him right.

"Why?" I ask.

"Just get in the car, Margo." He circles the car and slides into it without preamble.

Into the passenger seat.

I shake my head. He can't be serious. A heavy feeling comes over my limbs, making it hard to open the driver's door and lower myself into the car.

"Adjust the seat."

When I don't move, he leans over me and does it for me; a little button on the side slides the seat forward and up. His head is even with my breasts, but he doesn't even glance at them.

"Put your foot on the brake and press this button." He's still close, his head tilted so he can meet my eyes. He takes the key fob from my hand and drops it into the cup holder.

I try not to inhale. The car smells like his cologne—the same scent in my bed. It's familiar and distant at the same time. It carves a hollow space in my chest where my heart should be.

He sits back, watching me like this is just another fucking game.

"Why?" I ask.

"Because it's cold out, and if we're just going to sit here, I'd like to be warm." He shrugs. "Your choice."

That didn't answer anything. I put my foot on the left pedal and press the button.

His hand snakes out, covering mine. "No need to hold it there. Gentle with this baby."

I release the pressure, and the engine catches with a purr. Heat pours from the vents.

"A nighttime driving lesson," I murmur. "Probably not the greatest place to start."

He lifts his shoulder. "Even if we don't go anywhere, I figured you'd be more comfortable in the driver's seat."

I keep my eyes on the dash. "Why?"

"Because you're in control."

A secret admission.

I tighten my grip. It's confusing—one minute he's brash, angry, spiteful. And the next he's trying to get me to kiss him back and telling me I'm killing him, and giving me control...

Which version of Caleb is the truth?

"I can't—" I grab the door handle. I need to get out of

here and sort through my feelings on my own. Away from his influence.

"I'll tell you anything you want to know," he says. "But only tonight. Only if you stay."

I twist toward him, shaking my head. "There's always a catch."

His gaze remains solemn. "No catch. Not tonight."

I drop my hand into my lap and lean back, getting comfortable. I remind myself that this is my choice—*even if it isn't*—and I can go back inside at any moment.

"Why did you mess with my previous foster homes?"

"I didn't want you to be happy." He appraises me. "When did you find out about...?"

"Well, Claire recognized you from the foster house we were at together, although she didn't realize. And I figured you had to be behind some of the others."

"All of the others," he replies. "Minus the one where the guy hit you. I didn't get a chance to report him before you were out of there."

I shudder. I was thirteen, then. He's been following me for that long?

Longer.

I roll my head to the side and look at him. Am I expecting to see something different? It's no surprise that he's already watching me. I don't think he's taken his eyes off of me.

"Why?"

"Because I haven't been happy since you told."

"Since I *told*? Told what?"

"Careful, Margo," he murmurs. "I'll tell you if you want to know. But there are some things you probably aren't ready to hear."

I press my lips together. "Was there a field of tall grass that we used to go play in?"

"Not that I remember. Just the park. Why?"

"I had a dream," I say. "You and my mom were arguing. Maybe it wasn't you, and it was your dad. It looked like you, though, but older. Mom got so mad, she threw a glass."

"You were hiding outside."

I blink at him. "That was real?"

"Yes. They argued sometimes. Chefs are known to have hot tempers... and my dad had one, too." His expression darkens. "Not always, mind you. I think he was good to me. But if the right button was pushed..."

I take a breath.

"What else happened in the dream?" His fingers twitch on his thigh.

"Mom came into my room and shook me."

He nods like that, too, is normal. Or *real*. "She held in a lot of anger until she couldn't."

"Because of something I did?"

Caleb's lips part in slow motion, and I regret asking. He already gave me the warning that he would answer any question.

I lunge across the seat, slapping my hand over his lips. "Don't answer. I don't want to know."

His lips move against my palm, and his eyes crease. A smile. Even if I can't see it, I know it's devious. He's a wicked boy, playing wicked games with my heart.

Slowly, I remove my hand. I brush my thumb along his lower lip, and his smile fades. He doesn't come toward me like he might've before. Something's changed between us in just a few days.

"Kiss me."

I shake my head. There are more questions, but right

now, every beat of my heart is screaming at me to lean forward and touch him more. And every ounce of my brain begs me to run away.

The heart can only win so many times.

I fling the door open and jump out, running back toward the house. It's easier to sneak in. I haven't been gone long enough for them to come down and lock me out. I kick off my shoes and shed my jacket in the mudroom, then grab a glass of water—a plausible excuse if I've ever heard one.

And it's a good thing, too, because Robert appears at the top of the stairs.

"Everything okay?" he asks.

I nod, plastering on a smile to hide my alarm.

"Yeah, I just woke up with a dry throat." I lift the glass as evidence.

"Okay, honey." He ambles away.

Back in my room, I scan it and close the door. Would I put it past Caleb to come in? Not in the slightest.

I cross to the window. His car is still there, idling. But as I watch, it pulls out onto the street and speeds away. I exhale and close my curtains, falling back into bed.

I can't let Caleb suck me back to him.

Chapter 16
Margo

The rest of the week is uneventful. There's not much happening at school. Football has moved almost exclusively to away games, and the hockey team is traveling this weekend, too.

The snow stuck to the ground, leaving an inch or two for a full day before melting away with the rain.

Caleb comes up to me when I'm at my locker on Friday. "Come to our scrimmage after school."

I snort. "No."

Once you get in the habit of standing up for yourself, it gets easier and easier to *keep* standing up for yourself. Not letting people run over you feels good. Great, even.

"We leave tomorrow." He ducks his head toward me. "Half the school travels to the away games, but the half that *doesn't,* goes to the scrimmage. And since you seem determined to stay here..."

"I've never heard of that being a thing. *Half* the school goes to the away games?"

He shrugs. "Ask anyone. They love hockey and they're rich. Obviously they don't mind driving their parents' sports cars a few hours away, dropping a thousand bucks on a hotel room, getting absolutely blasted at a random party they find, and then heading back the next day."

My gaze cuts to him. "What do you know about that?"

He smiles.

"You're joking." The idea of spending that much on a hotel, to see a silly sports team play a meaningless game, knots my stomach.

"So, the scrimmage," Caleb continues. "It's today after school. It's just our team divided into two, but still exciting."

"Good luck," I say absently. I grab the last book I need and slam the door shut.

"Wait—"

I pause and turn back around. "What?"

"Why are you telling *me* good luck?" He gets closer, his expression sharpening.

"Are you even playing?" It's fun to push his buttons. "I thought you were still suspended. So... good luck convincing your coach to let you play."

He stares, but I hurry away. I make it to class right before the bell rings, slipping into my seat. It's the one class I have with no one else. The teacher is talking to one of the students at the front of the room, so I open my messages with Riley.

ME

Caleb wants me to go to the scrimmage.

RILEY

Is he playing?

That's what I asked.

"Let's get started," the teacher calls.

RILEY

Too late.

I stuff my phone into my bag.

Now... well, nothing I can do about it. Just a little way to dig Caleb farther into the pit with his hockey coach. Maybe it's not a great time to be making an enemy of Caleb Asher, but I just can't resist.

After all, this is a drop in the bucket compared to what he did to me.

Nothing happens the rest of the morning. I meet Riley at the doors to the library, and we eat in nervous silence.

Waiting for another shoe to drop.

We thought about targeting Amelie and Savannah, but I'm still unfortunately blanking. And Unknown has remained silent—for which I'm grateful.

The doors open, and footsteps approach.

Ian saunters toward us, a weird smile on his asshole face. "Caught you."

I scowl. "Caught us doing what? Eating lunch?"

"I knew you were up to something fishy. Coach is on a rampage."

Uh-oh.

"No one knows, yet," Ian adds. "I just happened to be passing by his office when he started cursing. Rage like that doesn't stay contained for long, though."

His gaze switches to Riley.

"Do you ever speak? Or just shoot withering looks everywhere?"

She glares at him.

He sighs and picks at his nails. "I admire the way you get under Caleb's skin so easily, Margo. It's the kind of move I wish I had more finesse in. Because you were buried in there, and when you left, you damn near ripped his heart out."

My mouth drops open.

"I don't think you understand how cruel a hurting boy can be," he adds. "And I'm not going to rehash everything, but let's just say, he was a feral animal until Eli, Liam, and Theo came along. Somehow, they managed to get him under control."

"They don't control him," I say. "They just..."

"They get it," Riley says. "Eli—"

"Oh, bore." Ian pretends to fall asleep. "Save the psychoanalysis for someone who cares. I just wanted to let you two know that whatever you're planning, it's too late to stop."

He leaves us to sit in silence.

"The people in this school are sick," Riley murmurs. "I thought I knew the extent of it, but I had no idea."

Right.

Suddenly, the library doors crash open again, and the hockey coach appears around the corner.

"You," he barks at me.

I jump.

"With me. Right now."

"I have to get to class..."

"I'll write you a fucking note."

I exchange a glance with Riley, then scramble to grab my bag and follow him. He doesn't go toward the athletic wing, though. We head into the cafeteria.

The bell rings, and students suddenly stream around us.

Okay, around *him*. I do my best to stay right behind him. Did he see right through the note Riley put on his desk? And now he's going to expel me.

Wait.

Can he expel me?

Maybe he's just going to find the principal...

We *pass* the principal, whose attention locks on to Coach, then jumps to me. "Ms. Wolfe?"

"She's with me," Coach snaps.

Not something I hear every day. And that rules out my immediate expel theory.

We get into the cafeteria, where the only lingering people happen to be the cheerleaders and the hockey team.

They all go quiet at our arrival. Although it has less to do with me and more to do with Coach.

"Asher!" Coach roars.

Everyone stops moving—except Caleb. His brow is furrowed on approach. It's the only indication that he's not sure what's happening.

Coach turns, and I trail after him. Caleb stalks behind me like a shadow. Down the hall, past students—including Riley, who stares at me with wide eyes. Into the athletic wing and right into Coach's office.

"Shut the door." He takes a seat behind his desk. "And sit down."

I hurry to one of the two chairs, perching on the edge of it. Caleb follows more slowly, shutting the door and dropping into the seat next to me. He kicks his legs out, then leans back. His arms fold over his chest.

Now is the time to act like my life depends on it—but there's no need to fake nerves. I'm so anxious, I might throw up.

"Not sure what this is about, Coach," he says.

I glare at him. "And you think I do?"

His eyes cut to me. "Well, you were chasing after him—"

"Quiet." Coach leans forward. "Do you know what I had on my desk today? Hmm?"

Caleb pauses. "No, sir."

Coach looks at me, and I shake my head quickly. It's a lie, but I'm hoping my sudden terror—*I wasn't supposed to be dragged into this*—masks it.

He throws a picture across the desk. Caleb grabs it before it slides off and hits the floor, taking one glance at it. He winces. He doesn't even show me—he just tears it in half, and then in half again.

"I got rid of this," Caleb says in a low voice. "Where—"

"A note," Coach says. He holds up the piece of paper that accompanied the picture. "I'll read this out loud, and you can tell me what sort of bullshit we're dealing with."

He clears his throat.

"Coach Marzden," he reads. "Your teams are held to a high standard. I, along with the rest of the school—faculty and parents included, I'm sure—find this admirable. We've watched the determination and focus of your football and hockey teams go to national championships because they avoid distractions.

"Parties. Girls. Drinking. You understand best of all how detrimental this is to our athletes.

"I'm disheartened to report that your star hockey player, Caleb Asher, has been seen indulging in all three of the aforementioned distractions. His scandalous fling with Margo Wolfe was even caught on camera, as seen by the evidence. This photo was passed around the school, right under the administration's noses.

"If this is what student leadership is, then I am ashamed to attend Emery-Rose and be represented by such monstrous boys. Get your team under control, Coach.

"Sincerely, Unknown."

Caleb scoffs. "They didn't even sign their name?"

I swallow. It sounds worse read out loud, my name coming out of Coach's mouth. The foul accusations...

"What do you have to say for yourself, Ms. Wolfe?"

I am going to pass out. My chest is tight, my mouth dry. I am pretty sure I'd rather face the principal and Ms. McCaw *and* the Bryans in a room together before I ever considered putting myself back in front of Coach Marzden.

Honesty is the best policy... right? Especially when it comes to lying.

"I've been harassed by someone via text messages for months. Their number showed up as Unknown. It seems fishy that this person would sign their name as Unknown, too..." I lift one shoulder, my gaze staying firmly on the desk.

"You've been getting *harassed?*" Caleb whispers beside me. "What the fuck, Margo?"

"Language," Coach snaps. "Show me."

I bite my lip and find the thread. I hand my phone over, and he scrolls through the messages. His scowl deepens.

"What happened with Ian?"

I jerk. "What?"

"They say, 'this is the only time I'll help you,' with a photo of you and Ian Fletcher."

"Um..."

Caleb's gaze is on me, too.

I suppose I dug myself into this hole. "Ian..."

"Beat her in the woods," Caleb finishes, not looking away from me. "And I found her."

I blink back tears. This, at least, I don't have to fake. Caleb's hand lands on my knee, squeezing slightly. I shift away and use my sleeve to catch the tears before they fall.

Coach grunts. I have the feeling he doesn't often deal with girls, much less crying ones.

"The note is a lie," Caleb says. "The photo—"

Caleb's coach sighs and slides a travel pack of tissues to me.

I grab one and blow my nose.

"This type of thing will not get you into Harvard," Coach says.

I go still.

Harvard? He's going to Harvard? Or—no, he didn't say he was going. Just that he wouldn't get in with this behavior. Shit, he wants to go to college in Massachusetts?

I don't know why that's unsettling. It shouldn't be.

He and I are *not* endgame. We are *not* going to end up living happily ever after with kids and a picture-perfect life. I've got trauma, he's got anger issues. Our past makes the water between us murky.

As soon as I turn eighteen, I'm out of here. That wasn't always the plan, but it sure as hell is now. Less than three months to go.

Caleb refutes his coach's words, though, with a shake of his head. "I don't party. I don't drink. And Margo—"

I glance at him. Margo, what? What lie is he going to spin now?

"We're dating," he finishes smoothly. "What happens outside of that is our business."

Coach Marzden appraises us, and it's hard not to squirm.

"Could've sworn I heard a rumor that you two broke up."

Caleb raises his eyebrows.

I take a breath.

"We did break up, sir." I stand, straightening my skirt. "I've told him repeatedly, and he doesn't get it. Frankly, he borders on stalkerish sometimes."

Coach's mouth drops open.

I slide my phone back into my bag and stride out of the office. The door sounds with a solid *click* behind me, and I check just to make sure Caleb didn't chase after me.

The situation didn't unfold the way I imagined, but I still accomplished something. Still bit away at his coach's trust in him, just like he's been doing to me for years with my foster family.

Will Caleb believe that this mystery stalker is the one who sent the note? If he doesn't, I'm afraid I might be on the receiving end of Caleb's anger once again.

Chapter 17
Caleb

"What am I going to do with you?" Coach asks.

I make a face. "I wasn't lying. We're dating. She just doesn't want to see reason."

Every fiber of my being screams, *She's mine!* It isn't my fault she doesn't see it. That she doesn't agree. She eventually will. And I can't even be mad that she's finally showing a spine.

Not such a little lamb after all.

No, Margo's becoming a wolf, and damn, that turns me on. Even if it's at my expense.

I'm a sick fucker, thinking about Margo while Coach is glaring at me. I think he realizes that, because his face contorts.

"Do I strip you of the captaincy altogether?"

I focus.

"Maybe call your mother?"

He's fishing for a punishment that will hurt the most.

"Your uncle would probably have something to say," Coach says.

He's only saying that because he doesn't know that of all

of us, the true monster is Uncle David. Not my mother. Not holding their aspirations of which fucking college I should go to over my head.

I sigh. "Coach..."

"You're going to make me the list of colleges that you're applying to, and I'll have a chat with your uncle about your behavior. You're coming off the rails, son."

My body already hurts at the thought of that.

I stand. "That it?"

He stands, too. "The list by the end of next week, or you're off the team."

My eyes widen. "What?"

"You heard me. I'm sure the guys will be able to pick up the slack."

I bite the inside of my cheek. "You got it."

"I don't want to see your face until next week."

That means no scrimmage.

I stare at him, waiting for the punch line, but his face remains stoic. He's dead serious. He points to the door, and his dismissal is clear.

My whole body gets hot. I storm out without looking back, doing my best to control my fury. Everything is slipping out of my control.

I'm stacking up offenses against my uncle. Missing dinner, talking back, failing to rein in Margo's mom, and now this. He already keeps track of my hockey. He encouraged me to play a sport, to go full throttle. Threatened it, in fact.

He said I had to be the best, or I may as well not play at all.

The bell rings. That whole thing, and I missed sixth period entirely. If I was a normal student, I'd let my anger show. Maybe kick a locker, punch someone. I'd love to punch Ian in the throat just for existing. But since I'm me, I have eyes on me at all times. And if I were to break... well, that would be worse than anything I just endured.

Students automatically move out of my path, which makes me feel only slightly better. They still respect me, even if I've been missing games. I thought my suspension was coming to an end... and now this.

Let's not forget Margo dropping the bomb of someone harassing her. A blocked number threatening her.

I head toward Mr. Bryan's class. Margo will probably avoid me, right? Just because she has a spine doesn't mean she's had any practice using it yet. And that interaction with Coach probably seeped all her courage from her skin.

I stop dead.

If I go into that class and she doesn't so much as fucking look at me, I'm going to lose it.

"Caleb?"

I spin around. Margo is the *last* person I expect to see standing in the middle of the now empty hallway.

"Are you okay?"

Is she fucking for real? "Just dandy."

She moves around me, and I follow. Again. I can't help it; she may as well have me leashed and collared.

"You didn't tell me you were being harassed," I say.

She glances back. "Because I thought it might be you."

"What convinced you it wasn't?"

"Nothing," she says. "It could still be you."

I grunt. "It isn't."

She stops suddenly and shoves me against a wall. My breath catches in my throat, my hand automatically wrapping around her wrist and keeping her palm pressed to my chest.

Damn, that was sexy.

"Savannah texted you the photo of Ian and me," she says. "True or false?"

I narrow my eyes. "True."

"Unknown sent me the same picture." She bites her lip. "Does this Unknown person think we wouldn't talk about it? Or brush it off as coincidence?"

"I can't help you."

Amelie had said Sav texted it to her to get a rise out of her about Ian. Which clearly didn't work... because at the lack of response, Sav texted it to me.

But where she got it, I don't know.

Margo leans into me, rising on her toes to meet my gaze. "Why not?"

I lift my hand, wrapping it around a lock of her hair. "You're beautiful when you're mad."

She frowns. "I'm not."

"You are."

Her hair slips through my fingers. I touch her neck, and a slight shiver runs down her body. I doubt she even notices. But she's letting me brush my fingers down her shoulder and back up.

I cup the nape of her neck, and she exhales.

My chest aches.

I lean down, stopping just before my lips brush hers.

"You wrote the note," I whisper.

She tries to jerk away, but I hold her fast. I might be up against the wall, but we've traded control. It didn't occur to me until right this second. The hidden smugness—she *wanted* me to get reamed out, to get in trouble.

The pieces fall into place.

"You wrote it hoping to get back at me, didn't you? You wanted to pin it on the person texting you because it's the most believable lie." I lick my lips, and my tongue touches hers, too.

Her whole body hitches.

"I did," she says. "I wanted you to feel—"

"The pain you felt?" My grip on her neck tightens. "Newsflash, little wolf. I've been carrying this feeling around since I was ten. And you just—"

"I know. I *forgot*. You blame me for that, but I can't help it." She's fierce, even now, as tears roll down her cheeks. From furious to heartbroken in an instant. "I don't want to be blind anymore. I want answers."

"I know." I reach up with my other hand, catching tears on my thumb. I doubt she knew they were falling.

When she tries to pull away, I let her go. She takes a few quick steps back. Her eyes are wide, like she can't believe we actually had a conversation. I gave her answers. She gave them back.

Maybe not in the way either of us was expecting, but...

The bell rings, shattering my thoughts. The late bell for our final class of the day.

Poor Margo flinches again, then reaches for my hand. "We're going to be late."

She tows me down the hall and up the endless stairs to Robert's class. We duck inside, and Robert stops talking mid-sentence.

"Margo. Caleb," he says in a low voice. "You're late."

"Sorry," she says, releasing my hand. "Won't happen again."

He shakes his head but motions for us to take our seats. There are only two spots left, and they're not close to each other. If we'd gotten here on time, I might've been able to switch. As it is, her foster dad is glaring at me like I just ate his pet.

We make it through class unscathed, and I catch Margo in the hallway.

"Don't go to the scrimmage," I tell her.

"Didn't you invite me?" she asks. "Or do you not..."

"Coach told me not to go. So."

She sighs. "Good, because the thought of it sounded miserable."

I tilt my head. "We'll do something else instead."

"I need to go home first." She hurries away from me without looking back.

Home, huh?

I frown.

ME

Coach banned me from practice. Got fucked over.

THEO

??

LIAM

What'd you do?

Nothing. Just some bullshit. I'll be back to practice on Monday.

ELI

Me, too. I'll be back tomorrow.

I breathe a sigh of relief. It's been a little weird having Eli's entire house to myself. He went to Chicago with his parents. I contemplated throwing a party just to cure my nightly boredom, but I didn't want to deal with the clean-up and aftermath.

Once we get to their house, I kick off my shoes and head to the basement.

I make it halfway across the room when something hits me from behind.

My legs buckle, and I go down, barely avoiding slamming my head into the floor. A heavy weight presses on my spine, and a hand grips the back of my head.

"You little shit," my uncle breathes. "Can you do anything right lately?"

I exhale. "Uncle—"

"Shut. Up."

His knee digs between my shoulder blades, and I freeze.

"Here's how this is going to go. You're going to pack a bag and stay at my house for the weekend. We're going to work on your fucking respect."

I stay silent.

He gets off me. "Up."

I do as he says, moving slowly. I climb to my feet and pivot.

He looks at me like I'm worse than a cockroach. His nose wrinkles. His eyebrows pull down, and his lips twist. "You have five minutes."

And then he walks out.

Consequences.

I knew they were coming. I didn't expect them to all happen at once.

I grab a duffle bag I use for away games and shove clothes into it. My running shoes. A jacket and hat. It doesn't take me long, so I linger for a moment with one of my shirts in my hand. Margo wore it once, and it still smells faintly of her.

I thumb out a message to her.

Me: Something came up. I'll see you Monday.

I shut my phone off and leave it on the table, then jog up

the stairs and out the door. I lock it behind me, wondering only briefly at how my uncle was able to get in. I imagine the housekeeper let him in, or the Blacks gave him a key when I first came to live here.

Either way, I wish he couldn't find me so easily.

The car idles in the driveway. He never drives—just part of his fucking persona—and his chauffeur opens the back door for me. I hand him my bag and slide in, and he gently shuts the door behind me.

Uncle David scowls in my direction. "Were you raised in a barn, Caleb? Your disrespect has reached new heights."

"I—"

His backhand comes out of nowhere. My head whips to the side, the pain spreading from my cheek down my jaw. My face heats, but I don't move except to once again look forward. I watch him out of my peripherals.

He's breathing hard. He hasn't hit me in the face... which means he, too, is losing control. Either that, or he knows I won't be showing my face in public until the bruises heal.

I press my lips together, keeping my hands in my lap.

Only a few more months until I'm free of him. My birthday is in December, and then... no more chains holding me down. No more dealing with my family's bullshit. It's right around the corner.

"I was *hoping* Coach Marzden would be a good influence on you. Guide you the way we couldn't, since your mother was against our methods." His jaw tics. "It's only by your mother's grace that we didn't transfer you to Lion's Head after the *incident*."

"I'm sorry," I tell him, if only to ward off his anger for a little while.

Uncle grunts, pulling out his phone. It's clear enough. For now, the conversation is over.

But I'm in for one hell of a weekend.

Chapter 18
Margo

"Where's Lenora?" Riley asks.

She's sleeping over tonight, which is a first for me. She came over a little while ago with her own pillow and a bag slung over her shoulder, grinning like a fool. Robert welcomed her in, told her to make herself comfortable, and has so far left us alone in my room.

"There was some work emergency," I tell her. "They asked her to come in today, but I think she's coming back tonight."

"What does she do again?" Riley pulls books from her bag. Not textbooks—*romance novels*. I stare at them, but she doesn't seem to notice until she has four spread out around her.

"What?" she questions.

I just shake my head at her. "She's some sort of corporate liaison for merging companies. She explained it once, but it kind of went over my head. There's a lot of legal stuff she deals with, but also I think she acts like a therapist for the CEOs losing their jobs."

Or, as Robert once said, a rich adult's mother.

"Did she work with Caleb's dad's company?"

I blink. "Huh?"

"When it was bought out." Riley leans forward. "I was looking into it the other night. Was she the one who helped negotiate the Ashers' jobs?"

I don't even remember the company selling. "I don't really know what happened with that. When did it happen?"

She clears her throat, sitting up straighter. "I've done my research. Prepare to be blown away. Okay, so, Benjamin Asher was a big insurance and real estate mogul. He basically had a foothold in most of Rose Hill. His insurance company was bought out by Prize Industries, but they kept him on as a vice president of something or other after the merge. Some articles made it sound like a sympathy job. As if they didn't really want him around, and he didn't do shit, but they couldn't get rid of him."

"So Caleb's dad sold the company and negotiated to keep a well-paying job, on top of a payout?" I ask.

"You didn't know about that? I think it happened when you were still around."

"I don't remember my parents talking about it," I say faintly. I'm sure they must've discussed it. The Ashers would've rocketed from wealthy into billionaire status, right? A personal chef—ha, they could've hired four personal chefs.

"I don't know what to believe about the past or the present. It's all just so confusing." I rub my temples. "I keep having these dreams, and Caleb kind of inferred that one was actually a memory..."

My head hurts. Literally. The pulse of pain is right behind my eyes. All I want to do is climb into bed and pretend none of this is happening.

"What about your dad?" Riley asks.

I jerk back. "What about him?"

"I mean, your mom left, right? She was a drug addict. It's what people at school say."

"That's true," I admit.

"And your dad's in prison."

"What's your point?"

She holds up her hands in surrender, and I realize... I'm snapping at her.

"I'm sorry. It's a sensitive subject." I frown. "I know you're not asking to be cruel."

"What did he go for?" she asks. "There's a chance he didn't want to leave you."

I think back. I wasn't allowed to go to his trial back then, and I only remember snippets of what I picked up from my foster family watching the news. Even then, they'd turn it off if they realized I was there.

"He went to prison for something to do with drugs. My case worker said he was dealing and probably got my mom addicted."

Riley doesn't reply, but there's pity smeared across her face.

"Don't, please."

"It isn't—"

My glare stops her short.

She hangs her head. "I'm sorry. It's a shitty situation, and I don't know how you deal with it all without being a mess. I admire you for it, but as your best friend, I ache for you."

I soften. That is incredibly sweet of her.

I take her hand. "I'm sorry, too. I'm just used to pity... not sympathy. Or even worse, empathy." I smile.

She laughs. "Never pity."

"Thank you."

"Okay, so, what are these books about?"

She smiles and goes through the synopsis of each one. On the last book, she confesses she hasn't read it and reads the blurb on the back aloud. When she recites that the heroine has cancer, Riley's face goes carefully blank for a moment. She keeps reading, then clears her throat and sets it down.

"What was that?" I ask.

"What?"

"The book mentioned cancer, and you reacted weird."

She chews her lower lip. "Oh, that? Mom had it. But she's fine now. In remission." She forces a smile. "She has six-month checkups, but for a while it was a big thing."

I sit next to her. "The school knew?"

"I missed a lot of school my freshmen year. Someone found out and spread it around that Mom was going to die."

She pauses.

"Eli, actually."

I wince. "He told people...?"

"He wasn't very nice. But she didn't die, and that humiliating moment faded."

"Still," I say under my breath.

"I'm not feeling any of these books. How about a movie and popcorn?"

"Deal."

And that's just what we do. We finish off a carton of mint chocolate chip ice cream with Robert. Lenora comes home and joins us, murmuring how glad she was to finally be back, and catches the end of the rom-com.

Riley goes to the bathroom, and I step into my room. The curtains are closed, the window firmly shut.

Unexpected disappointment coasts through me, and then relief a moment later.

He had texted me that something came up. Don't go to the scrimmage game, he said, and then promised we'd do something fun. Then, his *something*.

His *see you Monday*.

Did he do that just so I would die of curiosity? Not knowing where he is or what he's doing tugs at my brain. It has since Friday afternoon. A full twenty-four hours of Caleb being off the radar.

ME

Are you okay?

A single text. Just to check.

He can't sneak in tonight, not with Riley sharing my bed. Unfortunately, this won't be the first time I've been let down by him *not* breaking into my room.

Stupid heart. Stupid childhood.

Stupid bracelet, glaring at me from my dresser.

I pick it up, intending to put it in my drawer. *Out of sight, out of mind*. But once it's in my hand, I can't let it go. He really did find someone to do a good job. The threads are protected by the cage. For the first time, I think of the irony.

Did he get it?

That we've imprisoned each other in a life sentence of heartache.

I keep the bracelet in my fist when Riley finishes in the bathroom, and we trade places. I carefully set it down to brush my teeth and wash my face, but it's right back in my grip again when I head to bed.

My heart and my mind are at war—to love him or to hate him. How can I possibly choose which one is right?

Chapter 19
Margo

Winter has arrived early, it seems. Not in snowfall—luckily what little we had melted over the weekend—but in windchill. The temperature has dropped into the teens, and the ground is frozen solid.

Lenora puts a hat on my head, patting my cheeks and smiling faintly. She opens her mouth to say something, then seems to think better of it.

Robert drives me today. Riley texted early—way too early—to say that her dad was giving her a ride, too. She didn't trust herself on the potential black ice. Robert gets to go straight to his classroom, while the students have been shuffled from the courtyard to the cafeteria before school starts. He drops me off there and waves goodbye with a wide smile.

Someone's feeling cheeky.

In the back, toward the windows, are the popular kids. Amelie is absent, but Savannah is there with her cheerleaders, leaning against one of the football player's arms. She's got a circle of girls and guys around her, acting like... like someone put a crown back on her head.

I search the room for a friendly face, but Riley hasn't arrived. And Caleb hasn't either. Not that I would call Caleb friendly, but whatever.

I'm still hunting for either of them by the time the bell rings.

Caleb doesn't show up for first period.

Between second and third I find Riley. She almost doesn't see me, walking by with her head down, so I grab her and tow her into the nearest stairwell.

"Hey! I missed you in the courtyard."

Riley winces. "Yeah, Dad was running late. He had to sign me in at the office. Eli is back, did you see?"

I did notice that, although I hadn't registered that as weird or noteworthy. "Savannah is acting like she did at the beginning of the year."

My best friend sighs. "I heard that Amelie is finishing the semester in France."

"It doesn't sound like a bad idea." I laugh. "Wonder if I can join her?"

She snorts. "Yeah, right."

"Have you seen Caleb? Or heard anything?"

She hesitates. "No."

She says it like a lie.

I stare at her for a minute, but I don't have time to question her. The bell is going to ring any moment, the only warning being the sudden emptying of the hallway.

"Okay... let me know if you do."

"I'll see you at lunch," she says, rushing away.

I hurry to my next class and keep my head down. I still expect Caleb to magically appear in the hallway, dodging students and sauntering up to me. I crane my neck, trying to see past taller students, but he's nowhere to be found.

And it's daunting.

Right before lunch, I spot Theo. I skid to a halt right in front of him.

"Little wolf," he greets me. His tone is always so even. Undaunting. He only lost it once—at that football game we went to at Lion's Head. But otherwise, he's stoic. His mask is impregnable.

"Where's Caleb?" I ask.

A muscle in his jaw jumps.

"Come on, Theo. Don't make me beg."

His eyes darken, and I involuntarily take a step back.

"Don't mistake our moment in the woods for kindness," he says. "And as for Caleb, it's none of your business. He's taking a sick day."

"A sick day," I repeat.

When has Caleb ever been sick? As a kid—never. Since then, I don't know. Something feels off about this. Something wrong. But why does everyone seem to know except for me?

Theo brushes past me. "Leave it alone, Margo."

If there's one thing I'm good at, it's *not* leaving something alone.

Riley waits for me outside the library, her foot tapping. "Eli invited us to sit with them," she says. "Caleb isn't here, so I figured—"

"That's fine." I speed past her. The encounter with Theo has me thinking... and plotting. This just solves the issue of getting in front of the rest of his friends individually. "What'd you bring?"

"Figured I'd get hot lunch today." Her cheeks flush red.

"Look at you, Riley Appleton." I elbow her. "Turning

into one of *them*. Does that have anything to do with Eli Black?"

"He might've offered to buy it. And who am I to mock hot lunch, when it means I don't have to eat another tuna fish sandwich made with 'love' from my dad?"

"Fair enough."

She's been griping about tuna for weeks. It's about time she's done something about it.

We go to the hockey table. Liam shuffles to the side and pats the seat next to him.

I sit, emptying my bagged lunch, while Riley slides in across from me. Eli already got their lunches, and the table fills in around us. Ignoring Theo's pursed expression, I turn to Liam. "Where's Caleb today?"

Liam coughs. "Um, sick."

"With what?"

"Huh?"

"A cold, the flu, pneumonia...?" I tap my chin. "There are just so many things, some more serious than others."

"Drop it, Margo," Theo snaps.

I raise my eyebrow. "Eli?"

He lifts his head.

"Why's Caleb out with a mysterious sickness?"

Riley groans. "This is why you didn't even hesitate—"

"You live with him, for God's sake," I continue.

It shouldn't bother me this much, but it's just another mystery that I don't want to deal with. I need answers.

He said he'd see me today.

When?

Why isn't he here?

When did I become a junkie? Addicted to Caleb—no better than my mother and her drugs—completely disregarding how bad he is for me.

It takes his *lack* of attention for me to realize it.

I'm such an idiot. My heart is winning the argument.

"I'm not sure he'd want me to tell you," Eli says. "And that's all you're getting out of me while he's laid up in bed—"

"His bed, I hope, and not a hospital?" I give Eli my best worried face.

"He wouldn't go to a hos—"

Theo punches Eli's shoulder. "You idiot."

I stand, smiling tightly. *Mission accomplished.* "Thanks, Eli. I'm glad *someone* is helpful."

And then... well, I don't really have a plan. I walk out of the cafeteria and keep going, straight outside. I don't have a car, but that can't stop me. I'll walk there if I have to. Come up with an excuse for Robert later—

"Wait," Riley calls, jogging up behind me.

I look at her.

"Why didn't you wait for me?" she asks.

"Didn't your dad drive you?"

"Yeah, but—"

"So, you don't have a car."

She rolls her eyes and holds up a set of keys. "I happen to know someone who does. And that person might not have realized I stole them out of his bag, so we should probably hurry."

Oh, shit. Okay.

We run across the lot to Eli's truck, and it feels a bit like we're breaking the law. We stay hunched as Riley fires it up and backs out of the spot, then guns it out of the parking lot.

"Do you want me to wait for you?" We're not even there yet.

My hands shake.

"Margo," she says. "Do you want me to wait for you?"

"Oh, um, no. Can you just tell Robert that I had an emergency? Not a serious one. Like, I got my period and bled through my skirt or something."

She exhales. "Yeah, sure. He'll see through it, but..."

"Maybe I'll be back sooner than expected." I've got about an hour before I would need to be in Robert's painting class. "I could call a taxi or bike."

Her expression pinches, but she pulls into Eli's driveway without a word. *Caleb's* driveway. I have to remind myself that he lives here—it's his home, too. Even if his real house is a few blocks away, filled with ghosts and dust.

She hits the button for the garage door. "You can get in that way. They usually leave the inner door unlocked. Good luck... I hope he's okay."

I grin at her to hide my sudden panic. I have a sick feeling in my gut that something is terribly wrong, and his friends' answers didn't set me at ease. I wouldn't be here if I could just ignore it and focus on schoolwork. But *no,* Caleb's stuck at the front of my mind like superglue.

More like crazy glue.

I jump out of the truck and shake out my arms. Riley waits until I open the door, then triggers the garage door to close behind me.

I walk through a large mudroom, then the kitchen. It's silent up here, and I kick off my shoes to move quietly through the house.

I get to the top of the basement stairs. There's a light on at the bottom, but everything else is in shadow. Television noises float up. I swallow, then take a deep breath.

Courage, Margo.

I descend.

He's on the bed. I can make out his shape in the dimly

lit room, but he doesn't react to my appearance. I steel myself and creep closer and closer. Blueish light from the TV is the only source of illumination, and it flickers constantly with a movie's action sequence.

My heart pounds against my ribs. I inch closer, until he's more than just a blob of shadow. He's on his stomach, his head turned away. Sleeping? He's not wearing a shirt, but it's hard to make out details in this light.

What happened to you?

I'm afraid to touch him, but I do it anyway. I put my hand on his shoulder, as gently as I can.

He reacts like I hoped he wouldn't.

He comes alive, twisting and grabbing my arm. He hauls me over him and pins me to the mattress between him and the wall. He grips my wrists with an iron hold.

"Caleb."

His eyes are open but unseeing, and his whole body is tense. Tremors run through him. He doesn't see *me*, just whatever nightmare he's trapped in.

"It's okay," I whisper. I rise and put my forehead to his. "Come back to me."

He said those same words to me. *Come back*. Earth to Margo.

Now it's him who needs to be pulled away from his nightmares.

I don't mind the harshness of his grip. I don't mind any of it. I breathe and wait, keeping my forehead to his.

"It's okay," I repeat. "It's just me."

Slowly, he crawls out of the darkness. He blinks rapidly, gaze moving from my lips to my nose to my eyes. "Margo. What are you doing here?"

I manage to smile. "I came to check on you."

He leans away, wincing. His hands slide off my wrists.

I stay where I am. Part of me is still in shock. That whole ordeal took a minute at most, but it feels like we were in that position for a lifetime.

"You're hurt."

He forces himself up, but he hobbles. His hand presses to his side, and he limps to the television. "You shouldn't be here."

"Why?"

He turns it off, and the room goes dark. I sense him moving past me, and the light in the bathroom comes on. He's already in it, the door swinging shut. Not all the way—a crack allows a slice of light to cross the basement.

I scramble out of bed. "Why shouldn't I be here, Caleb?"

"I wanted the Bryans to kick you out," he calls through the door.

I flinch, but he's not done.

"I wanted your life to be ruined. To make you fall in love just to squash it—your heart—like you did to me."

I don't believe it. For once, I can *hear* the liar in him. Every word that falls from his mouth is a goddamn lie. And enough is enough.

"You're mad that you want me." I shove the bathroom door open and stop dead.

Shirtless, yes.

Horribly, *horribly* bruised.

"Were you in a car accident?" I gasp.

He watches me, immobile, until I step forward. Only then does he step back. I keep coming, and he keeps retreating until he hits the counter. I don't stop until I'm right between his legs.

The need to catalog every injury swells in me.

A pair of black eyes. A bandage over his nose. Split lip,

swollen jaw. There are bruises around his throat and across his chest, but most is centered on his ribs and stomach. Fist-shaped bruises. Shapes that I can't comprehend.

While I was having a sleepover, he was...

"It wasn't a car accident, was it," I guess.

Oh God.

My hands flutter over him without touching. I pause over his heart and lower my palm. His heart is steady, while my pulse is out of control. One hand stays on his chest, and I let my other continue up. Over his throat, which bobs, to his jaw. I sweep my thumb across his lower lip. The cut has scabbed over, but that doesn't make it any better.

His eyes are dark blue, standing out even more against the purple-black bruises.

"You're mad that I *see* you," I whisper. "All of you. And I'm not backing down. I'm here because you can't get rid of me, even if you threaten me."

I'm in.

Two words and a mountain worth of clarity.

It's always been Caleb. It'll always *be* Caleb.

He hasn't moved, and his words from his car come back to me. He handed me control, and I still have it. His hands rest on the counter, supporting some of his weight. His eyes are on my face.

It's my decision.

"Touch me," I demand, then hesitate. "Unless you're in too much pain."

If anything, his eyes get darker. I suppress a shiver. His finger edges under the waistband of my uniform skirt, untucking my shirt. He slowly unbuttons it and tugs it wide open. And then he just... looks at me.

"Caleb."

He sighs. "You know what's fucked up?"

I raise my eyebrow.

"I don't want you to get hurt anymore—or get caught up in my mess."

"What happened?"

He shifts slightly, but it's enough to allow me a glance at his back in the mirror.

Oh no.

There are long welts crisscrossing his wide shoulder blades. The skin around each is angry red, and I can't imagine how painful it is.

No wonder he was sleeping on his stomach.

"Who did this?" I ask, keeping my voice level. I've never quite experienced the rage that I sometimes see on Caleb's face, but it's coming at me now, faster than a hurricane. My hands shake.

He lifts them, kissing my fingers. "You caring means a lot."

"Was it your dad?"

I can't stop thinking about the dream—the argument between my mom and his dad. The glass she threw. They had a temper, I've figured that much. Both of our parents.

"Margo..."

"Just tell me." I gnash my teeth. "I'm so sick of the bullsh—"

"My uncle," he blurts out. "Okay? Happy? He wasn't thrilled at my behavior recently and decided he needed to teach me a lesson. Something that wouldn't affect my game." He laughs, but it grates against my ears. "I'm pretty sure he cracked a fucking rib and briefly dislocated my knee, but that shouldn't stop me."

My eyes fill with tears. "I'm not *happy*."

"Don't cry for me, baby." He brushes his thumbs under my eyes. "I don't deserve those tears."

"I'm not crying." I'm absolutely lying, but he doesn't seem to mind.

His uncle did that to him—his uncle *beat* him. While I had a sleepover with Riley? While I complained about him going silent on me?

"Is that where you were this weekend? At his house—"

His hands go to my throat, then the back of my neck. He pulls me into his chest, injuries or no, and I press my lips together. His chest is hot under my cheek. I close my eyes, because this is what I wanted. This is what I asked for.

Touch me.

When his lips ghost along my neck, I shudder.

"You are crying," he whispers. He hugs me.

Caleb Asher is *hugging* me. He wraps around me like an octopus, infusing heat into my suddenly cold body. It's a little surreal—like the devil has shed a few layers, and he's not actually that bad. I've discovered a bigger monster—his uncle.

I'm dying to hug him back but afraid of hurting him. My hands twitch at my sides. Just when I think he might kiss me—he's got that *look*—he takes a step back.

"Can you wrap the..."

The welts.

I nod, and he tosses me a roll of bandages.

"Okay. Yeah, I can do this."

He snorts. "Good, because you're all I have."

My heart stops.

He didn't mean it like *that*, but my heart will not be convinced otherwise.

After some trial and error, I finally ask him to hold the starting point under his arm. I manage to set the gauze and wrap a long rope of bandages around his chest with his help, then clip it to stay.

"You should go home." He turns on the lamp next to his bed and slowly lowers himself onto the bed. He sits on the edge, pressing his palm to his ribs.

"What? Why?"

"You don't think I noticed you came here in the middle of the day?" He picks up his phone, taps out a message, then tosses it back down. "It's cute. You skipped school. But what would Robert say if you're not home when he gets back?"

"Wouldn't be the first time." I sit beside him. "Can't I just stay here?"

"I'm just imagining the wrath of your foster family." He shrugs. "On second thought, maybe you should stay."

"Now you're just being an ass."

"I already called you a car."

"This is what I get for trying to be nice."

"After you were so cruel?" He bumps my arm with his elbow. "Hot and cold, little wolf."

My cheeks heat.

"Fine." I can take his dismissal, especially masked as concern. "Is the car here?"

"Probably."

I stand and tuck my phone into my pocket.

"Hey, Margo?"

I turn back to him, quirking my lips.

"Might want to button your shirt."

My whole body catches on fire. Caleb's laughter chases me up the stairs. I close my shirt and tuck it back into my skirt.

Nothing even happened.

I mean, I just discovered Caleb's uncle is probably a sadist, and I'm way more head over heels for Caleb than I thought.

We can call that *nothing*, right?

Chapter 20
Caleb

Everything hurts. I barely made it home, sunglasses shielding the worst of my face in case I saw someone I knew. My uncle almost threatened to have me stay until I was presentable, but I begged off.

The Blacks are still out of town, handling a family emergency in Chicago. I didn't mention that Eli decided to come back early. I can't fathom why, besides maybe a certain junior girl who has his dick in a vise.

He didn't see me this morning, though. I called him on my way back to Rose Hill, but he was already heading to school. I hinted at my situation.

I didn't expect him to tell Margo.

Liam and Theo are the first in, turning on every damn light in the basement. I grimace and throw my shoe at them, not caring who it hits. Lucky me, I nail Liam in the chest.

He grunts, catching it before it drops.

"You had Margo freaked out," Liam announces. He does a double take, though, and lets the shoe fall from his grasp instead of throwing it back.

"I know," I say, ignoring the way both Theo and Liam are staring at me. "She showed up."

I can't say I'm mad about it. Not at her. It makes me actually *happy* that she came to me—a buzzing in my chest like a million wasps. But I am pissed at my friends for being so fucking transparent.

Eli shrugs. "She's a feisty one. Riley stole my car for the expedition."

"Margo interrogated all of us." Theo flops on the couch. "Guess who gave in?"

"Eli," Liam, Theo, and I all say at once.

I laugh, then groan in pain. I push myself up and relocate to the couch. My knee fucking *hurts*. I've never dislocated it before, but Uncle had a doctor in to set it. He blamed it on me. I can't even remember what he said to him, but a lot of cash changed hands.

In theory, my knee should be fine. But I can't put my full weight on it.

Eli follows me. "Look, man, she just was pouting, and then Riley was staring at me—"

"Softie," Liam says through a fake cough. "Do you wanna talk about it?"

I roll my eyes. "About the hell weekend? Not particularly."

"My parents will be back soon," Eli says. "This shit won't fly."

"It will until I'm eighteen. I want to see a single dime, I have to do what he says."

"That doesn't mean letting him treat you like a punching bag," Theo murmurs.

"It's in *your* name." Eli glares at me like this beating was *my* fault. And honestly, it kind of is. I instigate my uncle's behavior time and again. Push his buttons. Set fire to his carefully constructed plans with glee.

Every action has an equal and opposite reaction.

Consequence.

Punishment.

It isn't like he kept me locked in the basement, although I'm sure he's considered it. Between teaching me *lessons*, he paraded me in front of my aunt and mother.

Mother is thinner than normal, makeup creased under her eyes in an attempt to hide the dark circles. She picked at her food, much to Aunt Iris's disdain. I was surprised to even see Mother there. Usually she makes a quick appearance—a day, two—and then vanishes again. But maybe she's back for good while she tracks down Amber Wolfe.

Something I didn't even get a chance to ask her about.

Uncle David grilled me relentlessly, at any moment. I didn't give him anything except hoarse wheezes between punches that stole my breath.

"Dude." Eli waves his hand in front of my face.

I jerk back.

"Lost you for a second."

Come back to me. Margo often goes down the rabbit hole of memories, and her face always goes blank. I must've looked the same.

"December twenty-seventh," I say, shaking out my arms. My muscles scream, but I lean into the pain. Pain means I'm still alive. "I just have to make it until then."

It's not so long now.

I think that's what's making my uncle nervous.

"What was the ultimatum?" Theo asks.

I tilt my head. "Stay focused on hockey. Don't fuck up. Get straight A's, get into Harvard. Not a toe out of line."

And forget about Margo. I can't voice that part aloud. It doesn't matter anyway: it isn't happening.

Especially after her visit this afternoon.

If I wasn't half out of my mind on painkillers, I might've done more to make her stay. But we've turned over a new leaf. She's mine—she'll *always* be mine—but she has to come to me.

She needs to learn to walk on her own again. And walk *to me.* She already is. That buzzing in my chest returns. It's hard not to grab my phone, text her. Tell her to come back.

"Fuck," Liam grunts.

"It's fine. You bring home food?"

"We ordered pizza on the way," Eli tells me. "How do you—?"

"You're *not* about to ask how I feel," I interrupt. "I'd rather go back to my uncle's than answer that."

"Fine." Eli crosses his arms.

"Fine." I glare at him.

Still, I admit that the company is a nice change. I take my medication on time and eat as much pizza as I can, topping it off with ice-cold water that clears my head. They fill me in on everything that happened at school, the scrimmage on Friday, the party on Saturday that was a big fat bummer.

All in all, I didn't miss much.

Except Margo. She admitted—or close to it—she wished I had come to her over the weekend. And even if she didn't say it, I could see the hurt in her eyes.

We have a push-and-pull relationship. She shoves me away, I reel her back in. Always. Except now she's the one doing the reeling, and my heart thumps extra-hard at that. She's not getting rid of me, even if everyone wants to keep us apart.

Once my friends leave and Eli retreats to his room, I slip on a zip-up sweatshirt and shoes and grab my keys. I ignore the pain in my torso, the twinge in my knee climbing the stairs.

It doesn't take a rocket scientist to figure out where I'm going.

I park outside Margo's house and get out of the car. It's barely seven o'clock, so I stroll up to their front door. Who's going to be more upset by my presence—Lenora or Robert?

I ring the doorbell, tucking my hands in my pockets.

Lenora opens the door. Her eyes widen, and she goes to close the door in my face. I block it with my foot, trying not to smile. It's a mother's instinct—pure protection. Margo probably doesn't see it, but I do. They care about her. It's sweet.

My fucked-up face probably doesn't help matters.

"What do you want?" she asks. Her gaze goes to my foot blocking the door.

"To talk," I say. "To Margo."

She stares at me for a moment. "You hurt her. *Us*. Tried to come between our family."

"I did." I roll my shoulders back, letting the pain radiate down my spine. It keeps me from getting distracted. "And I'm sorry."

Her lips press into a thin line. "Tell me why I should let you in."

"Who is it?" Robert calls.

She glances back and tells him, "Caleb Asher."

She opens the door wider, revealing her husband.

He gapes. "What happened—? Are you okay?"

"Just got into a car accident," I lie. "It's why I missed school today. The airbags did a bit of damage."

"Caleb?"

They both turn. Margo stands behind them, bare feet, sweatpants, one of my t-shirts. When did she take that? The day after the masquerade ball?

A lead weight falls into my stomach.

"Let him in," she whispers.

Lenora frowns. "No—"

"You don't have to," Robert finishes. "It's unavoidable to see him at school, but here? This is your safe place."

Her eyes fill with tears. "I know you don't get it, but he..."

Push and pull.

"I regret it," I tell them. "It was none of my business. Just because I suspected, didn't mean I had to tell you. I did it to hurt Margo, not to help you."

Lenora swipes at her cheek. "It was heartbreaking. But not for us. We've done our best to put Isabella's death behind us. Our hearts broke for *Margo*, that she had—"

She shakes her head, looking back at Margo. I wonder if they've had this heart to heart before, or if I'm the catalyst.

Robert steps out of the way, waving me inside. "No use letting the heat out. We can have this conversation inside."

Lenora grudgingly moves aside, and I go straight to Margo. I cup her cheeks. Times like these, she wavers between fierce and ethereal. The girl I knew as a child lived up to her last name, but not now. I just need to pull her string until she unravels. Until she finds her center.

"Hold tight," I say under my breath, and then I turn toward Lenora and Robert. They're not going to like this. "I have something for you."

They watch me warily.

I take the folded note out of my pocket, handing it to Lenora. "It was in the back of a picture frame."

She shakes her head and doesn't take it.

My hand hangs in the air, the note pinched between my fingertips, while I wait for her to move. "It's a note from Isabella."

I ignore Margo's quiet exhale behind me.

Robert reaches out and snags it. "Give us a minute."

I nod, taking Margo's hand. I guide her away, up the stairs.

"What are you doing here?" she whispers. "I thought—"

I tap the last picture before her bedroom. The smiling Bryans. "While you were missing, I snuck up here. I was going to take this picture and see if I..." There's not a good way to explain this. "I was going to show it to your mother and see if she remembered Isabella."

Her gasp is a knife between my ribcage.

"You know where my mother is?"

I look at her. "I did."

Now I don't.

"Where is she?"

"She was at a motel." I herd her into her room, shutting the door behind us. "She's not anymore."

She goes straight to the window, holding herself. Is she searching for her mother out there? Wondering if she's watching, waiting for the right chance to take her back?

I get angrier by the second. Amber doesn't want Margo—far from it. She still holds resentment for her daughter. Gave her away when she was ten, before her dad even got arrested. She just woke up and decided, *I'm out.*

And now Margo thinks she's come for her?

"Your mother is a drug addict," I say. "She came for money and nothing else."

She flinches like I hit her.

"She comes back every so often to beg at the shoes of

the Asher family. Doesn't matter who. Once we find out she's in town, we do whatever we can to make her leave."

She presses her hand to the windowpane. "Stop it."

"I'm telling you the truth now, Margo. You asked for it, but I've been trying to save you from it."

I've been trying to get her to remember. But this particular instance? Watching Lenora and Robert shaken over a note from the past, and then Margo's instant grief at her mother being back in town?

Maybe I have a heart after all.

"What did the note say?" She glances over her shoulder at me. "I'm assuming you read it."

"She wanted her parents to forgive her."

Margo covers her mouth. "For what?"

"Drugs? Being a fuck-up? Does it matter?"

She goes quiet.

I step closer. "You want answers, don't you?"

"Sometimes I'm afraid of the answers I'll find," she admits. She inches toward me, too, until we meet in the middle of the room.

I lift her hand.

She's wearing the bracelet.

My heart screeches to a stop. I can't breathe. When did she do that? Before or after she left my house this afternoon?

"Why did you put it back on?"

"Because I won't let you go," she answers, meeting my gaze. "Okay? Go ahead and do terrible things, and I'll just hold on tighter. Sometimes I hate you, but I can't help myself. You're mine."

Triumph floods through me, plus something else. A white noise in my ears.

Goosebumps.

I lean down and do what I've wanted to since I saw her this afternoon, pinned under me. I grab the back of her head and touch my lips to hers. She pushes up into me and deepens the kiss. I nip her lower lip. She groans, sliding her hands up my arms. Her fingernails scrape the nape of my neck, into my hair. The only safe part of me.

She walks me toward her bed, and we both go down without tearing our lips away from each other. I hover over her. All the pain in the world couldn't deter me from this.

My dick hardens at her tongue stroking mine. I want to be inside her, foster parents be damned.

She lifts her hips, gasping into my mouth when she feels me. I shift, the head of my cock rubbing through our clothes. It's too damn good, and it isn't even the real thing. Her breathing changes, and I move against her. It takes all my willpower to stop myself from letting my dick take control. From tearing her sweatpants down and pounding into her.

I lean to one side and push my hand into her panties, sliding my finger through her wet folds. She arches into me, her head falling to the side. Her pussy squeezes around my fingers.

"My—"

"Hush," I whisper, my teeth grazing her earlobe. It's been too fucking long, but I'll have to wait a bit more. I work her higher, alternating between thrusting my fingers into her and stroking her clit with my thumb.

She tucks her face into my neck, her whole body shuddering as she comes. She bites my shoulder, her fingers digging into my biceps. And then it's over, and her body relaxes. She blinks up at me, frowning.

A fierce emotion goes through me—one that I'm not particularly familiar with—and it unnerves me. She's dug her way under my skin, buried herself in my bones.

She reaches up and grips my chin, forcing me to look at her.

"Don't do that," she says. "Don't hide."

I watch her face. "I'm not."

"You're trying to hide," she argues. "Don't."

I should've seen Margo's transformation coming. I broke a follower—the lamb nickname I mock her with—and she turned into a wolf.

Her phone buzzes, and fear flashes across her face when she scans the screen.

"Who is it?" I ask.

She hands it to me.

UNKNOWN

What will you do now that Caleb's out of the picture?

I stare down at the words, then slowly scroll through the rest of the messages that Coach looked through. They're taunts, every single one of them. She replied occasionally, but never to any degree of success. I didn't know they were *this* extreme.

She grabs the phone from me, reading the message again, then shuts off the screen.

"They seem to be operating on old information," she says slowly. "Someone who thinks you're going to leave me?"

I frown. "You're right."

Who would think that? Only someone who knew it would be in my family's best interests... and there are a few contenders there.

I trace her jawline.

"It could be Amelie," Margo says. "Or Savannah..."

I sit up, forcing her to move back. It *could* be either of

them. Both of their mothers are very much into gossip, and my aunt is notorious, too. One of my uncle's tirades about Margo Wolfe was at dinner. Would it be a stretch for her to have mentioned Margo to one of them?

"Have they threatened you? Physically?"

Her eyes widen. "No. Do you think they will?"

I have no idea.

"Tell me if the messages get worse. It could just be someone jealous at school, but if it isn't..." It could be someone from my family. I wouldn't put it past my mother or uncle to try to play mind games with her. But seeing the messages written out, those two drop on the suspect list.

It's too sporadic. Late at night and early in the morning. Midway through school. Whoever saw Ian taking Margo across the field had to be at school that day, had to send the picture to Savannah, who sent it to me...

Whoever's doing this is ruled by impulsivity.

"Margo? Caleb?" Lenora calls.

We scramble off the bed. She smooths it out and perches on the edge, and I move to the window, trying to cool my skin and calm my dick. I lick my fingers clean, and Margo gapes at me. Once they're wet with my spit, I shove them into my pockets.

Lenora opens the door and steps in, glancing at me before focusing on her foster daughter. "Maybe keep this door open when you have a boy up here, Margo?" She smiles, but it's shaky. "And Caleb..."

I straighten.

She blows out a breath. "Thank you for the note. Although I can't imagine how you found it."

"He was going to show my mother the picture," Margo blurts out. "To find out the truth. But then... he found that behind the picture frame."

Lenora comes in and sits beside Margo, wrapping her arm around her shoulder. "Honey, I'm so sorry. Robert and I talked, and we're afraid that our past with Isabella has affected our relationship."

"It has," I cut in.

Lenora glares at me.

"*But*, you should feel safe and secure in this house," she continues. "You're not going anywhere. I wanted to reiterate that to you."

Margo exhales. "Thank you."

"Now, it's late. And a school night. Caleb, I think it's time for you to head out." Lenora stands, brushing off invisible dust from her thighs. "Although I'm sorry to hear about your accident, and I hope you feel better."

"Of course, Mrs. Bryan. I'm already on the mend." I ignore Lenora's burning stare and catch Margo's hand, then press my lips to her knuckles.

Margo sucks in a breath, and it's the last sound I hold in my mind as I walk back to my car. Even through the pain in my back and the heaviness in my chest. She's worth it.

Chapter 21
Margo

Lenora smiles at me, dabbing at her eyes with a tissue. "You forgive him, don't you?"

"I don't know when it happened, but yeah. I think so."

"He looks at you how I always hoped someone would look at Isabella. But he hasn't always treated you well, has he?"

I sigh. "Our relationship is complicated. But I'm done letting him try to walk all over me."

"Robert and I just want to be a good example for you," she confesses. Her hand lands on my shoulder. "Of what a healthy, solid marriage is. We love each other, but we also respect each other."

"You are setting a good example." I force a smile.

Caleb only just left, but loneliness stretches out in front of me. Being dependent on him isn't what I had in mind when I told him I wasn't going anywhere.

Sometimes I think my feelings are too big to fit inside me.

She touches my cheek. "You should go to bed, honey. Get some rest."

It's easy to feel like an intruder in a foster home. There are kids who came before me and after me, and each one leaves their mark. In a way, it's comforting to know that I'm not the only one. That I won't *be* the only one.

But here, there's no echo of past children. There was only one foster child before me, and they aged out. Lenora and Robert never talk about them.

And Isabella isn't here anymore either. If this was her room, there's no sign of it. No holes in the walls from pinned-up posters, or spots of pulled paint from tape. No forgotten long strands of hair that don't match mine, or, *this used to be her bed.*

It was a true fresh start.

That should help me sleep, but it doesn't come easily. I toss and turn all night, wondering about the marks on Caleb's skin. The exact force used to cause them, but also the expression on his uncle's face as he enacted that violence.

When I do sleep, I have insane dreams.

My mom, half erased by time, stands at the foot of my bed. She eyes me with suspicion.

My dad in an orange jumpsuit, frowning at me.

I can't move. I'm trapped in the bed, unable to push away the blankets that are more like restraints.

Caleb's dad. He walks up to me and ruffles my hair. Crouches until we're eye level.

"Leave my son alone," he says, and it echoes.

Leave my son alone.

My son alone.

Son alone.

Alone.

My fingers sting. I lift them, examine them in the dim light. My nails are torn, and blood drips down my hands. A drop lands on my cheek, and I unfreeze.

I fall through the floor, into an office.

The social worker sits across from me, behind a desk. "You can't see him. He was arrested."

"B-but why?" I sob.

"He did something bad and now he's paying for it."

I don't ask what he did. I don't care. I just want my dad.

"Margo?"

I glance up.

"A new family is going to take you. We're going there now."

We dissolve into smoke.

A distant beeping sound drags me up. Up, up, out of the dream world and back into reality.

My eyes open, and I lie there for a second. I try to catch my breath. My heart races, my pulse thundering through my body. Whether it was a dream or broken memories, it's given me an idea. My dad holds the key. He's the only one who might talk to me, give me answers.

What he did and what *I* did... they must be related.

I grab my phone, texting Riley to come early, and then shuffle into the shower. The dream slips away, as they usually do, but I can't forget the sound of my own sobbing because they refused to let me see him.

That holds its own sort of trauma, doesn't it? Being taken out of my family, away from everything I knew, is one thing. But then never getting to see my father, who I loved with my whole heart, and being told he had done terrible things...

How would I ever trust again?

I'm still getting dressed when Riley knocks on my door and steps inside.

"What's the nine-one-one?"

I make sure the door is shut, then blurt out, "I had a weird dream."

She rolls her eyes. "This seems to be a trend."

"No—I think it was more than that. I was a kid sitting in my social worker's office, and she wouldn't let me see my dad. She wouldn't even tell me what he did."

She cocks her head. "I thought you said it was something drug related."

I nod. "Yeah. I thought the news said as much, but I also remember seeing Lydia at a later point, and she mentioned it, too. But why wouldn't the social worker just say that?"

"And Lydia is—?"

"Caleb's mom."

"I smell something fishy going on." She sits on my bed, pulling out her phone. After a few minutes of frantic typing and scrolling, she exhales. "He's been in prison since you were ten?"

"Yeah." I gnaw on my lower lip. It has me unsettled this morning.

"That's seven years," she mutters. "Was it a felony charge?"

I stare at her.

"I'm just searching general sentencing," she explains. "It's confusing without knowing what he was charged with. But unless he was found with a lot of drugs..."

"He was arrested in a park," I say. "He was with me."

"What about his lawyer?"

My eyes widen. "Oh fuck."

How the hell could I have forgotten?

"What?" She drops her phone and stares at me. "Margo?"

"You remember when we went to the city? Me and Caleb?"

"Yeah..."

My legs give out. My knees hit my rug, and Riley reaches out. Her hand on my shoulder steadies me. I grip her wrist and take a breath.

"We ran into a man—he was petrified to see Caleb... and then me. Caleb said he was my dad's lawyer. I can't believe I forgot."

"What the fuck," she whispers. "You're in the middle of a freaking conspiracy here. This lawyer recognized both of you?"

"Yeah."

"Margo." She eyes me. "You were both ten—and had maybe turned eleven—for the duration of the trial. And he immediately recognized Caleb?"

Shit, when she says it like that...

"What was his name?"

"Tobias. I don't know his last name." I cover my face. "What is going *on*?"

"I could probably find from the media coverage on your dad's trial.... Or not." She flashes me her screen, and what she had typed into the search bar: *Keith Wolfe trial.*

No search results.

"How is that possible?"

"I've heard that results can be removed from search engines. That would take a lot of time... or deep pockets. Maybe your social worker would know? Or Caleb?"

Ha. Caleb has turned over a new leaf in terms of opening up, but I'm still not one hundred percent sure he wouldn't lie. He lies so easily. Telling my foster parents that his injuries came from a car crash, for one.

"There's got to be another way. I'll get on one of the school computers at lunch and see if I can dig deeper." I slide on my shoes. "In the meantime, we just need to act normal."

"Right. Normal."

"Oh, and my mom is apparently in town."

Her jaw drops.

"She doesn't want to see me," I add.

"What?"

One thing about being a foster amidst 'normal' kids—they take for granted having parents. Maybe that isn't quite true—Eli's parents are always traveling, Riley's seems to have an interesting and unusual dynamic, and Caleb's family is insane. But a mom who rejects you outright? Goes so far as to give up parental rights?

It leaves a scar.

"She hates me," I tell her. "So... she's here for some other reason. Caleb told me last night, but he wouldn't elaborate. Or he didn't know."

"Wow." Riley wisely doesn't say anything else about it until we're in her car, armed with buttered toast from Robert. "I just can't imagine."

"Your parents are nice." I take a bite of toast. "It's easy for the alternative to be hard to swallow."

"Okay, so let's just make sure I have this right. Something weird happened in your past that you can't remember and no one will talk about. Your mom's back in town. We need to find your dad's lawyer. Caleb and you are back together—"

"Ish," I cut in.

"Back together-ish," Riley amends. "Whatever that means. You forgave him."

"Something like that."

"And what about your dad? Are you going to visit him?"

I flinch. "I don't know. Why would I?"

"Because from how your face gets weird when you talk about him—and I can count on one hand the number of times you've actually *mentioned* him—it sounds like you still..." She shrugs, pulling into the school's parking lot. "Like, I don't know. He was the good parent, wasn't he?"

"Forcibly taken away instead of choosing to leave me?" My mouth dries. "I guess. Except he *chose* to deal drugs. Or take drugs and get caught. However it happened. So, yeah. Even if it doesn't appear like he decided to leave, he did."

I can't think about this now.

"If the drug charge is true," Riley mutters.

"I'm going to the computer lab at lunch."

"What are we going to do about Savannah?" she asks. We get out of her car and head toward school. "I mean, she's basically in charge again since Amelie went back to France. And that probably means she's going to make a play for Caleb."

I whirl toward her. "*What?*"

Riley snorts. "You didn't see that coming? She wants everything Amelie had, which includes Caleb."

"Ah, fuck."

She elbows me. "But you and Caleb are back together-*ish.*"

We walk into the cafeteria and stop dead. Savannah is sitting as close as humanly possible next to Caleb. To his credit, he seems unamused. His black eyes look terrible under the harsh fluorescent lighting, but he's still devastatingly handsome.

His attention lands on me.

"Why isn't he moving away from her?"

"Maybe he's waiting for her to make a fool of herself." She snickers. "Or for you to do something about it."

I glance at Riley. "Unknown finally made a reappearance. Seemed under the impression that Caleb and I were done for."

"And last Savannah knew, you and Caleb were on the outs..."

Right.

I mean, I think rumors flew as soon as his coach practically dragged both of us into his office. I encountered him after that, but we only went to Robert's classroom. The art kids don't gossip much with the rest of the school, so that wouldn't have mattered.

Well. We didn't even sit together in that class, and then I went home instead of to his place.

Easy to misconstrue as *on the outs*.

Savannah stands, raising her arms above her head. Her uniform shirt stretches across her breasts. She's knotted it just above her belly button. Apparently Emery-Rose's dress code is slacking. Her skirt also seems to be about two sizes too small. It barely hides her underwear.

One of her manicured hands reaches out, grazing Caleb's face. He shakes his head and leans away from her, but it's too late.

I see red.

"I'm going to do something stupid," I warn Riley.

She only has time to raise her eyebrow, and then I'm off. I weave through the tables, stomping right up to Caleb. I'll have none of that bullshit with Savannah, Amelie, *anyone*.

"Hey." I catch Savannah's attention. Caleb's gaze hasn't left me, but I surprise her.

"Margo!" She puts her hand on Caleb's arm. "We were just—"

"Back off." I grab her by her wrist and fling it away.

"Excuse—"

"Yeah, excuse you," I snap.

I'm boiling over. She *touched* him like—like—

I'm about two seconds away from punching her in the face.

"Easy, little wolf." Caleb snags me around my waist and pulls me between his legs. His fingers stroke up and down my thigh casually, but it doesn't help ease the fire burning in me.

Savannah stares at us like we've grown three heads.

"He's mine," I reiterate.

I look her up and down slowly. All she did was want to replace Amelie. It shouldn't have surprised me that she took over Amelie's underhanded bitchiness, too.

Once a mean girl, always a mean girl.

Caleb kisses my temple. His lips twitch, and I'd bet he's barely hanging on to his passive expression. He's enjoying this, the bastard. He probably let Sav stay *just* close enough to get a rise out of me.

My ex-friend glares at me, but she seems to get the hint when Caleb's other hand winds around me. His arm fits snugly just under my breasts, locking me against his chest.

She slowly backs away, into her group of cheer friends. They're all staring at Caleb and me, but I don't give a fuck.

His fingers are inching higher along my bare skin, touching the hem of my skirt and moving back down.

I scowl over my shoulder. "What was that?"

He grins. "I like seeing your possessive side."

"If she so much as touches you—"

"No one will." He grips my chin when I try to look

away. "Hear this, Margo. I don't take your promise lightly. Our game is between you and me."

"That didn't stop you before," I whisper.

Something flashes across his face, but I don't recognize the emotion. "That was then. And while you were always mine..."

Yeah, I didn't want anything to do with his crazy ass. But now I do.

God help us.

He kisses my lips, then releases me. "Tell whoever your ride home is that I'm stealing you away after school."

I nod, unable to speak. Part of me still hates him, and I don't know how to grapple with the loathing that rises like bile in my throat. It comes out of nowhere.

I step away from him and clear my throat. "I'll see you later."

The rest of the day, I have the inexplicable urge to avoid him. Except, he's everywhere. Leaning over my chair in first period, his lips on my shoulder. Watching me move down the hall with Riley after second period, then third. Haunting my locker before fourth.

And I know, I just *know*, he'll be waiting for me before lunch. I duck out of the class five minutes early, claiming to have cramps—it shuts up the teacher nicely—and hide in the bathroom outside the computer lab until the bell rings.

I wait until it's silent, then tiptoe out. For a split second, I'm shocked that Caleb isn't leaning against the door, my plan foiled.

Nope. Empty hallway.

I open the door and slip inside, scurrying to the back row of computers. Time flies by as I turn on a computer and begin my search. I pull out my lunch, giving it a fraction of my attention.

I'm lost in the interwebs when the computer lab door opens, and I instinctively duck down.

"It's just me," Riley says, laughing. She closes the door behind her and drops into the chair next to me. "Why are you in here with the lights off?"

"I figured Caleb would come searching for me," I murmur. "Keep your voice down."

I picked the last row strategically. Even if Caleb were to pop in here—which he wouldn't—we're out of sight of the window. I'm not taking any chances.

"Did you find anything?"

I shake my head. "There are fourteen attorneys named Tobias who practice in New York City. I'm going through the law firm websites right now, trying to find their pictures."

Riley turns to the computer next to me. "Give me half, we can work through it until we have to go to class."

I grin, pushing the paper between us. "You start at the bottom?"

"Deal."

We work in silence. She has me glance at pictures when she finds them. By the time we get through the list, there are two who don't have headshots online.

I stare at the two highlighted names. Tobias Hutchins and Tobias E. Rodrigues.

"What now?" Riley whispers.

A shadow falls across the narrow vertical window on the door, and we both duck behind our screens. It disappears after a second. While there's no proof it's Caleb, I'd put money on it.

"He's kind of a stalker." Riley laughs.

"If that was even him." I know it was, though. After this morning, he probably assumed I would hide. Luckily for me, I still have tricks up my sleeve. Including hiding in places he'd never think to check.

Riley groans. "Did you eat, at least?"

"Yeah, I ate with one hand and Googled with the other. You?"

"Yep, I sat with Eli for a bit."

Well, *that's* a lie. There's no way she'd be able to get into the academic wing once she went to the cafeteria. Not until the bell rang. But her cheeks are flushed, and I'm not in the habit of exposing my best friend's secrets.

Even if it kills me.

We gather our things slowly. The bell is going to ring any moment.

I grab Riley's arm. "I need to get to New York City. It would be better to confront this lawyer face-to-face, don't you think?"

"Right." She swallows. "I'm guessing you don't want Caleb to find out?"

"Something like that."

She chuckles. "Okay. Great. Let's do this."

Chapter 22
Margo

Past

I tapped on Caleb's door. It swung open without resistance, revealing an empty room. His bed was made, the pillows smoothed. And no sign of the boy I was searching for.

Instead of calling out for him, I left the doorway and crept down the hall. Voices were coming from his parents' room. I paused, unsure for a split second, then continued on.

"You're being unreasonable," Mrs. Asher hissed.

I froze again.

"Me? I'm the unreasonable one?" A male voice... but not Caleb's dad. "This is insane, Lydia. You can't expect me to go along with this."

"I can, and I will," she snapped. "Lord knows we pay you enough."

"There isn't enough money in the world to help us if we get caught," he answered. "Something I'm sure you're well aware of."

She sighed. She often sighed at Caleb and me. We did ridiculous things just to get a sigh out of her—her whole body moved with it, an exaggerated slump. She was an actress in a former life, she often told us. Dramatics were etched into her soul.

"We've come too far to turn back." Her voice got louder, and the door opened.

With a start, I realized I was in the middle of the hall, about to be caught eavesdropping. I ran back to Caleb's room, pressing myself against the wall behind his door.

"Lydia, I don't think—"

"Quiet."

I held my breath.

Her footsteps came closer and closer to Caleb's room, slowing down. She was visible through the crack between the door and the wall. She paused, taking a step into the room and vanishing from my sight. Any second, the door would fly closed and my hiding spot would be revealed.

"Mom?" Caleb called.

Mrs. Asher retreated into the hallway. "Ah, there you are. Where have you been lurking?"

"I was getting a snack. Amber said it was okay."

Lydia hummed at the mention of my mom. "Fine."

"Nice to see you, kid," the man said.

He flashed by the crack in the door as he walked past Lydia. His footsteps hammered down the stairs. And then he was gone, and Lydia was retreating, too.

Caleb walked into the room and swung his door shut. He stared at me, frowning. "What are you doing?"

Fear wrapped around my throat. "Shh!"

"Were you hiding from Mom?"

"No!"

My first lie.

❄

Present

"Parker, Wheeler, and Smith. How can I help you?"

"Can I speak with Mr. Rodrigues?" I twirl a piece of my hair in an effort to keep calm.

"Are you a client?"

"It's regarding an old case," I say.

Riley sits across from me, her eyes wide.

"Name?"

"Margo—er, Appleton."

Riley hits me with the back of her hand. "Hey!"

"Hold, please," the receptionist says. There's a click, then classical music fills my ears.

"Sorry. She put me on hold."

"Naturally."

The music cuts out, and the receptionist says, "I'm transferring you over to Mr. Rodrigues's line now."

"Thanks—"

A click, and then more ringing.

"Tobias Rodrigues. How can I help you, Ms. Appleton?" His words come out in an impatient rush. It might be because this phone call isn't billable.

I grab the notebook Riley has on her lap and clear my throat. "I was wondering if you could help me. My friend's dad had a public defender about eight years ago, and all she can remember is the name Tobias—"

"No, no. I came from a prosecutor's office four years ago, and my law firm mainly handles civil cases."

Dad was tried in criminal court, and this guy wasn't even a defense attorney at that point.

"I'm sorry to have wasted your time. Thank you." I hang

up and drop the phone, falling back on the bed. "Well, that leaves... *one*. Not very good odds."

She makes a face. "One is all we need. You'll recognize him, right?"

"Yeah."

"Well, let's go to New York City then." She stands, pulling me up with her.

"Wait, now?"

Riley snorts. "I mean..."

My phone rings. Caleb's name flashes across my screen, and I promptly turn it facedown. I'm not avoiding him, per se... but we're investigating why he knows my dad's lawyer.

I don't want to lie to him, and I can't exactly tell the truth. What if he tries to stop me? He could. He has the power to stop me in my tracks, at least temporarily. Distract me. Or worse, lie to me. And so, we're avoiding. *Big time.*

"He's going to get suspicious," Riley says.

"I'll deal with it later."

Her eyebrow lifts. Almost as soon as my phone goes quiet, Riley's starts up.

She frowns. "Eli? Um, yeah, she's with me—"

I shake my head fast. "No, Riley—"

She hands me the phone, looking apologetic. "Caleb."

"Obviously." I take the phone and put it to my ear, announcing, "You're interrupting girl time."

"Girl time."

My breath hitches. I haven't heard that dangerous edge to Caleb's voice in a while.

And yet, I continue on. "Yep. Riley and I were enjoying the peace and quiet. Catching up after a long day at school—"

"Where were you at lunch?"

I flashback to the first time he asked me. Then, it was to embarrass me.

Let's play a game.

"Busy." I grind my teeth together. "Why?"

I can practically hear his shrug. "Let's say I care."

"That'd be a new one."

"You're on dangerous ground here, Margo."

I roll my eyes, turning away from Riley. If I push Caleb to his breaking point, I'll know where we stand. "Maybe I like dangerous ground."

It strikes me that I did something similar when we were kids. Showing up at his house in a white dress, asking him to marry me... The motive was the same. I push until he gives me a definite answer.

He's silent. Then, "Enjoy your girl time."

The line goes dead, and I blink down at it. He just hung up on me without an argument.

My pushing didn't work.

"Did your ploy backfire?" Riley laughs at my expression.

"He said to enjoy girl time." I hand her phone back, shaking my head. "I never know what to do with him."

"It sounds kind of menacing. Oh! I just had an idea."

"What?"

She grabs my hand and tows me downstairs, into Robert's study.

He looks up at us and smiles. "You seem a bit on the mischievous side, Riley. What's up?"

"My dad is taking me to the open house at NYU next weekend," she tells him.

My heart drops into my feet.

"So I was thinking that Margo should come with us. You know, get to tour a college." She glances back at me, ignoring the panic I'm sure is on my face. "She hasn't really spoken much about it, and deadlines are coming up for seniors."

"Riley." I slip my hand from hers and put some distance between us. "I'm not going to college."

Both of them pause.

This has been a reality since I was ten years old. Before then? I had a plan. A loose one, of course, but a plan nonetheless. Kid-Margo was a planner, but that side of me got destroyed by the foster system. Now, the best plan is no plan.

"What are you going to do after you graduate?" Robert leans forward on his desk and watches me closely.

I shrug, shifting. "Well, you're only obligated to keep me until I'm eighteen, which is coming up kind of fast. January twenty-eighth." I laugh nervously. "Maybe I'll be a waitress? They make good tips. There's housing for aged-out foster kids, like a transitional sort of thing. Ms. McCaw can help me with it."

Robert slowly closes his laptop. "No."

"Huh?" I blink at my foster dad.

"No, I'm sorry." He stands and brushes past me. In the hallway, he yells, "Len! Come here, please." And then he's back, and he glances at Riley expectantly.

"Right, er, okay. I'll see you later, Margo." She pats my shoulder and scurries out.

Robert and I stare at each other. He's scowling, but it's not directed at me, exactly. I mean, he's looking at me but he's not *angry* at me. By now, I've learned how to tell the difference.

Lenora hurries in and stops short at his expression. Then my worried one.

"What's wrong?" She reaches out and touches my cheek. "You're flushed. Are you okay?"

"She doesn't want to go to college," Robert bites out.

This is the first time I've seen him upset like this.

It scares me.

I shrink away from both of them, rubbing my arms. "So? It won't be your problem."

Lenora clucks her tongue and goes to one of the plush chairs in front of Robert's desk. "Let's start at the beginning. Sit down, honey. Both of you."

We do. Robert perches on the edge of his chair behind the desk, and I sink into the one next to Lenora. I guess it's about time we discuss my plans for the future.

"All I said was, once I'm out of the system, I'll apply for community housing and get a job." I pull my leg up to my chest, wrapping my arms around it. It's safer that way. "I don't have the money to put myself through college. They require the tax forms filled out ahead of time, so I guess I could take a few classes the following year... I turn eighteen on January twenty-eighth, and then I'm out."

"Unacceptable," Robert says. "First of all, you are bright. You have a future ahead of you that I refuse to see you throw away."

My skin feels too tight. I've been avoiding this since I got here—it's terrible timing to be placed with a new family so close to eighteen. I struggle to take a deep breath and have to flatten my hands on my thighs to stop them from shaking.

"I get it," I say softly. "You wanted the best for Isabella. But me? Once I leave, I have nothing. I'll be starting over—*again.*"

Lenora puts her hand on top of mine. "Don't leave, then."

The whole world screeches to a halt.

"What?"

She smiles at me, but it's tentative. "We want you to stay."

"Even when you age out," Robert adds. "And..."

"If you want to go to college, we're going to support you. We're not abandoning you the moment you have a birthday." Lenora reaches out and wipes a tear from my cheek.

I didn't even realize I was crying, but everything is blurry, and my heartrate is going too fast. I'm still shaking.

There's a very specific decimation of a child's hopes when they enter the foster system. The kid I used to be knew my parents would've taken me to visit colleges, helped me fill out the form, co-signed on a loan. They would've urged me to get a job to help fund it, maybe given me rides or taught me how to drive. It's not something I actively thought about, it was just there. Existing.

And then Mom abandoned ship and Dad was taken away.

One of the first foster homes I was placed in was horrific. Eight kids, severe rules, no freedom. No friendships. School and home. No dinner if we were bad. The older kids made lunches for the younger ones, tucked us into bed. Everything was spotless and orderly when Ms. McCaw dropped me off, but it was a mask.

I don't remember their names. I do remember telling on them as soon as she came to check on me. They said I was a worthless liar, and they didn't want *me* either.

Another home, and then another. Some were abrupt, only meant for short periods of time. Others were longer. Ms. McCaw was either my saving grace or the devil that I didn't want to see coming.

She represented change.

Caleb almost destroyed my relationship with the Bryans. And only a few weeks later, they're asking me to stay... *permanently*.

"I don't..." I wet my lips. I don't know what to say or how to react.

The plan since I was a kid was to just survive until eighteen. Then keep surviving, but on my own.

So, what now?

The fear that this could end surges. They could change their minds and send me away.

"We would never want to come between you and your father, Margo," Lenora says, "but we would adopt you if we could."

I shake my head. "It's only been a few months. How do you know? Why...?" *Why do you even want me?*

"You're smart and kind," Robert says. "And you fit in with us. You've had a hard life, but we see the good in you with every decision you make. We want to be your home, kiddo."

I can't tell if I'm on the verge of a panic attack or something worse. A heart attack?

But I squint at Robert, who has since lost all of his ire. Instead, his expression is soft. So I was right, earlier. He wasn't scowling at *me*—just what I believed to be true.

I look to Lenora. "What did you mean, come between me and my father? We don't have a relationship."

They exchange a glance. She raises her eyebrows at him, and he frowns.

"You could have a relationship with him if you want." Lenora holds up her hands. "We're not pushing this on you, Margo. I want to be very clear that this is your decision. But if you wanted to see him, we're supportive of it. You haven't seen him since the trial?"

"I wasn't allowed to go to the trial. The last time I saw him was at the park when he was arrested."

She covers her mouth. "Oh, hon."

Do I want to see him again?

Behind bars? Seven years older?

No. No, I thought I did, but I really, really don't.

I stand. "I'll think about it. And I really..." My throat closes. I swallow sharply, then continue hoarsely, "I really appreciate you both."

Robert stands, too. "Do you want to go to the NYU open house next weekend?"

It'd be an excuse to go into the city—then Riley and I wouldn't have to think of another reason. And as much as I hate to admit it, I'm curious. *College.* What would that even be like?

"I do." Even if I can't get in, or afford it, I can live in the pipe dream for a day.

"Great. It's settled, then. We'll all go."

My mouth drops open. "Us?"

"As a family." Lenora nods. "I went to NYU for graduate school. It'd be lovely to go back."

I grin. "So you'll know your way around? And the best place to get coffee?"

"Yes. Oh, this will be so much fun!" Lenora claps and jumps up. "I'm going to get dinner started."

"I have homework to finish," I say.

"Me, too," Robert adds, looking down at the stack of papers. "Who knew an art teacher would assign homework? How terrible of me."

We laugh, and Lenora hooks her arm around mine. She pulls me out of the room, leaving Robert to his silence.

Once I'm back upstairs, I grab my phone. Since the text from Unknown asking me what I'm going to do with

Caleb not interested in me anymore, there's been radio silence.

I only hope it lasts.

Chapter 23
Caleb

I climb out of my car and circle to the front hood. I lean against it and wait. It only takes a minute for the other car to arrive. It parks beside me, and Mother gets out. She comes toward me, spreading her arms, but I shake my head.

She sighs. She doesn't react to my black eyes because she was there. Her arms fall, and she follows my line of sight.

"I'm curious if you saw your life going in this direction from the beginning," I comment, staring at the diner across the lot. It's run-down, and only regulars venture in, and I'm sure some stay all day. It's the kind of diner that's open twenty-four hours. One of Beacon's only sources of entertainment in the middle of the night. Not that she's here in the middle of the night. I can't imagine the great Lydia Asher agreeing to such a thing.

But she *does* work here.

Her life has certainly changed.

"It really picks up for brunch on Sundays," she says. "Surely this isn't the reason you wanted to meet?"

"I'm mostly curious about why you let your brother-in-law run the show?"

She glances at me. "Your father wants it that way."

"What a fucking joke."

"David and Iris have done more for our family—"

My glare cuts her off. Honestly, I've had enough of them. Uncle David holds my entire life over my head. He interferes with hockey, he meddles at Emery-Rose, and he will not shut up about *college.*

I need space, and I need Mother and I to be on the same page. If she reports back to my uncle that I'm staying on track, then all will be well. For a little while, at least.

But first, I need answers.

"Do you know where Amber is?"

Margo's mother has been eluding me for too long, but not without help. Mine said she'd take over with the search, and then... radio silence.

She straightens her maroon uniform shirt. She's due to start her shift soon, but she tuts and examines her nails. All nervous actions meant to distract from the truth. "Rose Hill isn't good for the poor woman."

Which means she's more than likely seen Amber. Talked to her.

She cups my cheek, forcing me to meet her eyes. Mother looks rough: circles under her eyes barely concealed by makeup, loose skin hanging off her frame. She lost weight recently. It's been falling off slowly in the past seven years.

Guilt has a way of doing that.

"Tell Uncle David that I only have one college on my list, and Harvard isn't it."

She raises her eyebrow.

"I'll tell you when you tell me where Amber Wolfe is."

Her lips part, but no words come out. I step back, and her hand slips off my skin. It hovers in the air between us for a moment, then falls.

Chapter 24
Margo

My floorboard creaks.

I open my eyes just as someone presses down on top of me, a hand wrapping around my throat. Caleb doesn't squeeze. There's barely any force applied to my skin.

I'd recognize him even in the pitch-black. As it is, moonlight filters through my curtains, casting strange shadows across his face. We don't speak. He peels back my comforter, and I put my hands on his wrist. My fingertips catch his quick heartbeat.

He drags my shorts and panties down my legs. I kick them off, unable to look away from his face. It isn't just the shadows—there's darkness in him tonight. His fingers find my center, sliding into me.

"Soaked," he whispers.

It's an automatic response to him. Always.

"Did you enjoy your girl time?"

I don't answer. Can't, since he squeezes my throat for a second, then goes back to the gentle hold.

I release his wrist and go to his pants. I unbutton them

and shove them off his hips. He stands, removing them, then comes back. I cast a quick glance to the door. It's closed this time, at least. He doesn't climb back in bed like I expect. Instead, he pulls me to the edge of the bed by my thighs. I sit up and grasp his dick, stroking slowly. It twitches a bit under my touch.

Caleb releases a hiss of breath. He bats my hands away and lifts my legs. My ankles go on his shoulders, the backs of my legs pressed to his chest. He wraps his arm around my thighs, keeping my legs together from hip to knee, and plunges into me without warning. This new angle makes me arch off the bed. He goes deeper, hitting a new spot, and the way my legs are together creates even more friction.

He stares down at me, and my cheeks heat. It's dark, but I think he can see everything. He slams into me over and over again, our skin slapping together. It's good the door is shut—he's not being quiet.

It's also...

Not intimate.

Still. I let him continue, writhing below him, although any sign of orgasm remains out of reach. He eventually slows, and he loosens his hold on my thighs.

My legs fall open, and I grab him by the front of his shirt. I scoot backward and take him with me. He crawls over me, our bodies pressed impossibly close. And when he pushes into me again, we both shudder. I wrap my legs around him. My arms around his shoulders, keeping him against me.

He buries his face in my neck. At first just lingering there, but then I feel his tongue. His lips. His *teeth.*

I groan.

"Your plan failed." I slide my fingers into his hair,

tugging until he looks at me. "Lenora and Robert want to keep me."

I kiss his neck. He stays completely still except for the slight roll of his hips.

I move up his jaw, along the edge of his lips.

"*You* failed to get rid of me."

He lets my lips explore his cheek, his temple. Over his eyelids and nose.

I'm learning him all over again.

"I didn't want to get rid of you," he finally whispers back. "If you thought that was my goal, you haven't been paying attention."

We took his darkness and put it into a new shape.

Me.

I let my hand wander up inside his shirt, over his muscled abs, to the bandages still wrapped around his chest. I wish I knew why someone would do such a thing to him. Why family can be so cruel.

"Kiss me." An order issued softly from his mouth.

I lift my chin, aligning our lips. He tastes sweet, and he kisses me like he can't breathe without help. Sometimes I feel like that, too. Before him, I just had one lung and half a heart.

Now I'm complete.

His hips move again. His hand slips between us, finding my clit with ease. He knows how to play my body like an instrument, winding me tighter and tighter until I explode. His tongue dances with mine, our lips, his fingers working magic on my bundle of nerves.

It's all too much.

He swallows my moan, chasing it a second later with one of his own. I rake my nails along his scalp, and he pounds into me, faster and faster. He flicks my clit, and the sudden sharpness of it sends me over the edge.

He pulls out and flips me onto my back. I let out a huff, but then he's right there again, sliding inside me. He bear hugs me from behind. His teeth score my neck. His movements become more erratic, almost frantic, and he finally stills inside me.

My birth control is working overtime.

"That was overdue."

Once he's slipped free, I roll onto my side. He brushes my hair off my face.

"Are you staying?" I ask.

"Do you want me to?"

I nod slowly. Carefully.

"Then I'll stay," he replies.

"Robert and Lenora want to keep me," I say again. "Like... for real."

I glance up and find him watching me.

"We're going to NYU for an open house this weekend."

His smile is quick. Too quick? Or maybe I'm paranoid.

"New York University, huh?"

"I never allowed myself to think about going to college," I admit.

"Margo," he admonishes.

"What?"

"You're going to college," he informs me. "But what about... They're *keeping* you—does that mean they're adopting you?"

I frown and flop onto my back. "No. Dad still has custody."

"You don't think he'd forfeit his rights?" Caleb scowls. "He should've done that already."

"I don't know if I want him to." That would be the last

straw. Dad giving up on me—*willingly*, after everything else that's happened.

"He's in prison, Margo." His voice is hard. "Why do you still care about him?"

This is the first time we've talked about him, and all the animosity Caleb used to throw at me is now back in his voice. I barely suppress a shiver.

"Because he's my *dad*."

He grunts.

"Caleb?"

"Come here," he says instead.

I twist on to my side to face him again. His finger runs up my arm, over my shoulder and along my neck. His thumb brushes my pulse point. Slowly, he leans forward and kisses my forehead.

My heart flutters.

"Sleep." After a long moment, he adds, "We'll discuss the pitfalls of your father later."

Chapter 25
Caleb

Margo's phone buzzing wakes me out of a sound sleep.

My eyes snap open. Her cheek is pressed against my upper arm, hers slung across my chest. Her legs are tangled with mine. It must be early—there's just the barest amount of light coming through the window. Slowly, so I don't disturb her, I reach out and feel for her phone.

I was right about the early. It's barely five o'clock in the morning.

UNKNOWN

Do your foster parents know Caleb sneaks into your room at night?

That he fucks you while they sleep down the hall?

What the hell?

Another text comes through while I'm holding her phone.

There are things you need to know about the Asher family. Things only I can tell you. Do you know who you're letting into your bed?

Rage coils in my throat.

Who the *fuck* do they think they are?

ME

I will find you and put an end to this.

Silence.

I delete the whole thread. Margo doesn't need to see this kind of filth. This person is getting out of control, and I'm going to stop it. Her phone goes off again in my hand.

UNKNOWN

Hello, Caleb.

I stare at the text, then jump out of bed. Margo whimpers, rolling over into the space I leave behind, while I stare around her room. I'd understand if we were on the ground floor—at least that would explain a peeping Tom. But this?

Maybe a camera?

I tug on my boxers, glaring around the room, then set to work.

I move things. Lift baubles. I'm well aware that people make tiny cameras nowadays. It could be anywhere.

"Caleb?"

I glance behind me. "Shh."

"What are you doing?"

"You have another hour to sleep," I tell her, pushing books aside on the shelf. My eyes lock on to a ceramic mermaid. Raising it, I contemplate if it's actually heavier than it should be, or if I've officially gone crazy.

I look back at Margo. If she's asleep, I'll leave it alone.

She's not. She's risen on her elbow, hair a mess, and she watches me with wide eyes.

"Where did you get this?" I hold it up, making sure not to aim the face at her. One of the eyes is too shiny—like glass. And when I use her phone's flashlight, I can make out the tiniest little lens.

Shit.

"Where did you get this?" I repeat.

"I don't know."

She's not the mermaid type. Someone must've given it to her.

"I don't recognize it," she says. "Where'd you find it?"

"On your bookshelf." I breathe in through my nose and out through my mouth. Years of therapy didn't do shit—except teach me how to breathe like a lunatic. A *calm* lunatic. I'm going to find this stalker and beat the living shit out of him.

It has to be a guy. Watching her in her bedroom?

Watching her *change*? Or have sex?

Hell, *I* feel violated, and I'm only here in the dark.

She just stares at me, so I toss her the phone. She reads the single message, and her lips twist. I resume my inspection of the mermaid. It seems fully encased, which makes me think I'd have to break it open to get anywhere.

I grab one of my socks from the floor and drop the mermaid in, then twist and wrap the excess around until there's no way it can see out.

Does it have audio, too?

I stuff it into my bag and plant a kiss on her lips. "I'll see you at school."

Once I'm dressed, I go out the window, down the side of the house. I jog across the lawn and down the street to my car. I know someone who might be able to figure this out for me.

I leave the wrapped mermaid in my car and stay outside. I lean my hip on the closed car door to make the phone call.

"Bit early, Caleb."

"I found something weird," I tell him. "Mind if I stop over?"

Pause. Then, "Fine."

I hang up. He'd never voice the million questions he wants to ask over the phone. I drive in silence, not even playing music. Who knows what's inside that thing? Does it have GPS tracking?

The way I'm regarding it like a bomb is a little ridiculous. I blow out a slow breath and shake out my nerves.

Finally, I pull up to a mansion's front entrance. The gate swings open ahead of me, and I park off to the side.

Matt Bonner, Lion's Head's star hockey player, meets me at the front door. He's still in his sleep clothes, and he scowls at me.

"This—"

I hold up my hand, silencing him, and he waves me in. Once we're in his room, I hand him the sock.

He takes it from me, wrinkling his nose, and shakes out the mermaid.

His eyes light up, and he gets to work.

I lean against the wall, arms crossed, while he examines it. It takes a lot not to hover, but he'd probably punch me for it.

Matt and I became friends in middle school. His parents were going through a nasty divorce, and he was put at Emery-Rose's middle school for a year while custody agreements were sorted out. He fell in with me and Eli. We hadn't yet met Liam or Theo yet.

His dad owns a cyber security firm, and Matt either picked up the skill through genetics, osmosis, or some weird idea that he had to be good at computers to impress his dad. Who knows. Either way, it came in handy to track Margo down.

He was doing deep-dive searches while the rest of us were learning how to swim. How else was I supposed to find her?

Eventually Matt's parents' divorce finalized, and Matt's dad relocated to a new house. This one, actually. Unfortunately for Matt, the closest private school was Lion's Head. He transferred out the next year.

We hype up the rivalry when we're under a microscope, but we're still cool. Who gives a fuck if I can't stand his teammates or we crush them on the ice?

"It's just a camera," Matt tells me. "No audio. Where'd you find this?"

"Margo's room. How does it work?"

He swivels toward me. "That chick you were with at the football game."

"Yeah."

"Interesting. Weren't you dating Lucy's sister?"

He means Amelie. But he'd know Lucy better from Lion's Head.

"Absolutely not." I motion toward the figure in his hands. "Explain how it works."

"It connects to Wi-Fi periodically and sends the video it collected. I think it's motion activated, which is pretty standard, but it only records for a limited time to preserve life. Think like those doorbell cameras? You can tap into them and watch live, but it drains the battery. Unlike those doorbell ones, this doesn't have audio. So in theory, it would last a lot longer."

Freaking hell.

I rub my eyes. "Can you find out where it was sent? And what the last video was?"

"It has a setting in here to send a data dump once a day, then it erases. Pretty nifty, actually, but quite ordinary. You could find something similar in any tech shop in the city."

"How am I supposed to find out who's been *spying* on us?"

Matt shrugs. "Silver lining?"

I stare at him.

"The person would've had to connect it manually to their Wi-Fi. First, whoever put it there would obviously need the home's password to get on, and then they'd have to set up this figure to connect."

I mull that over. "It would be someone who had the house's Wi-Fi password."

"Yep."

"She has a small network of friends." I sigh, because I'm pretty sure I'm back to square one.

If Savannah or Amelie is Unknown, it would make sense that one of them would try to infiltrate Margo's life.

So... which one did it?

There's a sinking feeling in my chest. This has to end.

"Can you track it?" I ask him.

He shrugs. "Yeah, I can probably rig a virus in. They'll open the most recent video, and it will let me get into their computer."

"You're a fucking genius, man." I slap his back and stand. I've still got to go home before I can make it to school. "Let me know what I owe you."

"Undying gratitude," Matt replies. "I'll cash in a favor someday."

At this rate, we trade exclusively in favors. What he'll need in a day, a week, a year is anyone's guess. But the same could be said for me.

"Call me when you get answers."

And in the meantime, I'm going to set some fucking ground rules with the Emery-Rose student body.

Margo is off-limits.

Chapter 26
Margo

"We're here!" Riley yells, sprinting across the parking garage. She knocks into me, her arms squeezing around my back for a quick second. And then she jumps back, bouncing up and down. "This is a lot more imminent for you, Margo, but I'm so excited! If we like it, we can both go here, and I'll only be a year behind, but I think I could probably graduate in three years if I take extra classes, then we can graduate *together* and—"

"Whoa," I mumble. "I have to get in first."

Sometimes I forget that Riley is a year younger. Besides the fact that we share no classes together, she doesn't act like a junior. I've been pushing off the fact that she still has a full year left at Emery-Rose.

"It's going to be so lonely next year." She sighs. "I don't suppose you want to get held back?"

I snort.

We link arms and head toward the elevators. Her dad follows behind us with Len and Robert.

Another new development: Lenora asked me to call her

Len. Less formal, and apparently her friends and family call her that, too.

"Did you tell Caleb you were coming?" Riley asks.

"He was glad."

"Because he wants you to go to college."

I shrug. This last week has been... interesting, to say the least. Caleb finally told me why he was worried about the mermaid figurine. The fact that someone—Unknown—was spying on me creeps me out. Either he or I have done sweeps with this device he got that alerts you to transmitting devices. Like cameras or bugs... the audio kind.

He says he disposed of it, and I didn't need to worry. *Ha.* Of course I'm worried. Someone got it into my room. It's already too easy for him to scale the house and get in, so how hard would it be for someone else?

The suspect list is long.

And the scarier question: Why didn't I notice it? It was so small, but it was obviously out of place. I pay more attention now, cataloging everything on my bookshelves and desk, but it's getting overwhelming.

The rabbit hole I fell down...

People can hide cameras in *pens*.

Needless to say, I haven't got much sleep this week.

But today... *today*, we're in New York City, and we're going to take a tour of the NYU campus. Riley and I are going to sit in on a class while the adults go to a seminar on financial aid. And after that, we get to meet some professors, talk to current students, and then we need to pull off the ultimate trick: convince our parents to let us take off by ourselves for an hour.

It's better than sneaking away, we reasoned. Less risk.

We locate the admissions office, where a bunch of other high school students are gathered.

Lenora—*Len*—squeezes my shoulder. "Excited?"

"Terrified," I whisper.

After a tour that leaves me awestruck—the campus is huge—and an international law class, Riley and I find our families to get lunch.

On the quad, the Bryans are chatting with a man with an NYU lanyard around his neck.

Len grins at us. "Margo, this is one of my old college professors, Eric Marks."

"Old," Professor Marks says, shaking his head and trying not to smile. "You always knew how to make a guy feel good, Len. Pleasure to meet you, Margo."

I shake his hand, suddenly shy. "Hi."

"Your parents have been raving about you," he continues. "Grades are good. You're going to get involved in an extracurricular activity?"

"Yes," I agree, although I'm still stuck on *parents* and not *foster parents*.

"And the school newspaper," Riley inserts. "To cover the hockey team."

I bite my lip, but the professor just smiles.

"Riley Appleton," she introduces herself. "Currently a junior but eager to join your university, sir."

They shake hands.

He dips his head. "I appreciate the enthusiasm, young lady."

Riley's dad joins us. We finally break away from the professor, who wishes Riley and me good luck with our applications, and load plates at the outdoor buffet. There are clusters of chairs and tables scattered around, and we end up at a freshly vacant one.

"There's another seminar about housing," Riley's dad says. "We were hoping to attend that. While the school has some housing for freshmen, we'd like to be prepared in case there's a more reasonable option."

Riley turns to me. "Imagine, we could *live* together!"

Oh my God.

I offer her a weak smile. "Sounds great."

She doesn't notice any hesitancy, and the conversation sweeps away.

"You guys should go," I say to Robert. "Riley and I can keep busy for an hour. Maybe get a little taste for the city?"

Len and Robert exchange a glance.

"You want to go wander?" Robert confirms.

I nod.

"I rented an apartment for grad school," Len says. "But you're a lot younger, and we'd worry if you were completely on your own. So maybe we should check it out..."

I'll be honest—time moves slowly until the three of them depart for the housing seminar.

"We'll meet you here when you're done!" Riley calls after them. To me, she says, "I pulled up his office on my phone. It's only ten minutes from here."

My stomach erupts with butterflies. "What if he isn't there?"

"He will be. I made an appointment under a fake name."

Oh my God. I'm pretty sure that's against some law... or maybe it's an ethics thing.

We head down the street, following the map on Riley's phone.

This part of the city is different from Times Square. Less busy, more trees spaced evenly down the sidewalks. No glaring screens over our heads. Just regular storefronts and tall office buildings once we get out of the residential section.

Finally, we round a corner and stop in front of a large building. It's noisier here. Cabs and cars rush by on the street. Businessmen and women flood the streets. There's a smell of burning coming from the grates beneath our feet.

"Tenth floor," Riley says.

We go in. Unlike the office building Caleb and I went to, this one doesn't have much in the way of a lobby. Just a few rows of metal benches facing glass walls. No receptionist desk. We go to the elevators, then up.

Tobias Hutchins. I don't know if he's going to be the same man Caleb and I ran into, or if he'll recognize me. Maybe I can lie about who I am, get him to open up before I ask him about a seven-year-old case.

"Good afternoon," the receptionist greets us once we push through the frosted-glass doors to the law office. "Are you here for an appointment?"

"Yes. Under Amy Lawson."

I snort and quickly cover it with a cough. *Law*son? Really?

The receptionist eyes me with disdain.

"Margo?"

I spin toward the voice.

The lawyer.

Tobias.

Oh, shit. He's the right one. And he recognizes me. *Again.*

"Mr. Hutchins—"

"It's okay, Sandy. I've been expecting Ms. Wolfe." He looks... defeated. Maybe he was hoping I wasn't me. Wouldn't be the first time someone wished that. "Follow me, girls. It's best if we talk in private."

The receptionist makes a vague noise in the back of her throat.

Riley and I trail him down the hall. There are private offices and conference rooms, and then the hall opens into a bullpen. Some are empty, but the greater majority are occupied. On a weekend.

That's dedication.

He stops in front of an open door and waves us in. He has a view of the city. Not a corner office, but nothing to sneeze at. I figured he would be one of the ones in the center, fighting with his colleagues for elbow room. His name is on the glass door in gold lettering, the word *partner* just under it.

"The couch?" he directs, closing the door behind us. He busies himself with drawing a shade down over the door, giving us another layer of privacy—or secrecy.

There's a framed newspaper article on the wall from five years ago about Tobias's promotion to partner. It's surrounded by other accolades and family pictures. A bookshelf on one wall holds law books and plants. In the corner by the floor-to-ceiling window—one of them anyway—there's a cozy setup of two couches and two armchairs, a glass coffee table between them.

We take a seat on one of the couches, and Tobias relaxes into the armchair next to me. He crosses his legs. He seems the picture of ease, and it irks me.

"You know who I am," I say.

"You resemble your dad a bit." He nods. "And I figured you would track me down after I ran into you and Mr. Asher."

"How do you know Caleb?"

Now he fidgets. "Through the trial, of course. He was present, even if you weren't."

I sit up straighter. "I was kept away. But... He was at my dad's trial? Why?"

Tobias pauses. "Why wouldn't he? It involved his family—"

"Because my dad was dealing drugs while living there?"

He stares at me, his expression contemplative. "Right. What did they tell you?"

"He went away on drug charges. My social worker wouldn't let me go to the trial. I didn't get to see him again after he was arrested."

"I'm afraid that was your father's doing." Tobias's expression morphs into practiced sympathy. "He was adamant that you not see him like that."

I exchange a look with Riley. Would he have done that? Our last interaction was horrific. Wouldn't he have wanted to reassure his terrified daughter that everything was going to be okay?

"Can you walk us through the case?" Riley asks.

"It was a long time ago." He *sounds* apologetic, but he doesn't seem it. The sympathy is glued on his face like a mask. "Is there anything else I can help you with?"

"It was a long time ago," I echo. "But you know Caleb—and you keep calling him Mr. Asher. That's a lot of respect for someone you've known since he was ten."

He shakes his head. "Listen, Margo. These things happened in the past. It's best to just leave them buried."

"I refuse to accept that." There has to be more here.

He stands. "Unfortunately, I don't think I can give any suitable answers. Attorney-client privilege is a tricky thing to navigate."

"One last question." It's weird to be open about the desperation clawing at me. I need answers—I'll do anything to get answers. And Tobias Hutchins is my last hope.

He waves for me to continue.

"You were a public defender. And soon after that case,

you left that office to come here." I point to the framed newspaper clipping on the wall. "And you were made a partner in just two years? That's a little fast, isn't it?"

His face slowly turns red. "It's time for you to leave."

Riley takes my hand and squeezes. "We're going. Thanks for speaking with us."

He doesn't answer. His eyes follow us to the door, which Riley yanks open. We get the hell out of dodge and don't speak until we're on the street.

"That didn't answer anything." I groan. "He didn't give up any information about how he knew Caleb, or why he was afraid, or what happened with Dad's case."

"Except maybe..." Riley bites her lip. "I think it *does* prove something. It proves that he's involved. And not in a good way. Did you see the way he started fidgeting when you brought up Caleb? And he seemed surprised about your dad's charges."

She still hasn't been able to find anything about his trial.

Everything feels hopeless.

"Margo..."

I meet her eyes.

"I think you need to talk to your dad."

Chapter 27
Caleb

"Tell me again," I say evenly.

The receptionist and I stand in an abandoned floor of a high-rise. It's Sunday, mid-morning. I got the call from her two hours ago, because the only thing left on her desk was my phone number scrawled on a ripped piece of paper.

Only twenty-four hours ago, this floor was occupied by Tobias Hutchins' law firm.

And now it's empty.

"I arrived for work like I always do. I work Sundays to catch up on paperwork and get some extra hours. Mr. Hutchins never minded." She swallows. "I scanned my fob to get up the elevators since the building isn't open on Sundays. That's normal. But everything was dark. The door"—she's talking about the glass doors right off the elevator—"wouldn't open. I had to call maintenance, who let me in. I propped open the door just in case."

"And everything was cleared out?"

"Just like this. No one's been here. I saw the number on my desk and called you."

"Did you leave early yesterday?"

She nods. "He let everyone go after he had a drop-in visit after lunch."

Interesting.

"Who was the visitor?"

"The appointment was under Amy Lawson, but he didn't call her that."

I go still. "What did he call her?"

"I didn't catch a last name. But he called her Margo."

Fuck.

"Call this number," I tell the woman. I give her my uncle's business card. If there's one thing he's good at, it's cleaning up other people's mess. "He'll have you compensated for the trouble—but the details remain with me. Do you understand?"

"Y-yes."

"Speak a word of his last visit, and I'll strip away everything he gives you," I promise.

"I understand. Thank you, Mr. Asher."

I leave her standing in the middle of the bullpen. Forgotten cubicle dividers, desks. But no computers, no paperwork. Tobias Hutchins is officially spooked, and it all comes down to whatever Margo Wolfe said to him.

What are you up to, little lamb?

Chapter 28
Margo

Past

"Ready to go, kid?"

I raised my arms in the air, and Dad obliged me. He scooped me up, up, up, placing me on his shoulders. Mom said I was getting too big and I was going to break Dad's back one of these days. He told me to ignore her.

I was still his little girl. Always would be.

We approached the door, and I ducked, curling myself around his head. He tickled my foot, and I giggled into his hair. He carried me out of the school, past all the other kids waiting for the bus.

I loved the days Dad picked me up. It meant Mom was out, either with friends or on a supply run for Caleb's house. We got to do fun stuff. He played music in the car and sang along like a private concert.

He put me down beside his car and ruffled my hair. I fought the impulse to hug him before he opened my door and held out a hand to help me climb in.

"What's for dinner?" he asked when he sat behind the wheel. "Pizza?"

"Duh," I answered.

"Are you okay with Caleb joining us for dinner? His parents are having a party."

"Is that where Mommy is?"

He met my gaze in the mirror. "Yeah, she's catering it. It's gonna be a late night."

"Caleb likes pizza," I said quietly.

We grabbed the food on the way home, and I ran into my room to change out of the uniform. The front door opened and shut. Dad's and Caleb's voices drifted down the hall toward me.

It wasn't often that I was tempted to eavesdrop—barring that one time last week with Mrs. Asher and the mystery man—but any conversation between Dad and Caleb was worth its weight in gold.

Caleb idolized my dad. I didn't know why, and deep down, it irked me. He was *my* dad. Caleb had his own. But he was always asking him questions, hanging around when Mom wasn't here. He didn't like to be in our apartment if my mom was home, but my dad was another situation entirely.

"Where's Margo?" Caleb asked.

"Getting changed," Dad said. "How was school?"

"Fine. I caught Amelie and Ian kissing in the hallway. They both paid me five bucks to keep my mouth shut."

Dad chuckled. "You're going to be quite the businessman."

"They should pay for me to keep secrets," Caleb muttered. "Amelie says she's Margo's friend."

"Is she?"

"Well, she's not a very good one."

I stormed out into the living room with only one sock on. "She's a fine friend! You don't know what the hell you're talking about."

"Language, Margo," Dad commented.

"He insults my friend, but I have to watch my language?" I was so mad it hurt.

"*I'm* your friend," Caleb answered, balling his fists. "And she's not. Just watch, she's gonna turn into a mean girl, and when she does, I'll say *I told you so.*"

He stuck his tongue out at me.

Tears sprang into my eyes. "Stop it."

Dad stepped between us, pulling me into his side. "Enough, Caleb." He knelt in front of me. "Margo, kids can be mean at this age. Caleb, Amelie, the bullies… Take everything with a grain of salt."

Grain of salt. He explained that one to me last week. Be cautious about everything, he said. Don't just blindly believe everything you hear.

"How about you go put your other sock on and we'll eat this pizza."

He patted my head, and I rushed away. I batted at the tears, the anger diminishing the farther away I got.

Dad always knew how to make things better—even Caleb's harsh words or Mom's weird moods. He was my favorite. He carried me on his shoulders and made up bedtime stories, checked in my closet for the boogeyman. Never raised his voice. Not at me.

But he did yell at Mom…

Grain of salt. Maybe she deserved it.

Maybe she deserved everything that happened.

Present

I can't go into my room.

It's been over a week since Caleb found the camera, but this fear seemed to have crept up after we got back from NYU. Maybe it was that all three of us were out of the house on Saturday? It left it vulnerable. Last night, when we got back from the city, I forced myself to go in.

Today, not so much.

Robert and Lenora are out doing some errands, and I've been working up the courage to talk to Dad. I figured I could write him a letter or something. That's about as minimal contact as I can get.

I'm *angry* at him, but I didn't realize it until now.

Or rather, I had shoved it down until now. He went to prison on a drug charge. He put *drugs* ahead of his own child.

Who does that?

The great man I knew as a kid is nothing more than a drug dealer.

And now Unknown has made it virtually impossible to go into my room without being held captive by terror.

I hold my breath, creeping into the room. Sunday morning light streams in, but everything else is untouched. My window is locked. The closet door is shut. My bookshelf seems the same. I compare it to a photo I took before I left, but I'm not convinced.

I flick the light on, inhaling sharply. "If you can hear me, I'm going to find you."

And then I get to work. I use that wand thing on everything, and when that doesn't soothe my fears, I tear my room apart.

And yet, I find nothing. Absolutely. Nothing. I guess I

should be grateful that the only thing spying on me was a mermaid figure. But how long will it take for Unknown to get back in here and plant something else?

I sink to the floor, leaning against my bed.

My phone rings. A blocked number.

"Hello?"

There's a click, then, "You found my gift."

It sounds off. Not quite human. Kind of like the GPS navigation voice.

"I wouldn't really call it a gift, since you were using it to spy on me," I answer.

When they remain silent, I say, "You've never called before. What prompted the change?"

"Texting is so... impersonal," Unknown says. "Wouldn't you agree, Margo Wolfe?"

"I can't say I particularly agree with any of this."

"You've always had bad luck picking friends. How do you know this time is any different?"

There's a click, and the line goes dead.

I bring my phone away from my ear, and it vibrates a second later with a text.

CALEB

Are you home?

My stomach flips. It's just coincidental timing—that's all. I don't answer him and crawl into bed instead. It's still early, but I don't care. There is a pile of things in the center of my room that I will reorganize tomorrow. And I *can't* deal with Caleb's judgement right now.

I should've known that pretending to sleep wouldn't keep Caleb away. I don't know how long I doze, but soon enough, he pulls back the covers and slides in behind me.

"Are you avoiding me?" he whispers.

"I'm avoiding life," I mumble. I roll into him and bury my face in the crook of his neck.

He always smells so good. It's unfair. He could be sweaty from a run and he'd still smell like sandalwood and pine.

"And apparently the mess in the middle of your room."

"I was searching for other..."

He hugs me tighter. "Did you find anything?"

"No. But I'm questioning everything. I was just thinking about the time you said Amelie was a bad friend."

He stiffens.

Then I stiffen.

Because it coincides so much with what Unknown just said...

"Do you remember that?" I peek up at him. "One night eating pizza with my dad—"

"I try not to think about memories with your dad, baby," he says. "But Amelie *was* a bad friend, even when we were kids. You refused to believe me."

"I like to think the best of people." I exhale.

"A weakness I'll help you overcome."

I tip my head back, squinting at him. "Really."

He smirks. "You thought I wasn't a monster... Hell, you even convinced me to marry you." His finger traces the bracelet on my wrist.

Half the time, I forget I'm wearing it.

"Stuck with me now, Wolfe."

I try to hide my frown. My fears. I flip onto my back and stare at the ceiling, my chest tight.

Life is fragile. Hadn't I learned that from my parents?

But that day is blocked. What I did to make Caleb hate me is still gone, scrubbed free from my mind. There's a wall I keep mentally running into, even in my dreams.

And I'm afraid I might misremember something.

"Do you trust your memories?" It's easier to ask when we're not looking at each other.

"Sometimes I don't," he admits. "But most of the time, yes. I've got to trust myself, or no one else would."

I shake my head. "I don't. The little pieces I do remember—like the pizza night, or eavesdropping on your mom—"

"You eavesdropped on my mother?"

I glance at him. "You found me in your room hiding behind your door."

He turns his head and stares me down. "Is this a new memory?"

My cheeks get hot. I wonder if he can tell, even in the dark. "I don't know."

"The football team is going to the state championships," he says suddenly. "They're playing against Lion's Head, and they haven't made it so far in a while."

"So?"

He chuckles. "So, we're going. It's at Lion's Head. They won last year."

"You can't just order me to go to a football game."

"It'll be fun," he says, rolling toward me. "It's only a few weeks before my birthday. Think of it as an early present."

His fingers walk down my stomach, dipping into my panties. He swipes across my clit, and my back arches off the bed. It's a lazy assault, and he watches me squirm under him.

We're alone in the house. My heart jumps into action at the thought, but he doesn't change the urgency. This kind of attention—the slow, meticulous kind, where he sees *everything*—only makes me wetter.

Maybe it's because no one else has looked at me like he

does. His expression tells me I'm the source of every ounce of pain... and his redemption.

He presses his lips to my cheek, just below my eye. His tongue flicks out and tastes my skin. "Why are you crying?"

"Because I'm broken." My axis is tilted, spinning me off course.

My mind has been filled with friendship and love and thoughts of a future. And *Caleb*, promising forever. But that's not all. There's also darkness and deceit and horrible skeletons swinging in my closet.

"You're not broken." Every word is another brush against my cheek. "Even if you think you are. Even if I've tried to break you. You're stronger than you think, little wolf."

He makes me come, but he doesn't try to press his advantage. Does he know I'm scared to be in this room alone?

I don't feel strong.

I feel empty.

Chapter 29
Caleb

Matt refuses to let me drive. He's practically vibrating with excitement, and yet...

"Just spill it, would you?"

He swerves onto a side street and hits the gas pedal, the engine whining. He grins, flexing his grip on the steering wheel. At this point, I'm just along for a ride. And I'm not sure, with the way he's driving, I'm going to *survive* this ride.

"I got a location," he finally says.

About time. It's been two weeks. We're a few days into December, and I was losing my patience.

I lean forward. "How?"

"Got into the computer. It only connects to one network periodically, otherwise it's completely shut off." He grimaces. "Basically, it was a waiting game. Whoever it is, they're smart. This must be a device designated for this. I didn't find any personal documents stored on it. No clues. Sorry, man."

"Did you see any of the videos?"

He shifts. "Yeah. They kept two."

"Of what?" I want to punch Matt at the thought of him watching Margo in her room, even though he's helping me.

He eyes me. "There's no audio. But there's one of you sneaking into her room through the window—hey, man, I stopped it after that. I don't need to see your naked ass fucking your girlfriend."

I glare at him.

"And the other is her and Riley. I'm not sure what's so special about it. They sit on her bed and make a phone call."

"But you can't hear what they say?"

"Nah, it's just video. I guess you could figure out what they're saying if you were a lip reader. Otherwise? Just two girls making a call."

"Send them to me." Maybe there's something he's missing.

"We're almost there. I'll check my laptop and see if it's active. If it is, chances are good that we'll be able to find Margo's stalker."

My blood rushes hot and cold. It's true—she has a stalker. Someone obsessed with her... and her relationship to me.

Matt turns onto a familiar street, then into a parking lot. "The Wi-Fi comes from that restaurant," he says, pointing to the diner on the corner.

My stomach drops.

I was just here, talking to my mother.

Matt puts the car in park and reaches into the backseat for his laptop. But I can't wait. My mom's car is in the farthest corner of the lot. I don't even spare him a glance as I climb out and stride across the road, up the concrete steps. Into the diner.

I'm on autopilot.

My gaze sweeps around, trying to find someone with a

laptop, a cell phone, a tablet... nothing. The place is filled with old people sipping coffee and young families enjoying brunch. No one notices my abrupt entrance except the hostess, who has frozen by the podium.

"Caleb, what are you doing here?"

I don't spot anyone I know. No Amelie—the girl is supposedly in France anyway—and no Savannah.

I point at her. "You know something."

"What?"

The door bangs open behind me, and a hand lands on my shoulder.

"They're not here." Matt sees who I'm locked in a staring contest with and coughs. "Holy shit. Mrs. Asher?"

"Matthew," my mother comments. "Did you boys come for dinner?"

"Ah, no, ma'am," Matt says. His face reddens.

Mother's eyebrow goes up. "Then what are you doing here?"

"Did you deliver my message to Uncle David?"

"About your college choice?" She tilts her head, confusion washing over her features. It's an act—every emotion she reveals is an act. She's much more calculating than that. "Of course I did."

"Great. Just checking." I shove Matt out the door ahead of me.

"Caleb, wait—"

I ignore her. All she had to do was tell me about Amber. She knows where she is—I'm growing more certain of it by the day. But she hasn't called me, hasn't shown up at Eli's house, *nothing*.

Which means Amber Wolfe is still in town, and she can't admit it.

Once we're outside, I let out a growl.

"What the hell was that?" Matt grabs my arm and stops me. "Dude. Why is your mom working at a shitty diner in Beacon? I honestly didn't even know Beacon *had* shitty diners."

"There's just the one diner." I yank free. "And it beats me."

He shakes his head, following me back to his car. "This is so fucked up."

"You're telling me?"

"Well, whoever normally connects there, I guess maybe your mom would know?" He unlocks the car. "Damn. I didn't think this was going to be a wasted trip. I was ready to spring on this stalker... I guess we could camp out here, see if anyone you recognize shows up."

I grunt. "Fine."

We sit and wait. Every person who comes into the diner isn't right. Matt and I get antsy, and eventually we decide to head home.

I try not to take the day personally, but it comes down to one thing: we failed. And somehow I'll have to go pretend everything is fine with Margo, knowing Unknown is just going to make another attempt to spy on her.

That gets me thinking. Plotting.

She might just be safer with me.

"You have a gleam in your eye," Matt comments. "Care to share?"

I don't.

"Just take me back."

We drive in silence toward Eli's house. A black car is parked in the driveway, and dread laces through me. Just the person I didn't want to see.

"You okay?"

"My uncle." I climb out and pat the roof. "Don't forget to send me those files."

"See ya next week," Matt says, lifting his hand.

Right. The championship game at Lion's Head. I only just invited Margo, and it already evaporated from my mind. I guess Uncle David has that effect on me. Now I just have to hope he doesn't drag me back to his house to teach me some lesson—how to properly inform your family of college choices, perhaps.

My mind is torn in two different directions. I walk into the house and search the first floor for any sign of my uncle, then go down the stairs. He's leaning against my dresser, holding the picture I had taken from my house the same night I took Margo's bracelet.

It's the two of us as children, our arms hooked around each other's necks. We were young and happy.

But judging from my uncle's expression, he doesn't care that it was a happy memory. He cares that it's *Margo Wolfe*. The destroyer of our families.

She'll never win in his eyes.

I used to think the same way. If Margo came back, I'd make her life a living hell. And for a while, I fed on that energy. She came back to Emery-Rose for senior year. But then she got under my skin, and she's stayed there ever since.

It was my uncle who shaped my opinion of Margo. My uncle who poisoned me against her.

I should've known.

Uncle drops the frame to the floor and takes a deliberate step forward. The glass crunches under his heel.

I cringe, but that's all that slips out.

"I tried to warn you. But you just. Don't. Listen." He sighs. I can only imagine what goes through his head in times like these. How much does he want to throttle me, and how much does he care? "People are buying your car accident story?"

I jerk my head in some form of a nod, but I don't trust myself to speak just yet.

"Good, good," he muses. "I received an interesting phone call tonight."

I raise an eyebrow.

"Receptionist at Hutchins' law firm. He cleared out?" He eyes me. "Why is he running?"

I shake my head. "Something spooked him."

"Obviously. Who?"

The last person I'm going to name is Margo. "Maybe my mother?"

He stills. "Why's that, Caleb?"

I lift one shoulder. "You'll have to ask her."

He stares. Upstairs, the front door slams, and Mr. Black's voice calls out for me and Eli. I move out of the way of the stairs, my expression wary. He can't do anything with Mr. Black here, right?

There's a layer of protection embedded in being around adults who would act.

My best friend's father definitely qualifies.

"I'll see you for dinner next week," my uncle says.

He straightens his tie and brushes past me, his shoes grinding the bits of broken glass into the carpet. And then he's gone, without a word to Eli's father, and I sag against the wall.

Chapter 30
Margo

The portrait of Caleb is half completed, and I'm running out of time to finish it. December has arrived, which means the due date is quickly approaching. It's starting to resemble him, although it's missing his eyes and lips. The two most defining features, and... *difficult*. I've been hemming and hawing over how exactly to do it.

At the beginning of the project, Caleb was simple in my mind: vicious. The devil incarnate. A bully barely holding on to his demons. The slant of his mouth reflected that, but the closer we got... I painted over it, determined to start it again. Perhaps not a smile, but something similar.

A smirk?

He has moments of softness and kindness. He has demons, but there's light in him. He's a liar and a jerk and sweet and the most heartbreakingly beautiful boy I've ever laid eyes on.

How do I paint a liar's lips?

How do I paint the devil's eyes?

Len enters the dining room, where I've been hunkered

down since school got out an hour ago. "I hate to interrupt, but you have a visitor."

She tips her head toward the front of the house.

"Who?"

"Go see for yourself." She takes my brush from my fingers and sets it down. "This will wait a little while. Go on."

I exhale and stand, sweeping invisible lint off my thighs. I walk through the kitchen, toward the front door, and catch a glimpse of my mystery visitor in the living room.

My foster sister sits on the couch, her leg jiggling.

"I'm so sorry," she blurts out, throwing her arms around my shoulders. "I was cruel to spring that on you at your Fall Ball."

I hug her back tightly, leaning into her. The vanilla scent surrounding her is familiar. It brings back memories—most of them good.

"You don't have to apologize," I tell her.

"No, I really do. I've felt guilty ever since, but I couldn't bear it if you spent one more night with that monster." Her attention goes over my shoulder, then back to me. "Can you come with me? Maybe go for a ride?"

"You have a car?" Something dark flutters in my chest.

"My foster parents taught me how to drive." She bounces on her heels. "Isn't that cool? I just was able to get my permit last week! It's kind of against the rules, but they don't mind if I take the car out by myself. I just have to promise to be careful."

It stings like lemon dripped into a fresh cut.

Luck of the draw. It's always that way with foster care. Kids either get lucky or... *not*.

And I'm not saying I'm unlucky—I'm just saying...

I have a flash of Caleb dangling his keys out in front of

me. An offer to teach me to drive. I sat behind the wheel and didn't even touch the gas pedal.

Without a doubt, I know I can't get in the car with Claire. It's not the principal of the matter, it's the raging jealousy. I don't want to see what kind of car her foster parents let her drive. She wouldn't brag. Her excitement is genuine.

But that doesn't make it easy to swallow.

"Let's sit on the sun porch," I offer. "It's warm this time of day."

Lenora lets out a slight exhale behind me. I suppose I'm not the only one who was uncomfortable with that offer.

"Fine," Claire huffs.

I roll my eyes, and we go to the sun porch on the side of the house. It's a three-season porch generally, with big glass windows all the way around, but like I said: this time of day, when the sun's been heating it all afternoon, it's pleasant.

I sink into one of the cushioned wicker chairs, and Claire mimics my movement.

"How are things besides learning to drive? How's Hanna?"

Her face softens, and she grabs my hand. "I'm sorry, Margo. I just feel awful that I gave you that clipping and told you I recognized Caleb, then left."

Claire might've been the catalyst of my realization, but Caleb dug his own grave.

"You were just trying to help."

"Still." She pouts. "I miss living with you. I miss seeing you at school. We ended up so close to each other. But now I can see you so much more. And, well, I wanted to show off my driving skills. I couldn't get away before now."

Claire, the wild child. Always a rule breaker. I don't bother pointing out that she shouldn't be driving alone with a permit, and she *especially* shouldn't be driving someone else around without a license. A little thing like the law wouldn't stop her.

"How's Hanna?" I ask again.

"She's good. She's really enjoying that school. She's made some friends, which used to be difficult for her. I think she doesn't feel like such an outcast in the uniforms. There's no bias. Even her shoes are new, and our foster mom makes sure her hair is done up really nice every morning."

"That's nice," I murmur.

There were a few instances of Hanna coming home sobbing, some mean girl in the grade above picking on her for her threadbare shoes or shirts. To hear that's not happening anymore...

"She's at Lion's Head's middle school, right? Caleb and I are going to the championship game. Are you going?"

"Oh my gosh, Margo. I got asked out on a date!" Her cheeks pinken. "I don't think I'm ready for it, though. He's nice and all. He wanted to go to the football game together. Do you and Caleb kiss?"

I blink. "Um—"

"I just don't know what to expect," she murmurs. "Do guys expect to kiss on the first date?"

"I don't know," I answer. "I can't say I've gone on too many first dates."

Let's just call it none. Caleb made sure of that, and he doesn't count.

"Well, if you go, you can meet me there."

I have the sense of time lost between us, and I don't know how to get it back. So much has happened since September.

"Maybe," she hedges. "I'll have to accept the date first."

"Is he a nice guy?"

"I said he was." Her expression flickers from uncertainty to annoyance. "I just don't know if he's a good kisser."

"Jeez, Claire, is that all you care about?" I laugh. "Do you remember when we first met?"

"How could I not? Hanna and I weren't expecting anything other than a shitty foster home that'd been coerced into taking both of us. We got the surprise of our lives when you joined us."

"Me, too." Reminiscing doesn't help that sinking feeling in my chest.

"Are you and Caleb together?" she asks suddenly. "I only ask because there are a lot of rumors at Lion's Head about the ERE hockey captain. It's actually shocking how much people gossip. I'd love to dispel the rumors for you."

I squint at her. "In a way..."

"That means you're fucking him, right? Even though he's an awful person?"

"Seriously?" I get up. I need something—a glass of water to drink or chuck at her head, I'm not sure.

She follows me through the dining room, pausing in front of my easel.

"Wait," she says. "What's this?"

"A painting." I continue on, making a beeline for the fridge. I pour two glasses of water and carry them back, and she's still staring at it. "Claire."

She jerks. "Yeah?"

I force a laugh. "I know it's bad, but there's no need to gawk."

"No, it's pretty good, actually. Sorry. I didn't sleep well last night." She bounces on her heels. "Why are you painting Caleb?"

I narrow my eyes. "How do you know it's him?"

"Because I've seen him, dummy. And who else would you paint?"

"We had to partner up for an art class," I tell her. "He has to paint me, too."

She takes a sip of her water. Then another, and another, until the glass is empty. "I thought you might've painted him a little more gloom and doom. Based on what happened anyway."

"A lot has changed."

Between both of us. I don't know what I'm doing right now, with her. I don't know how to navigate this conversation. It's dancing around, out of my control, and every time I think I've got a grasp, she throws a curveball.

It's the kind of shit she used to pull with our foster parents, although she once said she had no idea she was doing it.

Her attention tears away from the painting, to my face. "A lot has changed for you?"

She must feel the same way I do—that we've slipped away from each other. We used to be inseparable. Now look at us.

"I should get going," she says abruptly. "Return the car before my foster parents notice I'm gone."

Ah, see? She didn't actually ask them.

Same old, same old.

"It was good to see you." I wrap my arms around her. It takes her a second to hug me back, but I ignore the hesitation. It's just normal weirdness. "Next time, bring Hanna."

Claire giggles and pats my cheek. "Sometimes I think you like her more than me."

I rear back. "What? No."

Her expression turns serious. "You're always asking about her."

I do—because Claire is solid in front of me, and I have no way of knowing how her twelve-year-old sister is. One of us has to bring her up, or else I'd never know.

"I'm sorry you think that means I care more about her than you." My voice is stiff, and I'm suddenly glad that Claire is on her way out. I take the glass from her hand, set it down next to my painting, and lead her out. At the front door, I pause. "I hope you know it isn't true."

Her face falls. "I know. I just get moments of jealousy sometimes."

I stifle a sigh.

She throws her arms around me one more time. Her lips touch my cheek briefly, and then she pulls away. I stand in the door and watch her trot to the sleek black car parked at the curb. It's fancier than I imagined.

She revs the engine and takes off, tires squealing, and it proves that not getting in the car with her was a smart decision.

I return to my painting. My groove is thrown off, so I don't even try. I cover the paints on my palette with plastic wrap and leave it where it is, determined to try again tomorrow. Instead, I flop on the couch and close my eyes. There's pain in my chest from her judgment, like a steady second heartbeat.

I just need to put it out of my mind.

Past

Two scrawny girls entered the house. They carried black garbage bags with them, and they held on to each other with grubby fingers. I tried not to analyze their stringy, greasy hair, or the way the older one's eyes darted around.

She found me hidden on the stairs, but she didn't say anything. Her attention just snapped back to my foster mom and the case worker standing next to them.

I was rather abruptly yanked out of my last home and placed with Cindy and Jeff. I'd been here a few weeks and was settling in well according to Ms. McCaw. I sometimes had nightmares of people in gray suits forcibly removing me from the home. One or two nights, I woke up sweating. But they had been kind to me so far, and the nightmares were easing.

But now... more kids.

Cindy mentioned it the other day at dinner. Two girls were on their way from upstate New York. A ten and fourteen-year-old. She pointed her fork in my direction, making me promise to be good. Kind. To show them the ropes.

We had chores and a curfew, which wasn't just for out of the home. If we weren't in our bedrooms by nine, there was a promise to remove our door. I said *we*, but really, it was just me for a few weeks. They were certified respite housing, too, but no one came through while I was adjusting to their household.

I saw a therapist once a week, talking about the issues I had. I'd been carrying around a *runaway* label for about a year, and it hung heavy every time Ms. McCaw spoke it into existence. She didn't get it, though. I had to get out of that house.

Not this one, though. Threat of bedroom door removal or no, they were nice.

"Margo!" Cindy called.

I jumped up and ran down the stairs, pausing at the

bottom. I put my hands behind my back and picked at my fingernails where she couldn't see.

"This is Claire and Hanna," she introduced. "How about you show them to their room? The one connected to yours." She smiled at me. To the case worker, she said, "As we showed the woman who did the home inspection, we have a jack-and-jill bathroom that the girls will use."

She left out that they just removed the locks on the outside of the doors.

"I can show you, if you'd like."

"Not necessary," the case worker said. "You know the drill. Girls? Call me if you need anything."

"Sure," the older one said.

I didn't know if she was Claire or Hanna. She grabbed her sister's hand.

With wooden legs, I led them up the stairs. Once we were out of earshot, I whispered, "I'm Margo."

"Claire," the older one answered. "And this is Hanna."

"Margo is an old lady name," Hanna blurted out.

It broke the tension I didn't realize was forming.

Claire and I grinned down at Hanna.

"Yeah," I said simply. It wasn't worth arguing. "This is your room."

Bunk beds in the corner, pink curtains covering the window. It was definitely meant to be a room for girls. Claire and Hanna wandered in, dropping their bags by the beds. They exchanged unspoken words.

Hanna went to the window while Claire turned toward me.

"You get your own room?"

I shrugged. "We share a bathroom. My room's on the other side."

She appraised me, then stomped through the bathroom

and into my room. I followed her. She stopped dead, threw back her shoulders, and turned to me. "Switch with me."

I regarded her. *Did I seem like a pushover?* Too many kids had tried to force me out of things that were mine. I rubbed my wrist, where my bracelet used to sit. I lost that a few homes back and still felt the ache of its absence.

"No," I said, inching past her. It was *my* room, the first one I'd ever had of my own. And I was not about to let some skinny kid walk into my home—and all over me.

I tried not to flinch at my line of thoughts. Did I really just call this place home? Even in my own head, it was alien.

"No?" Claire echoed. Her lips pushed down. "B-but why—"

"Because I was here first," I snapped. "You don't get everything your way."

Her chin wobbled, and she stared at me. Her eyes filled with tears.

All at once, it stopped. She shook her head and inhaled a deep breath, then stuck out her hand. "Fine. Truce."

I shook her hand, if only to maintain a bit of peace. No use starting a war on their first day.

Hanna shoved into my room. Her attention latched on to our hands. "Claire didn't cheat you out of this room, did she?"

I snorted, and Claire groaned.

"Has she done it before?" I asked Hanna.

The younger girl laughed. "She's good at getting her way."

"Not here," I said. "I'm not a pushover—and neither are our new foster parents."

Claire just smiled. "Yeah? Well, you passed. But *they* haven't met me yet."

Famous last words.

Present

I wake up to Robert sitting on the coffee table, facing me.

He glances over at me when I stir. "You okay? You were muttering in your sleep."

I sit up and take the water bottle he extends in my direction. "Yeah, I think I was dreaming about the first time I met Claire. She tried to trick me out of my room."

"This was at your last foster home?"

I nod and take a sip. "She was always on the wild side. Some kids get to be like that. You know."

"Our last foster was like that," he says. "She liked to push our buttons."

"With the curfew," I mumble.

"And other things." He smiles at me. "Don't let that dissuade you from going through a wild phase. Although I think dating Caleb might give Len enough of a heart attack to last until we're old and gray."

I crack a smile. "Yeah, he's..."

Robert mirrors my expression. "I get it. I've had him in a few different classes and never had a problem with him. It's just the perception of him that Len has an issue with, and possibly his last name. That, and he purposefully tried to turn us against you—which isn't going to happen."

"Lapse in judgement," I hedge.

What else are we going to call it?

"Your social worker called," he says. "She's going to swing by this evening and chat with us. I invited her to stay for dinner."

I tense. "Why do we need to talk to her?"

"It's nothing bad," he assures me. "We just want to see what the next steps are to make you a member of this family. Len asked about it a few days ago, but we wanted to have the chance to talk to you."

"It still seems..." *Out of reach.*

"Impossible?"

"Yeah, maybe."

He looks down at his hands, then back up at me. "Len might have a harder time saying this, but I don't. We love you, Margo."

We love you. The words echo inside me, banging around my chest. It hurts, but it isn't bad pain. It's a sore muscle stretching for the first time. A heartbeat I thought had died long ago.

But there's always another shoe to drop.

Chapter 31
Caleb

I'm losing control. If this was a chessboard, my uncle would be maneuvering me toward checkmate. Even though I'm fighting it, I get the sense that there's something I'm missing.

As soon as I'm done with this dinner, I'm going straight to Margo's. It's the only solace for attempting this dinner alone.

I've barely walked into the house when my uncle pounces. His palm lands on the back of my neck, gripping firmly and guiding me down the hall. He's shorter than me by a fraction, and thinner, too. I'm stronger than him, but years of bending to his will has left me unable to strike back. My body still remembers the pain he's inflicted, and it seizes up.

That, and he still controls everything else in my life. The constant threat hangs over me at what he *could* do if I tempted him badly enough.

"You've been visiting your mother?" Uncle David asks.

He gives me a light shove into his study, and I stumble forward. I did the same thing to Margo on one of her first days at Emery-Rose. Guilt washes through me, feeling the humiliation of it. The helplessness. I straighten and face him, meeting his mocking smile with a blank expression.

He wants to pick a fight—or just get his anger out on his human punching bag.

He grabs the front of my shirt and twists the fabric. My collar bites into my neck. He gets in my face, his cold blue eyes burning into mine.

"Answer me," he grunts.

"I didn't realize there was a rule against seeing my own damn mother."

Only a few weeks to go until my birthday, and then I can be done with him.

He's been in a foul mood ever since Margo reappeared at school, but it's only gotten worse in the last few weeks. I'm not fool enough to think it's unrelated to either of those. My birthday *and* the girl from my past.

A feminine cough draws my uncle's attention.

Aunt Iris stands in the doorway. Her blonde hair is coiffed, her long dress perfectly pressed. There's not a wrinkle or misplaced piece of lint in sight, just as my uncle prefers her.

She pauses at the state we're in. "David, is everything okay?"

"Does everything look okay, Iris?"

She murmurs something. The click of her heels on the floor indicate she is abandoning me to him. *Again.*

"I've done what you asked," I say, while on the inside I plot his demise.

One day, he'll get what's coming to him.

"Oh? And what's that, exactly?"

He was never supposed to bear the brunt of my father's company. Even after the merger, Dad owned a percentage that he passed on to me. But because I was so young, Uncle David inherited it in my place.

He was never supposed to support his nephew or guard my inheritance. I imagine he had plans of his own that were tossed to the wayside. It broke something inside him.

All because, as Mother likes to say, "It's happening the way your father wants."

Bullshit.

"College," I grit out. "Hockey. Grades."

"For one—you're not even *playing hockey*. And how about the part where you don't fuck that Wolfe girl?" He shoves me backward. "You're so stupid, Caleb. Are you destined to repeat your father's mistakes? You're going to break off all relations with her. You're not going to see her. Touch her. Communicate with her."

Shit.

I laugh, because he's lost his mind. "Or what?"

Uncle David has a few telltale signs of extreme anger. But the best indication I've ever seen is the redness of his ears. If it were possible, the next step would be steam coming out. Right now, his whole face is mottled red. Including his ears.

I know why he hates the Wolfes, but it's more satisfying to make him say it out loud.

Instead, he goes to threats. "You won't see a dime from me. You will get nothing. No help. No support."

"My inheritance doesn't revolve around your *permission*. As soon as I turn eighteen, I don't need anything from you. So what's stopping me from marching into the Prize Industries offices on my eighteenth birthday and explaining to the Board exactly what you've been doing?"

His red face turns white.

I've never threatened him before, but it feels good. Satisfying.

Aunt Iris gasps from the doorway, her hand raised to cover her mouth. "Caleb, honey—"

"Shut up, Iris," her husband snaps.

The last time, when I was trapped here for a weekend, he wanted me to leave Margo alone. It was part of his conditions, layers of rules cast down on me that are meant to suffocate my free will. But I didn't do it. It isn't the hockey, or refusing to pick out a college, or my failure—my mom's failure—to get Amber to leave town.

It's *Margo*.

I shake out my arms on my way out. I've read through the paperwork multiple times, but it's clear. Even Mr. Black, a prestigious defense attorney, has concurred. My father, through the company holding my trust fund, put *no* stipulations on my inheritance except age. Uncle David, as my legal ward, got a stipend every month to cover my expenses. I assumed he passed along at least a slight portion of them onto Eli's family. They were the ones who fed me and gave me a place to stay, after all.

But now... I kind of doubt that.

"You walk out that door, you don't get to come back!" Uncle David roars behind me.

It's a pity that family has a way of disappointing you—even when you expect it.

"If I never see your face again, I'll die happy." I salute him and walk out the door. Something crashes behind me. I keep going, liberated by my choices, until a sharp pain spikes through the back of my head. My vision goes dark, and I distantly feel myself falling forward.

The impact with the floor finishes the job of knocking me out.

Chapter 32
Margo

Caleb has disappeared—*again*. I swear to God, I'm going to kill his uncle. I was expecting him last night after their family dinner. With no texts, no calls, and no climbing in through my window, I've surmised something is terribly wrong.

I even made Eli show me Caleb's basement room, which was empty, to make sure they weren't doing a better job of lying to me.

And now I'm outside the Asher mansion.

I freeze at the door, my body unwilling to go any farther. I'm pretty sure the family hates me for reasons I can't remember. And a little thing like memory loss wouldn't hold up against years of anger.

So if this is fight or flight, I'm choosing *freeze*.

Riley climbs out of the car behind me. "I don't think anyone is here."

I blow out a long, slow breath and glance back at her. "Why?"

She shrugs, joining me on the wide, covered front steps. "It's getting dark out, and there are no lights on."

"Right." I ring the doorbell and hold my breath.

Because I suffered through the full day at school, just to make sure that Caleb wasn't going to spontaneously show up.

And when he didn't, my worry only deepened.

Eli, Liam, and Theo echoed my concern. But they're at hockey practice, so Riley and I are here alone.

No one answers the door.

"So... you ever going to tell me what happened with your social worker?" she asks.

I grimace. "She wants me to see a therapist. I guess this kind of transition can be delicate, or whatever. The Bryans didn't think it was a terrible idea, so we scheduled an appointment for after Christmas. Also, I'm going in."

Into the house, I mean.

"Margo—"

The door is unlocked. I pause with it open a crack, expecting sirens. Nothing. A huge place like this doesn't have a security system?

We creep into the foyer. Riley follows close behind me, almost touching my back. When no one comes running, we both straighten.

"That was a little anticlimactic," she murmurs. "Plus, a therapist? You can't just say that and then walk into someone else's house. It kind of proves that you do need one."

"Caleb is in here. I can feel it."

"I'll stand lookout, I guess. You search for him." She shivers. "I'm picturing him tied up somewhere. Is that awful?"

I elbow her. "Don't even think that."

Eli saunters in through the open door, and both of us jump.

"What are you doing here?" Riley whisper-yells.

He rolls his eyes. "Have you met David Asher? He's terrifying. You guys should not be breaking into his house."

Our eyes go wide, and he laughs.

"Kidding. I meant, you shouldn't be breaking in *alone.* Which is why I'm here. I moved your car, too, by the way. You should never park in the driveway to burgle."

Well. He does have a point.

"I'm still keeping lookout," Riley tells us.

She stays in the foyer. Eli and I split up. I take the first floor, and Eli jogs up the stairs to the second floor. The house is giant, I'll just say that. There are rooms upon rooms, each more extravagant than the last. But more than that, they're *old.* Antique furniture and dark wood on the walls. Rugs that have probably never been stepped on, chairs and couches that've never had kids bounce on them.

It's cold. Worse than Caleb's house. Winter is upon us, and it feels like the heat has been shut off.

I find an office-looking room, with a chessboard on the floor. The pieces are scattered across a thick rug. I shiver and keep moving.

I get to a closed door and pause in front of it. Up until now, everything has been open. I hesitate for a fraction of a second.

A low moan comes from the other side.

I shove the door open and go still at the darkness inside. After a moment of feeling along the wall, my fingers hit the light switch.

Blinding lights flicker on in the ceiling.

My gaze flies around, searching for the threat. It's a game room with a pinball machine, a pool table, and other various games, but only one person in it.

Caleb.

He's on the floor, his back against the wall. Like he was sitting and then fell over. His eyes are closed.

There's blood on the wall. Just a smear, but enough that my heart hammers.

I rush to him, falling to my knees. "Caleb, wake up."

His eyes flutter open.

For a long moment, I question whether he recognizes me. He blinks slowly, squinting, then touches the back of his head. "Little lamb. What are you doing here?"

"Coming to rescue you, of course."

His fingers come away wet with blood. "What day is it?"

"What?"

"The day—or night, judging from the dark room behind you."

"Glad you're with it enough to notice it's dark out," I grumble. "It's Tuesday evening. I got worried when you didn't show up last night after your family dinner."

He smiles. "Just wanted to see how long it took you to notice."

"You're really going to dissect the time it took me to find you?"

He shrugs and climbs to his feet. He staggers a bit, catching himself on the wall. I grab on to his waist, steadying him. He's *bleeding*. From his head. And he's watching me like he's worried about *me*.

He rubs his thumb between my brows.

"What are you doing?"

"Trying to erase your concern."

I scoff. "I found you on the floor in a dark room. I'm not supposed to be concerned?"

He shrugs. "Nope. I'm fine."

After a little wobble, he straightens and manages to

walk without falling over. He leads me out of the room, into a hallway that cuts straight to the kitchen. He locates a bag of frozen veggies from the freezer and puts it to the back of his head, winking at me. "Let's get out of here before my uncle decides it's time for round two."

"Eli is wandering around upstairs," I tell him.

He pauses. "Is he now?"

"Nope!" Eli calls. He propels Riley in front of him into the kitchen. "Your aunt and uncle just got home. Aren't you glad I moved your car, Ri?"

She tries to scowl, but the fear bleeds through.

"We need to leave right now," Caleb barks. He leads us out the back door and around the corner of the house, to the side of the garage.

The vertical opening is loud from our position, and we wait until it's silent for us to make a break for it. We hurry along the tall shrubs dividing the property from their neighbors, and I take a moment to cast a silent thank you that Eli moved Riley's car. We slip past the slowly closing gate and onto the sidewalk.

Around the corner, we pile into Riley's car. Eli in the driver's seat, the keys in his hand, Riley beside him in the front, and Caleb and me in the back.

All of us let out relieved sighs. I lean into Caleb's side, wrapping my arms around him.

"Didn't take you very long at all," he muses. "Eli?"

He glances back at us. "Well, we all know what happened last time..."

I shudder.

"I told him to shove it," Caleb informs us. "And then he hit me with something... I don't know. I was on my way out the door. He didn't like that very much."

We're on the road, but I still push up onto my knees and

move the frozen vegetable bag out of the way. He leans forward slightly, letting me inspect his scalp. There's an inch-long gash of oozing blood just above where his neck meets his skull.

"He could've killed you," I whisper.

Eli growls. "This is ridiculous. I'm telling my parents—I don't care what you say."

Caleb doesn't react.

"They won't let David come back. We'll change the locks—"

"I just have to last four more weeks," Caleb says woodenly. "That's all."

"At the rate he's going?" Eli mocks. "You'll be dead in three."

I imagine this isn't the first time they've had such a conversation.

We end up back at Eli's house, and the four of us head inside. I hang back a minute, sending a text to Robert and Lenora. Ms. McCaw made a point about good, open communication, and I want to do well. A part of me fears any more missteps could have me sent away. So much has gone wrong, already.

Hence the texting.

A minute later my phone buzzes.

ROBERT

Len and I are fine with you sleeping over.
We won't tell. ;) Have fun with Riley!

Okay, so maybe my communication isn't the best... And yes, a sleepover is technically breaking foster kid one-oh-one. But with a month and a half left, there's low risk for great reward.

"Come on, Wolfe!" Eli yells from the doorway. "We're ordering pizza!"

I tuck my phone away and go in, taking a deep breath. Riley and Eli are in the kitchen. I peek into the living room and dining room, then make my way down to the basement.

Caleb is standing in the middle of the room. His attention is focused on his bed.

"You okay?" I ask.

He turns toward me. His eyes are dark. He lowers the frozen bag from his head and beckons me closer. "You came for me."

I shift, taking a small step in his direction.

"Margo."

"Don't make it a big deal."

He meets me halfway, his hand sliding around my neck and into my hair.

I melt. Can't help it. I hold on to his waist and tip my head back. He leans down, and my heart pounds, tremors spreading through me. His lips are millimeters away, and he pauses.

"It *is* a big deal. Can you admit that?"

I press my lips together.

He smiles, twisting to the side. He kisses the corner of my mouth.

I'm already winded.

"You care so damn much," he goads.

"Stop."

"Is it a bad thing?"

Is it? Caring about people gets them taken away. *He* taught me that.

Caleb's body is flush against mine, so I can feel just how much he *cares*. His lips travel down the side of my jaw, to my throat. I jump at the scrape of his teeth on my skin, the feeling sending sparks through me like runaway firecrackers.

"God," I moan. "Fine. It is a big deal. I hate your uncle for hitting you. I wish you didn't get hurt. I—"

I almost just confessed my heart because he's kissing my neck.

Grow up, Margo.

I grab his face and drag it to mine. I capture his lower lip in my teeth, nipping and releasing. He growls deep in the back of his throat, but he lets me have control. I walk him backward until his knees hit the side of the bed.

He lowers himself, and I straddle him, opening his lips and sliding my tongue into his mouth. His hips raise ever so slightly, his erection rubbing against my core.

"I need to feel you," I whisper. "Is this going to hurt?"

"Fuck, no," he says.

I yank off my leggings and climb back on him. He unbuckles his pants, then tugs them down far enough for his erection to spring free.

I scoot backward and bend forward. I take him in my mouth. My eyes close, and my fingers dig into his thighs, as I suck. His groan is an encouragement, and I swirl my tongue over the head of his cock. I take him deeper, sucking, and his thighs automatically tense. I open my jaw wider. Something inside me chants, *more, more, more*. He hits the back of my throat. I choke a little but keep going. My nostrils flare.

Deeper.

He hisses out a breath. I come back up, sucking and stroking him with my hand. His fingers wind in my hair, taking back an ounce of power.

"Fuck, Margo," he grunts.

I keep going until he can't control the movement of his hips.

He abruptly yanks me up onto his chest. "If you keep doing that, I'll come, and where would that leave you?"

I barely have time to catch my breath while he situates me on his lap, then he drives up into me.

I put my hands on his chest and lean back. He completes me. And yeah, that's some bullshit we could go over in therapy, but right now? I let my head fall back and I *feel* it. It's like a soulmate thing, I think. I rise, thrilled at the sight of him between my legs, then slowly lower back onto him. I'm shakier than a newborn deer, every micro-movement sending waves of electricity through me.

Once I'm steady, I move faster. Our thighs slap together.

His grip tightens on my hips, slamming me down onto him.

"Look at me." His hand slips to my clit.

I gasp, holding on to him. It's too much. There's too much emotion assaulting me. He's hitting a spot deep inside me, working me up higher. I freeze, and an orgasm crashes over me. It's barely slowed when he flips me onto my back and thrusts into me.

His pace is brutal, but it doesn't last. He shudders above me, letting his head fall to my shoulder as he comes. His whole body jerks, then stills.

"Did that make your head worse?" I ask.

"Maybe. But it was worth it."

"Come on, lovebirds," Eli yells from the top of the stairs. "Pizza is here!"

"Perfect timing." Caleb kisses the tip of my nose. He rocks his hips again, humming under his breath, then slowly withdraws.

I follow him into the bathroom, and we clean up in silence.

Upstairs, Eli and Riley laugh at us.

"Couldn't wait until after we ate, huh?" Eli throws an ice pack at Caleb.

My face heats up. We were pretty quiet, but—

"You reek of sex," Eli continues. "Seriously, guys. It's kind of turning me on."

Riley jabs him with her elbow.

I go to the boxes of pizza and ignore their chatter. I'm still tangled in a web of worry. He probably has a concussion. *I just fucked a concussed person.*

I don't have an appetite. I stare down at the pizza, inhaling the scent of cheese and garlic, and my stomach turns over.

It isn't just finding Caleb bloody and alone in his uncle's house. It's that plus the fact that he kissed my nose and my heart skipped a beat. It's that Ms. McCaw visited and she asked how I was doing, and for the first time in a really freaking long time, I was able to say, *Great!*

We talked about long-term fostering, going to court to petition for the Bryans' right to adopt me, the steps we'd have to take. She mentioned restarting therapy, and Robert and Lenora agreed. Even if I'm not a hundred percent sure I want my father to give up his rights.

Do I ask?

Does someone else?

I exhale and close the lid on the pizza.

Caleb comes up behind me, one hand coming around my waist, and his hand splays over my stomach, pulling me back against him.

"Not hungry?" he asks. "After that?"

I shrug, glancing away.

Why can't I just lean into happiness? It's right there, begging me to take it.

"What's wrong?" His breath hits my neck, followed by his lips.

I tilt my head to the side. His other arm comes around me, dropping the ice pack on the counter, then locking around my chest. I'm thoroughly encompassed.

"You can tell me."

"Everything," I whisper. "Everything's wrong. Do you ever just feel sad for no reason?"

He twists me around, cupping my jaw and tilting my head up.

I keep my gaze on his chin.

"Margo."

I press my lips together. My chin wobbles, though. The traitor.

"You have every reason to fall apart. It's my fault—when you first got here, I wanted you to break. But I changed my mind." He frowns. "*You* changed my mind. Because you're still..."

I'm hanging on the edge of a knife.

"You're still good. A bit devious." He winks. "But in your heart?"

"Stop." I push away from him.

He doesn't let me go. His fingers dig into my neck, and he tugs me even closer. "*You* stop. Don't run away."

I wasn't is on the tip of my tongue, but I can't voice it.

He releases me and grabs the box of pizza.

"I don't think I can be vertical for much longer," he announces to Riley and Eli.

They pause their conversation. Riley's eyebrows jump up.

"Come on, Margo." And then he just leaves. His feet pounding down the steps to the basement.

"You okay?" Riley asks me.

If only people would stop asking me that. I force a smile. "Super okay."

"Don't let him push you around," she says.

I scoff.

"She's been on a roll standing up to him," she adds, glancing at Eli.

He glowers at her.

"On that note, I'm going home." She slings her purse over her shoulder.

Eli jumps up. "What? Already?"

"I still have a curfew."

"Fine," he snaps. "You need to drive me back to my truck."

Her eyes round. "In *Beacon*?"

He shrugs.

I watch the two of them walk out, and suddenly I'm entirely alone.

It doesn't feel good.

I hurry to the basement and stop on the third-to-last stair. Caleb suddenly appears at the bottom. At this angle, I'm just a little taller than him.

"Eli and Riley leave?" he asks.

"Yeah."

"And you?"

I shake my head. "What about me?"

"Do you want to leave?" His eyes are impossibly dark.

"You should get some rest." I go up a step.

He follows me. One for one. "They say the opposite for a concussion. *If* I have one, which is doubtful. I've had a few concussions in my life."

"From your uncle?"

"From hockey." His smile doesn't linger.

"What do you remember?"

He huffs. "I'll tell you if you're naked."

I hesitate.

"Clothes off. All of them this time."

In our haste, we hadn't removed our shirts. But now... I grab the hem of my shirt and lift it off, letting it fall from my fingertips behind me. My bra is next. He drags my leggings over my hips, and I hold his shoulders to step out of them. Then panties.

He hops off the step and stares at me.

"Your turn," I mumble, trying not to let my self-consciousness overwhelm me. I haven't had this feeling before—shaky. The last time we had *good* sex, in the hotel room after the ball, I trusted him. We've had crazy sex since then, but... I don't know if I trust him now.

He captured my heart so slowly, I barely realized he was taking it. But my heart is just a fraction of the picture. And now, letting him peruse my body, it's obvious there are still broken shards between us.

He wants it that way. He thinks *he's* broken. The thought comes on suddenly, out of nowhere. But he's so wrong.

I will file you smooth, I vow to him. *One sharp edge at a time.*

"Strip," I demand. "Fair is fair."

His eyebrow jumps up. "Have we ever played fair?"

I raise my chin. "Starting now."

He just watches me for a moment, then nods. He unbuttons his pants and lets them drop around his ankles. Then boxers. He hesitates on his shirt, but I have no such reservations. Not when it comes to him.

I walk to him and take over, pulling his shirt over his head. I drop it on the floor and run my finger down his chest. He has hard abs and faint white scars. I circle around him, tracing an invisible path with my index finger, and he stands perfectly still.

I touch a pink, raised scar. This was a welt not too long ago. A welt at his uncle's hand.

He shudders. Goosebumps rise on his skin.

I suck my lower lip between my teeth and keep going. There are old scars, barely visible in the low light. Circular ones that catch the light.

"Did he burn you?"

He sighs. "I don't know what's worse—growing up like you did, or like me."

I lean forward and kiss one of the scars. He shivers beneath my lips, and my chest aches like he just punched out my heart. He had family, but at a steep cost.

"I wish I remembered what happened."

He turns around and lifts my chin with his finger. "Do you?"

"You could tell me," I whisper.

He shakes his head and pushes my hair off my shoulder. "You'd never believe me."

My mind goes back to ten years old. One minute we're happy kids chasing each other through his house. *Blank.* I'm scratching at the door. *Blank.* I'm at the park with Dad.

The gaping holes will drive me mad.

I open my mouth to ask another question.

"Leave it for tonight," he says. "I wasn't lying about my head hurting."

Well, then. I climb into his bed, folding myself into a little ball with my back against the wall. I pat the space beside me. "You said you'd tell me what you remember."

He joins me, picking me up and putting me on his lap. I wrap my arm around his shoulders. The room is a bit chilly, and goosebumps break out along my arms and legs. He draws a pattern on my thigh.

"What do I remember?" he muses. "Yelling at my uncle. Telling him enough was enough."

"Yelling at him about what?"

"My right to live my life."

It's a bit cryptic, honestly, but I don't question him further. We just sit in the quiet for a few minutes. My eyes track the pattern he's drawing on my thigh. A circle, a cross, a loop. *A word.*

B. R. A. V. E.

"Who are you calling brave?"

He pauses. "I heard a woman screaming. It's weird, right? Aunt Iris is used to her husband's... outbursts."

"Does he hit her?"

He flinches. "I doubt it. Uncle David has other ways of keeping her and my mother under control."

The last time I asked about his dad, I got shut down. I keep my questions about him to myself this time. There will be other days to ask where his dad went. Did I drive him away? I know something had to have happened with my mother. I didn't just make the Ashers hate me—I made her *leave* me.

What kind of child does that?

"You're in your head again."

I meet his eyes. "Misery loves company."

That gets a smile out of him. He kisses me softly, but it doesn't last. We weren't meant to be soft. So I let him push me onto my back and take away the aching in my bones.

Chapter 33
Margo

Riley picks me up from Caleb's house the next morning. She wiggles her eyebrows at me, laughing. "How was your night?"

I glare at her. "I should be asking you the same thing."

Her smile widens. "Yeah, you definitely should. Damn, Eli is good in bed."

"Stop."

"Nope, you asked." She backs out of his driveway with a shit-eating grin. "He does this thing where he kind of rotates—"

"Riley!" I yell, finally laughing. "I really, *really* don't want to hear about your sex life. Not the details anyway."

She shrugs. "Okay, okay."

"I'm glad you're happy, though."

She goes quiet.

I tilt my head. "You are *happy*, though, aren't you?"

"We're not talking about me, we're talking about you."

"Hmm." I don't trust her glossed-over non-answer, but I let it go. I tip my head back and close my eyes. We had mind-numbing sex. Multiple times. One of us woke up in the middle of the night and the other just knew. We needed each other.

Hands reaching toward each other in the darkness.

Our faces so close we shared breath.

"Earth to Margo," Riley says. "Where'd you go?"

"I want to remember what happened to me," I whisper, my gaze on the houses flashing past us. "But I think it's going to be traumatic."

Riley's family didn't move to Rose Hill until I'd been gone a while, so no one was talking about it at that point. I don't think anyone in our class actually knows the real story except Caleb. And a piece of my mind I can't access.

I want to know why he hated me and how he was able to stop.

She glances over. We're almost at my house, and she instinctively slows.

"What do you want to do?"

I inhale. "My old house brought back memories last time."

She makes a quick turn. "Roger that."

I left Caleb eating breakfast with Eli. There's no way—hopefully—he'll pack up his stuff and go to his house. Why would he?

Besides, I don't think he'd mind us breaking and entering...

All too soon, she pulls in the driveway and shuts off the car. "Now what?"

"Now we hope the place doesn't have an alarm."

"Was one burgle not enough for you?"

"What did you think I was going to do?"

She rolls her eyes. "I don't know, just sit in the driveway for a minute?"

I laugh. "You didn't have a problem with it when it was Caleb's uncle's house..."

I get out of the car. Either she'll come or she won't. But Riley is faithful, and a second later her car door creaks open, too.

"This way." I show her down the secondary driveway that leads to the guest house. I've done this too many times recently for it to be shocking, but I still get flickers of a younger me running past us.

Riley's head swings around, trying to take everything in. It's a bit overgrown, but winter is upon us. No one cares about landscaping in November.

I point to the guest house that comes into view once we're past the garage. "I grew up there."

"Literally in Caleb's backyard. Damn."

I nod.

"Okay, so where do you want to go? In there?"

"Yeah..." I scan the yard and pause on the pillar by the sliding glass doors of the main house. My feet automatically carry me in that direction, an old dream rearing its ugly head.

I crouch and stare through the window.

"What are you doing?" Riley whispers.

"I had a dream that I hid here while my mom and his dad argued in the kitchen." I shake my head, hunkering lower. I duck my head and close my eyes. "I couldn't hear what they were saying."

The image comes back, but it's still without sound. My mom throws the glass against the wall. Caleb's dad storms away.

I grimace and open my eyes. Riley's watching me strangely, but she doesn't comment.

"I wonder..." I go to the sliding glass door. They used to

keep a key on the top of the frame, which didn't help Caleb or me on the off chance we got locked out—we had to make a big production of dragging a chair over, teetering on it precariously—but now... now I'm taller.

I run my fingers along the top of the frame, pausing when they trip over something cold. Metal. My chest erupts with butterflies, and I pull down a grime-covered key. It fits in the lock, audibly turning the latch on the sliding door, and then... we're in.

I spare a single glance at the kitchen counter and go to the stairs.

"Caleb lived here?" Riley whispers. "What happened?"

I shrug. "I don't know."

He moved away. In with Eli. He doesn't talk about his parents, just his uncle. Something happened here.

At the top of the stairs, I have a choice. Go left to Caleb's room and bathroom, or go right, down the hall to the master and guest bedrooms. I go left.

His room is virtually untouched, the same as mine. It's neater, no clothes lying on the floor or in the hamper. I guess he had more time to pack than I did. Still, it's a ten-year-old's room. Blue walls. A train set in the corner. Toys stacked on top of his dresser.

We used to play with this stuff.

I hid behind this door once.

Riley follows me in. "It feels eerie to be here," she admits. "Do you remember anything?"

"Just stuff I already knew."

I drag my finger through the dust on top of his dresser. Every other room in the house has been swept clean, covered in white sheets.

Why is Caleb's room different?

I reach for the door, intending to close it, and am

gripped with a sudden sense of déjà vu. Grabbing the door to hide. I did that once... but then, there's the sense I did it again.

More than once.

Past

"You have to run." Caleb hauled me by my shoulders and shoved me toward the stairs.

His dad was on a rampage. His yelling echoed through the kitchen and dining room, to the living room where Caleb and I had been trying to learn chess. It came out of nowhere—peace one second, then an earth-shattering roar.

I trusted Caleb, and now, I listened. I bolted for the stairs, flying up and to the left. I made it to the safety of his room and grabbed the door, ready to slam it closed behind us... but Caleb hadn't followed me.

I waited a moment, breathless and terrified. His dad was still hollering about something, the sound of breaking glass and wood haunting my ears.

If Caleb got caught...

I tiptoed out into the hallway, just as he appeared on the staircase. He looked at me oddly, like he was confused why I wasn't in his room.

"Caleb!" his dad screamed. "What the fuck is this mess?"

"The chessboard," he whispered, more to himself than me. His shoulders slumped. "I'll be right back. Margo. *Stay here.*"

He pushed me back into the room. Behind the door, which he left open.

I latched on to the knob, and I couldn't pry my fingers off of it. Not until Caleb was back. Fear wormed its way up my throat, choking me. My dad never got angry like that. Never screamed. Mom did, but Dad said it was the chef in her. She learned how to use her voice in a kitchen, surrounded by men.

I didn't know what that meant, but I always nodded.

At any minute, Caleb was going to appear in front of his dad and take the blame for the chessboard and pieces spread across the floor in the living room. But before it had even begun, everything screeched to a halt. Something had distracted Caleb's dad.

"I'm coming to get my daughter." My father's voice carried upstairs. "Jesus, Ben. I could hear you from my house."

"*Your* house," Caleb's dad sneered. "It isn't your house. It's mine. And who do you think you are, coming in here like you're welcome?"

"I came for my daughter," Dad answered. Even. Maybe annoyed, but definitely not showing it.

The fear loosened its grip on my airways.

"She's not here," Caleb's dad snapped.

"Margo!" Dad called. "It's okay, honey. Come on out."

I ran out of Caleb's room, down the stairs, and launched myself into Dad's arms. Caleb was on the floor at his dad's feet, scrambling to pick up the chess pieces. I tried to help, but Dad held me fast to his side.

"Caleb was going to teach me how to play," I whispered into his shirt.

Dad looked from me to Caleb, then Caleb's dad.

"What did she say?" Caleb's dad snapped.

"Caleb and Margo wanted to learn how to play chess," Dad said. He released me and bent down. He picked up the box, sliding the board inside. One by one, he took the pieces out of Caleb's hand and put them in their foam slots, his hands steady. Then that, too, was added to the box. "I think we can do it in our living room. Margo's mom was a chess champion back in her day. Maybe she can give us some pointers."

He straightened and tucked the box under his arm.

Caleb's dad stared at mine. "Well."

"Amber will be over soon, I'm sure," Dad said. "I'll send Caleb back with her. Or maybe later?"

"Well," Caleb's dad said again. The wind had been taken out of his sails.

Dad took my hand. I took Caleb's.

My first hero marched us out of the house, and we didn't look back. It didn't make it okay—it didn't erase the pops and flashes of terror the sight of Caleb's dad incited. But knowing Dad was just a minute away sure did help.

Present

"Riley," I choke out, sinking to my knees.

A tsunami wave of sadness hits me square in the chest. I didn't realize how much I missed my dad until I recalled that fear of Caleb's.

I dig my fingernails into the wood.

"Tell me," she says.

I lay out what I remembered. It wasn't necessarily a new memory, or a previously blocked one, but it was one I had shuffled to the very back of my mind. Caleb's dad had a temper. It matches what I dreamed about—my mom and him in an argument.

We go back downstairs, and she looks out the sliding doors to the guest house across the lawn.

"Your dad heard him yelling from in the house." Riley's face is pale. "That must've been terrifying as a kid."

"Yeah." More so for Caleb than me, I'm sure.

I lock the sliding door behind us and replace the key where I found it.

"Caleb invited me to the football team's championship game at Lion's Head," I tell her. "Well, I don't know if I can call it an invitation. He said, 'Come with me.'"

Riley glances at me. "That matches his personality."

"Did Eli ask you?"

"No. He'll probably just show up at my house and demand I go with him." She shrugs and gestures to the door. It's unlocked, but I haven't opened it yet. "Let's do this thing."

"It's weird in here," I warn her. "Like stepping back in time."

"Okay."

I shove the door open, ready to be assailed by memories.

But I'm not. It's empty.

I walk into the living room and spin in a slow circle.

Nothing.

"I'm guessing this isn't what you expected," Riley says. "This doesn't feel like a time capsule. It even *smells* clean in here."

What the fuck? "This place hasn't been touched in seven years! And *now* everything is cleared out?"

I yank open drawers in the kitchen. Swipe my finger along the counter. Check the fridge, then venture farther into the living room. No furniture. It's all *empty.*

I run to my bedroom, shoving the door open.

Every piece of my childhood has been removed except

the dresser—maybe it was too heavy? I go to it, yanking open drawers. Caleb did this. He had to. Who else would want to get rid of this stuff?

I find something in the bottom drawer. A note.

Cheers to the good times and the bad. May the hits keep on coming.

– a friend

"I'm going to be sick."

I drop the note and rush to the bathroom, falling to my knees in front of the toilet. I realize with vague detachment that the bathroom has been scrubbed clean, too. I heave, but nothing comes up. After a solid minute of my stomach rolling, I fall back and lean against the wall.

"You okay?"

I glance up. "Did you see the note?"

She holds it up. "A friend. Who is that?"

"You're my only friend. Was it you?"

"That's not funny."

"Humor is a good escape." I pick myself up. "Did you check the other room?"

"No, figured I'd wait."

I sigh and cross the hallway. My parents' bedroom door is still closed, and I'm not sure I even want to look. The last time I saw it, it was a wreck. But Caleb didn't give me a chance to really... *explore*. That, and I was on the verge of a panic attack last time.

Now, I'm much steadier.

"Ready?" I ask Riley.

She takes my hand. "Yep."

I push open the door, immediately sucking in a breath.

It's untouched.

Like a tornado went through their things, there's clothes everywhere. Broken glass from picture frames and a shattered lamp. The dresser is cracked, one leg missing, and it leans to one side.

There's a hole in the wall.

"What happened here?"

I pick my way through the room and squat next to the fallen frames. I carefully brush away the glass and slide the photo out. I was maybe four years old in it, running on the beach. Mom is behind me, blurred out, but I can tell her arms are outstretched.

—Hands reaching for me, shaking my shoulders—

No.

My hands tremble on the photo. White spots flash in front of my eyes.

"Margo—"

The darkness creeps from the corners of my vision. I manage to scoot away from the glass, grabbing the edge of the bed. "Sorry. This is too much... Fuck. I'm gonna pass out."

It swoops in, and down I go.

Chapter 34
Margo

Past

Dad rushed inside, his gaze flying around until it landed on me in the corner.

"Oh, Margo," he said. He was sad.

I was... something else. Not really in my body anymore.

Tears streaked down my face. My fingers hurt. My chest hurt. My head ached.

"You're okay." He scooped me up and sat on my bed, cradling me to his chest. "Let me see."

I sucked in a shaky breath, on the verge of tears again. My fingernails were torn, bloody. Every single one. I hadn't realized until I stopped screaming and dissolved into tears. Then I cried until I couldn't breathe.

Now I'm empty.

"We're going to clean you up and go to the park, okay?"

I nodded and closed my eyes. He left me on the bed and returned a moment later with a warm, damp cloth. He gently cleaned off each finger, wrapping them in Band-Aids. He helped me change my shirt and put on a zip-up sweatshirt. New pants, socks, shoes. He brushed out my hair, then stood.

"Come on, Margo. Time to be strong."

He took my hand, and we walked out the house. Straight down the driveway and into his car, which was the only one there. He buckled me into the seat, and I watched the sky on the way to the park.

"Where's Mom?" I asked.

He sighed. "She lost her marbles."

"Is she looking for them?"

He glanced back. "Yeah, kiddo."

We got to the park. Once we were free of the car, he took a deep breath. "I need you to pay attention to me, Margo. Things are about to change."

"Why?"

"Because you told me a secret, but I couldn't keep it. I had to tell another adult."

I had to keep the secret. Caleb begged me not to tell, but I did. I told my dad, because he was trustworthy. And now my dad told someone else?

"Is Caleb going to be mad?"

He glanced down at me, but then we were at our bench, and he looked away. Finally, he said, "He might be."

I sniffled. I ran my finger across the bracelet. I had told Dad we were married, but all he did was chuckle and kiss the top of my head. What was I supposed to do when Caleb was mad at me? When Mom was mad at Dad, she went to the Ashers' house.

Dad glanced over his shoulder, then back to me. "Listen to me, Margo."

I met his gaze.

"Don't believe what they say about you and me. Okay? You're a Wolfe. You're strong. Your—" He broke off and squeezed my hand. "Your grandmother would be proud of you."

I'd never met my grandma, although Dad talked about her a lot.

He revealed a small bag of bird seed. "How about you go feed the ducks?"

I grabbed the bag and hopped up. The ducks swarmed to the edge of the pond, crowding me without getting too close. They weren't that brave. And really, neither was I.

There was a commotion, and I spun around. A police officer was taking Dad away!

I dropped the bag and rushed back.

"Daddy!" I screamed.

A woman caught me by the shoulders. "Shh, Margo. It's okay. You're okay. Can we sit? We need to talk."

Things are going to change, Dad said. I didn't think he meant so soon.

Instant. One minute we're gasoline, the next we're aflame.

And I haven't stopped burning.

Chapter 35
Margo

Present

Dear Dad,

This feels weird. I told myself writing to you wouldn't be bad—it's better than a phone call you could reject or a visit you could deny. But instead, it feels like I'm about to bare my soul on the page.

I'm not sure I'm ready for that.

Do people keep you updated on my whereabouts? If not, the short story is that I'm back in Rose Hill, and I'm also back at Emery-Rose Elite with the same classmates I left when I was ten.

The not-so-short story is that I've always had memory issues surrounding the incident that put me into foster care, and I've started experiencing flashbacks.

Listen, I know you denied my request for visitation when I was a kid. I wish you hadn't done so, but I think I understand it a little. You didn't want me to see you like that... but all I wanted was to know it would be okay.

Maybe you couldn't have given me that.

Anyway. Because of the flashbacks, I'm left with more questions than answers. I'm going crazy trying to piece it together.

My foster parents think it would be a good idea to have some sort of relationship with you. I don't know if I agree with that, but... I do need you to fill in some gaps for me.

No one else is willing to do so.

I hope this letter makes it to you.

Sincerely,

Margo

Dear Margo,

You're welcome to visit any time.

Dad

Chapter 36
Margo

"The deadline to apply to NYU is coming up," Caleb tells me once we're settled in Robert's classroom. "You don't want to be stuck not having applied anywhere."

I set down my paintbrush. "What's this about?"

"You seemed excited to see the school."

"I always thought I'd just get a job after high school. What's the big deal?"

He meets my gaze. "What about your future? Don't you want to dream bigger?"

"That ended the moment I was put into foster care," I tell him. I had *dreamed bigger*—of course I did. But I stopped. I forced those dreams to go away, and now I can't remember them at all. "And yes, the Bryans keep telling me they'll help. But I don't know what I want to major in. Attending an expensive school before I figure that out seems silly."

Robert pauses in front of us. "Is there a problem?"

I blush. "No."

"Margo isn't sure she wants to go to NYU," Caleb tells him. "I was trying to convince her to apply."

"Margo," he chides. "You should at least apply. Give yourself some options." He's quiet for a moment. "I'm sorry, we should've discussed this more after the open house. Most deadlines are January first, which gives us a few weeks to tour more schools, if you wanted. NYU might be different. Or, you might change your mind after you talk to your dad."

I stiffen.

There's one thing I've managed to keep from Caleb. Two, now. The first is that I wrote my dad a letter a few weeks ago.

The second is that I got a reply yesterday.

After sharing with Robert and Lenora, they agreed that Robert could take me over to the prison for visiting hours on Saturday.

The big championship game is tonight, and I asked them if I could sleep over at Riley's house. Of course, I'll most likely end up in Caleb's bed... if he doesn't stop looking at me like that.

I dip my head to get Robert to move on, which he does, then peek at Caleb.

"What?" I question.

"Don't be so defensive, baby," he replies coolly. "You're allowed to see your dad."

"I know."

"Didn't think you would hide it from me, though."

I face him. "I was going to tell you tonight."

"Just blurt it out when I was fucking you?" He leans in, his eyes gleaming. "When I wouldn't be able to get pissed? Or, no, when me getting angry would benefit your pussy?"

My face heats. "That's not it. I didn't think you'd react this poorly in general."

He scoffs.

And, yeah, maybe I should've seen this coming.

"I just decided yesterday," I tell him.

I pick up my paintbrush again, dipping it into the sky-blue acrylic paint. We're working on cloud formations, using the actual clouds out the window as inspiration. It gives me an excuse to face away from Caleb.

"You're going to regret it," he says.

My shoulders lift a fraction.

The truth is, I don't really care if I regret it. My dad knows things—I'm positive he does. I'm not getting answers from anyone else. Tobias Hutchins' phone has been disconnected, all signs of his online presence wiped.

Caleb says my mom is in town, but I haven't been able to find her either.

He won't give me answers.

Which leaves *my father*.

I swallow around the lump in my throat, gazing at one particularly fluffy cloud and trying to figure out where to use darker colors.

"How's your portrait coming along?" Caleb asks. "Seeing as how it's due soon."

I eye him. "Almost done. You?"

"Finished." He smirks. "I can't wait for you to see it."

My cheeks heat. I don't know how Caleb sees me, and up until right now, I was eager to find out. I think I can hold off a bit longer, though.

I hum noncommittally, and he laughs under his breath.

The rest of the class flies by, and soon enough the bell rings to dismiss us for the day. I wave goodbye to Robert, who tells me to be home by noon tomorrow. In the hallway, Caleb takes my hand. Our fingers lace together.

The energy in the halls is palpable, kids rushing by in ERE colors. The football players are grinning, bouncing on their heels. They move in a pack toward the locker rooms.

And yet, no one knocks into us. They skirt around Caleb and me like we're protected by a forcefield.

The advantage of being Caleb Asher, I imagine.

Riley and Eli meet us at my locker.

"Are we all riding together?" Riley asks.

Eli bounds beside her. Caleb's energy is more contained, held like a jar full of bees in his chest. I feel the same way. My limbs won't cooperate, and we're on the edge of a cliff.

It isn't just the game either, or the night ahead of us. It's *tomorrow*. I'll be seeing my father for the first time in seven years. And if I let myself think about it, I'll work myself into a panic.

Like what do I say? What do I wear?

"Focus," Eli says to me, snapping his fingers in front of my face.

I jerk back and scowl.

"Yes," Caleb answers Riley. "We'll drop my car off at Ian's house and ride together. Then we'll be able to leave from the party whenever we want."

I nod at his rationale.

"Great," Eli hoots.

I slam my locker, books unloaded, and we join the throng of students exiting school. The pep squad—girls who weren't able to get on the cheerleading team, apparently—has decorated the front of the building with signs and balloons.

We're going to state!

Go get 'em, ERE!

Our mascot is a gold-and-black eagle, but it's only used for sports. Liam mentioned that the school prides itself on the silver crest logo that appears on all documents and emails, hiding away from the fact that it even has a mundane mascot.

"An eagle isn't *mundane*," Eli had yelled. "It's fucking *majestic*."

Right.

Off to the side of the lot, cheerleaders are decorating two buses. I nudge Riley and lift my chin in that direction, and she makes a noise in the back of her throat.

"Party bus and athlete bus," she says. "Football players and cheerleaders all ride together, and the party bus is for anyone who doesn't want to drive to the game."

"Ah."

She grins. "The state championships are a big deal."

"Right."

Caleb squeezes my hand, laughing as I wave goodbye to Riley. We'll see them in a few minutes anyway. Apparently the no-driving rule only applies when Mrs. Black is home to see Caleb leave for school.

I lean over and touch his cheek, guiding his mouth toward mine.

The kiss is sweet and slow, and I pull back slightly. His eyes are already open, focused on mine.

"What was that for?"

"I can't kiss you when I want?"

In truth, I have a weird feeling in my chest. I'm anticipating the distraction of tonight.

He smirks. "You can, but you don't usually kiss like *that*..."

I bite my lip and ignore the heat that floods through me. I press my thighs together, trying to be subtle about it.

His eyes darken. He misses nothing.

"Maybe we should take a detour," I suggest.

In response, he starts the car and pulls out, tires squealing. He takes me to the lookout we once went to and parks in the corner. There aren't any other cars. I thought, once, that he was going to leave me here.

He pushes his seat back and pats his legs. "Get over here."

Once I'm settled on his lap, my knees on either side of his hips, I kiss him again. I want the distraction. For him to take me to another place.

"Does this count as strenuous activity?" I tease.

His hands skate up my sides, over my uniform shirt. He undoes the buttons one at a time, revealing my white camisole and nude bra. He takes his time scanning me. His dick hardens against my thigh, and I can't hide my wicked smile.

I like turning him on. Affecting him as much as he affects me.

I'm also glad I wore the skirt today, even if it's freezing out.

He unclips my bra and pushes down the cami, exposing my breasts. He guides me forward and puts his mouth on my nipple, his tongue flicking out. I let my head fall back and suck in a deep breath.

He continues his assault, his hand going to my other nipple. He rolls it between his fingers.

"Fuck," I exhale. "You could make me come like that."

He chuckles, barely leaning back. "Yeah?"

He renews his assault. His teeth graze my breast, and

fire spreads through me. I grind on him, unable to stop myself.

"Caleb." I think we've just decided condoms aren't for us. I just... I know it's silly, but I don't want anything separating us. I take my birth control religiously, so... "Fuck me."

He tips his head back and grins. "Eager, are you?"

I grab his face and slam my lips to his, showing him just how eager I am. My hands go to his pants, unzipping them, then navigating his hard length out. He jumps in my hand.

He tugs my panties to the side.

I'm soaking wet. His finger pushes into me, curling, and my eyelids flutter.

His hands go to my hips, lifting me slightly, and he slides in. We both groan. He just... fits. Perfection.

"Fuck, baby," he growls, claiming my lips again in a quick kiss.

His teeth drag against my lower lip. There's no more talking after that. We stare into each other's eyes. He guides the pace, slamming me down on him. Our faces are close enough that we could kiss if either of us moved a fraction of an inch closer.

He leans me back and suddenly hits a whole new spot. My mouth parts. I hang on to his shoulders, letting him press me back on the steering wheel. He darts forward, leaving a trail of kisses down my throat, my collarbone. He bites my breast, then soothes it with his tongue a second later.

Kiss.

Bite.

Lick.

My fingers slip into his hair, tugging. I'm coming undone, thread by thread. Falling apart in his hands. He sucks on my nipple, and that's it.

His gaze flies up to mine. I shatter. My whole body pulses. He grabs my chin, forcing me to look at him as the orgasm sweeps through me. I don't realize we've stilled until I slowly come back.

"Hold on," he warns me.

He grips my waist and thrusts his hips up. I tighten my grip on his shoulders, and he pounds into me without restraint. Chasing a high.

A minute later, he freezes, his eyes on me. He groans.

We stare at each other.

I'm caught entirely in his web.

...and then reality returns. The game. The party. And *tomorrow*.

He catches my face in his hands. "Don't do that."

"Do what?"

"Disappear again."

"I'm not."

"You *won't*," he corrects. "You're trying to do it now."

Bossy as ever.

"Say it."

I sigh. "I won't disappear again."

He squints at me. "No matter what happens tomorrow. No matter what happens with my family or our past." He shakes his wrist, drawing my attention to his bracelet. "You promised."

I smile, running my finger over his bracelet. The fact that he wears it openly, unashamed, makes my heart sing. "I did promise."

He kisses me once more. "Good. Let's go have some fun." He looks down at his lap, where we're still connected.

"Unless you want to skip the game and do more of this?" I ask hopefully.

He laughs. "If we don't make an appearance, people will talk."

"Talk isn't the worst thing in the world."

"If only you believed yourself."

I climb off him and pitch myself into the passenger seat with a groan. He hands me my bra, then panties. He tucks himself back in his pants. Once we're both more put-together, he winks and drives out onto the road.

First to drop off the car at Ian's house, then onward to Lion's Head.

Why does it feel like we're about to walk into the enemy's lair?

Chapter 37
Margo

King Caleb has returned to his throne.

At least, that's what it feels like.

The Lion's Head football field, located behind the school, seems newly built. Crisp, white-painted lines. Bleachers on either side and a small building manned by two adults selling food and drinks. It's a giant campus abutting a state reservation, and it's much more peaceful than I would've guessed.

Caleb keeps me tucked next to him as countless people approach him from the top of the bleachers. He slaps guys' hands, waves off girls. Smiles and jokes. He's charming, which shocks the hell out of me. I don't know why I expected grunts and stares, which is what most people usually get out of him.

He squeezes my arm, and I'm reminded of the last time we did this. The first and *only* time we did this. It didn't really end well...

I let my head rest against his shoulder. We came prepared in winter gear. Ian wasn't exactly thrilled to let

Riley and me into his house to change, but Eli barged past him, Riley right behind.

Riley and I giggled to each other, shrugging out of the white uniform t-shirts and the dark skirts, putting on skin-tight black leggings and gold shirts she found at the mall. Mine shimmers like silk, and hers has a rough, purposefully ripped vibe. The outfits aren't for the game—it's too cold for that—but for the after-party. We painted on makeup and fixed our hair, and finally we were ready.

An impatient Ian stood by the door, periodically checking his watch.

Caleb and Eli thundered down the stairs, decked out in black and gold, and we were off.

I sink farther into my black coat, grateful for the hat Lenora gave me a few weeks ago. It's an Emery-Rose winter one, black with gold tinsel-like threads woven through, and an eagle stitched on the side.

Riley and Eli are just below us on the bleachers, and Caleb's teammates run interference for him a few rows down. They're sprawled out, being generally loud and rowdy, but also blocking a lot of people from reaching our bubble.

Liam and Theo, I suspect, will be here later.

"How does it feel?" I ask Caleb.

He glances at me. The game hasn't started yet, but he and Eli seem particularly keen on the Lion's Head sidelines. They keep staring like a monster is going to pop out.

"What?"

"Being so popular," I elaborate. "It must be weird, right?"

He shrugs. "I've always been popular. Even when we were kids. You just never noticed."

True.

"My parents prepped me for this type of lifestyle." He throws his shoulders back. "You think my dad was able to go anywhere without being recognized? His face was on billboards around town."

I raise my eyebrow. "I don't remember that."

"Well, Uncle took them down after a while. They lost their effectiveness."

Weird. But he has an odd expression, so I don't question it.

The cheerleaders run out across the field, shaking their pom-poms.

Two familiar people climb the steps, and I shoot to my feet.

"Claire! Hanna!" I race toward them.

Hanna's face lights up, and she crashes into me. I throw my arms around her, squeezing tight.

"I swear you grew five inches," I tell her. "How are you?"

She grins at me. "Good! Claire said she saw you, but I couldn't go." Her lower lip pops out. "I miss you, Margo."

"I miss you, too." I rub her arm. "Are you liking this school? Claire said you were making some friends."

Her hair is pulled back in two neat French braids, and the sisters are decked out in Lion's Head colors.

I touch the purple hair bands and smile. "You guys went all out."

Hanna beams. "Claire helped me with my hair, and she got me this shirt from school, see?" She unzips her purple jacket and shows me the purple-and-black shirt. *Lion's Head Forever* is scrawled across her chest. "My friends are sitting on the other side, but we saw you."

"Aww, well, I'm so glad."

Claire steps up and hugs me. "You guys really got prime seating, huh?"

I glance back at Caleb, but he's talking to someone else. The boy dressed in purple and black is vaguely familiar.

I shrug. "I guess."

"We're on the other side." Claire hooks her thumb toward the field. There are stands on the other side, and it's very clearly divided: Lion's Head fans on one side and Emery-Rose on the other.

"Well, thanks for coming to say hi. I don't think I would've spotted you otherwise."

Claire shrugs.

"Hey, Margo."

I turn toward the Lion's Head boy who was just talking to Caleb. He towers above me. "Matt Bonner," he reminds me. "We met at a game a few months ago."

I nod. "Right..."

Claire clears her throat, raising her eyebrows.

"Oh, right. Um, Matt, have you met Claire? She's a junior at Lion's Head."

Matt grins at her, extending his hand. "Pleasure."

She blushes.

Ooh. So much for that nice boy who asked her out.

Matt takes a second to release her hand, and my attention bounces between the two of them for a hot second. Then Claire pulls away. She steers Hanna back toward the ground.

"Nice to meet you." Her voice is gruff. "Margo, I'll see you later."

"Maybe at the after-party?" Matt asks. "Fletcher's hosting."

"Lion's Head students are going?" I ask.

Matt watches Claire for a second, then turns back to

me. "Yeah, well. Depends on who wins and who's a poor sport. But I'm Caleb's friend, so I plan on going."

"I have to take Hanna home after," Claire says, stepping down. "So..."

I get it. Responsibility is bound to rear its ugly head for her at some point. Hanna pouts, but her older sister ignores it. They both give me a wave and head back to the Lion's Head side.

Matt pauses beside me. "She's a junior, huh?"

"A transfer." I eye him. "You're friends with Caleb?"

"You betcha."

"How's that work during hockey season?"

He coughs. Maybe he's shocked by my question, because he takes a long moment to answer. "We know to leave our friendship on the benches during a game."

I'm not surprised to find Caleb's gaze on me.

"Your school rivalry allows that?" I ask. "The games just... end when the timer reaches zero?"

The teams run onto the field, and the crowds have grown thicker. Matt's purple-and-black colors stick out like a sore thumb in a mass of gold.

Matt chuckles. "Is that what you're worried about? You think whatever game he's playing hasn't ended yet?"

I purse my lips. I didn't say that—and I don't really like having words put in my mouth.

An announcer's speaker clicks on, and they begin a welcome speech.

"Shit, that's my cue. See ya around, Margo."

I go back to Caleb, who's had a delivery of concessions. He hands me a soda and popcorn.

"Where did this come from?" I ask.

"You and Bonner have a nice conversation?"

I roll my eyes. "I just wondered if he saw Claire in

school. And then I asked how you two managed to be friends with the whole rivalry thing."

"Eh, Matt used to go to Emery-Rose. We were friends before he transferred, and it just stuck."

"That's sweet." I pop a kernel into my mouth. Salt and butter explode on my tongue. "Is Theo gonna go crazy again when he gets here?"

Caleb snorts. "Probably. See the girl with the camera? By the Lion's Head coach."

I squint, but then I see her. Her blonde hair is pulled back in a braid, slung over her shoulder. Dark-framed glasses. She's drowning in a huge black jacket. There's a camera around her neck, and she periodically raises it to her eye.

"What's his problem with her?"

Caleb shrugs. "I don't know."

"Why?"

"I didn't ask. But he might freak out on her."

Eli turns around. "Might? Hundred bucks says he'll do something stupid."

Caleb's eyes narrow. "Define stupid."

"Touch her in some way. Push her or break her camera."

"Maybe he'll just yell at her." I don't really want *anything* to happen to her—because I know how it is. I know what it's like to have someone gunning for you. Especially someone as dark as Theo. As dark as Caleb.

"Is that a bet?" Eli asks me.

"I sure as hell don't have a hundred bucks to give you."

Caleb snickers. "I'll pay if you're wrong."

Eli and Caleb shake hands, and I roll my eyes.

"He might not even react at all," I murmur.

"Nope. See?" Eli points.

Sure enough, Theo and Liam have arrived. They're

wearing mostly black, but they're on the Lion's Head sideline. And they stalk right past the players. Well, *Theo* stalks. Liam follows, seeming resigned.

"Ah, hell," Caleb mutters. "Game hasn't even started yet."

Theo stops just shy of her. She stands still. He waves his hands in front of her face, but he doesn't touch her. He might be on the edge of it, because I picture steam pouring out of his ears, but Liam grabs him and yanks him back.

Theo goes.

And it's over.

Caleb hoots. "Pay up, Black."

Eli grumbles and holds out a crisp hundred-dollar bill. More money than I've ever held at once, I'd reckon.

I eye it like it's kryptonite, and both boys laugh at me. Caleb takes it and tucks it into my front pocket, patting my thigh.

"Good call," he whispers, kissing my temple.

"Well, we did fake date. You really get to know a person that way." I realize the instant the words leave my mouth that I shouldn't have said it.

Caleb's expression drops. "Is that right?"

"Um, no..."

He takes the cup from my hand, setting it on the bleachers, then yanks me to my feet. "Let's go for a walk."

Riley watches me with wide eyes, but she doesn't say anything.

We're past the point of Caleb torturing me.

Right?

We get to the grass and keep going. The roar of the crowd quickly fades the farther away we get.

"Caleb, stop." I yank my arm, but his grip doesn't

loosen. If anything, he holds me tighter. "Oh, come on, I was joking."

The cold mask I had grown to recognize has settled over his features. Scary Caleb.

I was wondering if he would ever make a reappearance.

We round the back of the concession stand, and he backs me against the wall. He cages me in, leaning down. His lips brush the shell of my ear.

I stay perfectly still.

"Hearing you talk about dating Theo makes me want to go out onto the field and pummel his ass."

"Fake dating," I breathe. "Which we only did for about fifteen minutes to get a rise out of you."

"A rise out of me, huh?" He draws back, smirking, then presses his hips against mine. His erection digs into my belly.

My lips part.

Shit. He's really turned on.

"I guess it worked." He tugs on a lock of my hair. "Now what?"

Distant cheering, but I don't know if it's for our team or theirs.

As much as Scary Caleb is hot—in an intimidating way—I prefer the other version of him.

"Now..." I push up onto my toes and get in his face. "We go back to the game." I slip out from under his arm and walk away. I ignore the tingling down my spine.

If I were to look back, I'd see him staring. Jealousy suits him.

"Every action has a reaction, little wolf," he calls.

I shiver.

He follows me back up the bleachers. To our seats. He

grabs my hips before I can sit, though, and pulls me onto his lap.

After a failed attempt to get up, I loop my arm around his shoulders. We watch the game, the players moving up and down the field. Their grunts and the creaking of equipment, the way they crash into each other. Eli and Riley are absorbed in the game. Theo and Liam join our bubble, and they watch just as intensely.

Everyone is focused on the field.

Caleb's hand starts on my thigh. I think nothing of it until it slides up just a hair, under the edge of my coat. I ignore it. I ignore *him* and whatever game he's trying to play right now. In public.

"The thing I love most about your outfit, little wolf?"

"What's that?" I'm hyper-aware of his thumb's circular path.

"You can still feel everything through leggings," he comments. His hand climbs higher, and his thumb brushes my center.

I gasp, pressing my legs together, but it's too late. He's already there.

"You can't keep me out." He darts forward and kisses my neck. "I wonder who will notice your face when you come on my hand?"

He rubs my clit through my leggings and panties. I bite back a groan, already strung out on a wire from feeling his erection and standing up to him. It was an unexpected high. And now, it's too much.

I turn my face into his neck. "You're wicked."

"It's your game," he says into my hair. "Will you scream my name?"

I grit my teeth and shift, trying to get some relief. He's driving me wild. Every inch of me is focused on the drag of his finger on the most sensitive part of me. I dig my fingernails into his shoulder.

"Stop," I moan, but I don't push him away.

I've gone insane.

He reaches higher, to my waistband. I angle toward him, trying to shield myself. My coat is doing a pretty good job, but even then...

His hand slips into my panties, and the feel of his fingers on my skin almost undoes me. Two fingers thrust into me, and I yelp, burying my face back in his neck. I expect him to laugh, but he's silent, moving faster.

Something good happens on the field, because students below us surge to their feet. We alone remain sitting as the crowd goes crazy.

"Scream," he says, teeth on my earlobe.

The orgasm rips out of me, and I do scream into his shoulder, the noise getting carried away by the cheering. He pulls his hand out of my pants, straightens my jacket for me, and waits.

The crowd settles.

My heart seems to be bursting out of my chest, and then it goes quiet, too.

And shame trickles in. Burning embarrassment follows it.

Holy shit, I just had an orgasm on the bleachers at a fucking football game. Surrounded by students. The last time he fingered me in public, someone captured it on video and sent it out to *everyone*.

And our best friends are right in front of us.

As if on cue, Riley asks, "Is she okay?"

"Fine," Caleb says, shifting me closer to him. "Just overwhelmed."

"Margo?"

"Yep," I say into his chest. "Peachy."

"Peachy," she echoes. "Um, okay."

Caleb's chuckle rumbles in his chest. He doesn't force me to come out of hiding until my face has stopped flaming. I grapple with my anger, letting my hair fall in front of my face.

When I pick up my head, Caleb turns his attention away from the game and toward me. "A state championship we'll never forget."

I stare at him, shocked. A laugh bubbles out of me, and I clamp my hand over my mouth. It doesn't stop the giggles. I thought *I* was the insane one—turns out, we both are.

Chapter 38
Caleb

We won. We're on the field with the football team and their fans, jumping and cheering.

Well, not *all* of us are cheering.

Eli and I spot Theo a moment before Liam does.

The girls are with us, Margo's hand firmly holding mine, but I drop it to lunge toward my friend. I grab his arm and take a split second to marvel at the rage he must be feeling, because he throws me off without a thought.

He goes toward the Lion's Head girl.

Eli jumps in front of him, holding up his hands. "Yo, man, normally I wouldn't get between you and your business, but literally the entire school is here, and you're going to just start a—"

Theo growls, shoving Eli to the side. *Great.*

I haul Eli up, and we chase after Theo. I look ahead and see the reason he's pissed.

One of the Lion's Head football players has his hand on her hip. They're standing too close.

Liam runs past us, but even he isn't quick enough to stop Theo's charge.

Theo's fist slams into the Lion's Head football player's jaw, knocking him to the ground. He's on top of him in an instant, his elbows snapping back. He delivers blow after blow to the poor sucker's face.

"Fucking hell, Theo!" I yell.

People are noticing.

Eli and Liam haul Theo away, but it's too late. The Lion's Head football team swarms us. It's only a second before the rest of the Emery-Rose football team, who had been celebrating, leap into the fray. I catch an elbow to my stomach. Eli swings wildly, getting people away from us.

And in the midst of all of this, Theo's still struggling to get free from Eli and Liam. I push myself in front of him and slap him.

Theo's eyes finally focus on me.

"Calm the fuck down," I growl.

Eli drops Theo's arm. "Riley and Margo."

We're in the center of a shitstorm. On the edges, I spot Coach Marzden yanking students off from each other. It's become an all-out brawl. Not just angry or hyped-up football players, but the fans—students from both schools—as well.

"With me," I order. I drive my shoulder to get through the crowd.

The four of us duck flying fists and elbows, bodies being hauled across the grass.

She's not where I left her.

"Caleb!" she yells.

I spin around, searching. Someone hits me from behind, knocking me flat on my stomach. They're gone in an instant, and Theo helps me up. The last thing my concussed head needs is another blow. He meets my gaze and nods once. He stays behind me, shoving people away.

"There." He points toward the bleachers.

Students are running, and it takes me a second to realize why: the police have arrived.

Someone knocks into Margo, and she falls in slow motion.

I sprint toward her, shoving people out of my way. Screams follow us. The fighters realize the police are here, and suddenly everyone is sprinting past us. I tune it all out, focusing on getting to Margo.

She stands, and I arrive at her side a second later.

Eli reaches Riley, tugging her behind him.

"See you at Ian's!" he calls.

I almost drag Margo after them, but there's a higher chance we'll get caught. Margo *can't* get caught—they'd take her away for sure. Haul her in for questioning at the very least.

"You okay?" I ask her.

Theo is right behind me, still blocking us from getting hit.

"This is insane!"

I pick her up and put her on her feet. "Now's not the time to dwell on it. Ready to run?"

She smiles. "This feels familiar."

If I didn't know better, I'd say she was delusional... but I do know her, and I know she's referring to the time we ran through a field to hide from my father.

I pause. She had asked me about a field. But...

"Come on." She takes a few quick steps backward. "They're going to catch us, and the whole night will be ruined."

What else can we do?

We run.

She goes toward the parking lot, but I grab her arm and

steer her toward the woods bordering the school. There's a path somewhere along here...

"This way!" Matt comes from our left, Hanna on his back.

Claire jogs beside him, worry coating her features. "The path is over here."

We follow them along the tree line. The harsh lights from the police cars paint everything red and blue. It makes the earth weirdly pitted. Margo trips in a hole and latches on to my arm.

"Keep moving," Matt yells.

He finds the path and veers into the woods.

"Hey, stop!"

They found us.

Margo's palm is sweaty against mine, but I don't let go. I can't. She's slow behind me, but it doesn't matter. Matt and Claire have their phones out, flashlights illuminating the ground in front of us. All I can hear is Margo's sharp pants.

I drag her to a halt. "Get on my back."

"But—"

I drop to a knee. "Now."

She jumps on, wrapping her arms around my shoulders.

"Try not to choke me." I get to my feet. She's light—we should've done this ten minutes ago. I take off after Matt.

Margo lets go with one hand, reaching back. Her phone flashlight comes on, giving me enough light to see the path.

I catch up to them quickly.

Constant vigilance. Something Margo's dad used to say to me, trying to instill a general sense of awareness in my surroundings. The words ring in my ears. I glance around, trying to figure out where we are. It's a cross-country running path—it has to lead back to the school eventually.

"This way," Matt yells ahead of us. His light swings wildly.

We go onto a smaller path, mostly hidden by leaves. Ahead of us, Claire slips on loose stones and almost goes down.

"Where is he taking us?" Margo says in my ear.

"Somewhere the cops won't find you," I answer.

If she's caught, it doesn't matter if she was involved or not—they'd take her in. She's in the system. She's labeled a runaway. What next, a troublemaker?

Not on my watch.

Our jog turns into a walk, which turns into a climb.

And finally, we get to our destination. We're dumped out of the woods into a clearing. I spin in a slow circle, taking in the view. The water tower that supplies half the town is on the opposite side of the field. But beyond that is nothing but treetops, the city lights flickering in the distance.

"Beautiful." Margo wiggles until I release her thighs. She slides down my back. "We came all the way up here to escape the police?"

Matt puts Hanna back on her feet, and she rushes to Margo.

The two of them hug while Claire watches.

"How did you know this was up here, dude?" I ask Matt.

Theo and Liam didn't come with us—I suspect they peeled off and caught a ride.

Matt grins and heads straight for the water tower. "Our team parties up here sometimes." He unearths a cooler half hidden by brush. "Drink, anyone?"

"No," Margo murmurs.

"I'll pass, too," I say. To Margo, I whisper, "Plenty of time for that later."

She snorts.

Matt flips the cooler lid closed, shaking his head. "Just as well. It's probably not cold."

He types on his phone, then stuffs it back in his pocket.

"So, you two know each other?" Margo points from Claire to Matt.

"You told me to keep an eye on her." He raises his bottle, tipping it toward Claire. "So that's what I did."

Margo doesn't say anything, but her attention bounces between her foster sister and my friend. Trying to figure out a deeper connection? I don't know. I'd believe Matt over the foster girl.

My phone buzzes, and I reach for it eagerly. Honestly, this is the last place Margo and I should be—with her foster siblings and my friend who has probably watched a spy-cam video of Margo and I fucking. But I can't see a way out of here without being rude... or leaving Margo's foster siblings with Matt.

I'm not that big of a dick.

Liam is calling me.

"Yeah?" I answer.

"That was fucking wild," Liam hoots. "Police are gone. Coach sorted them out, although they hauled away like a dozen kids. Not sure how Theo got out—*ow*, okay, I guess the deputy recognized his last name—*ow*, fucking hell, Theo, stop—"

I snicker.

"Shut it, Asher," he says. "Where'd you go? Eli texted, said he and Riley would double back for you if you needed it."

I exhale, motioning for Margo to come closer. "We'll be

at the parking lot in ten. Doesn't matter who gives us a ride as long as someone waits for us."

"Over and out," Liam answers.

I stuff my phone back in my pocket.

"Cops are gone," I tell them. "We're going to head down."

"Yeah, we'll join you," Matt agrees. "Wouldn't want anyone getting lost."

Claire leads the way, and Hanna slips her hand into Margo's. My heart warms just a bit at the sight of the younger girl clinging to Margo. Of all the injustices, Hanna and Margo being separated seems like one of the worst.

And then Matt is beside me, and I glare at him.

"I'm just being friendly." He raises his hands in surrender. "Not my fault she's so damn pretty."

I chuckle. "Don't even think about it."

"Whoa, whoa." Matt's eyebrows hike up. We both turn on our flashlights. "Think about what?"

I sigh. "I'm gonna do this even though I might puke after. They're Margo's sisters. You can't fuck with them."

"*Them?* Buddy, my eye is just on Claire. And if she wants what I'm giving..."

"Don't make me punch you." I glance ahead, then pull him slower. "Any update on you-know-who?"

He groans. "No. It's been maddeningly frustrating. No activity. I think they know their figurine was found and they're lying low."

"Keep an eye on it," I tell him. And then I break away, jogging to catch up with Margo.

I've had enough people-ing for the day.

Chapter 39
Margo

Caleb and I climb into Theo's car. Liam has already claimed the front seat before we arrived, and he's still chuckling at our daring escape. Matt waves us off, Claire and Hanna close behind him.

Something spins in my gut, but Caleb trusts him. He told me they were friends. And after I hugged Claire and Hanna goodbye, Caleb said Matt would take them home.

As much as I kind of hate it, I'm letting it happen. Claire is old enough to make her own decisions. She's sixteen, after all. That's the age to be boy crazy *and* stupid.

"You seem tense," Caleb whispers in my ear.

I sigh. "Yeah."

"We could always just go home..."

He smirks. I'm pretty sure my face just lit up. There's nothing more I'd like better than to just... go to bed with him.

Caleb's presence has a way of shielding the nightmares.

"Hey, Theo, drop us at my place."

Theo grunts. "No partying with us, man? We just won fucking *state*!"

"Yeah, then you almost ruined it by fucking up a Lion's Head player." Liam shakes his head. "What the hell is it with that chick?"

Theo turns to him, glowering. "Shut up."

I whistle. "What could one girl do to deserve all your anger?"

"That, Wolfe, would be a long story," he says.

I wince.

Caleb shakes his head without taking his eyes from the window. "He's had a hard-on for that girl since sophomore year, but he hates to admit it."

Theo slams on the brakes. "You're damn lucky we're here, asshole," he says. "Get out of my car."

"Testy," Caleb says under his breath. He grins at me, flinging open the door and helping me out. As soon as the door is closed, Theo's tires burn rubber. We're left standing in the road, watching him go.

"Are the Blacks going to question why I'm here?" I ask, crossing my arms over my chest. The jacket and hat aren't helping against the chill anymore. It smells like snow.

"They're out of town this weekend."

I bite my lip and follow him inside. "I'm going to see my dad tomorrow."

"I know."

"Well, I felt the need to remind you."

He flicks on lights in the living room, the hallway, the kitchen. Soon the whole downstairs is lit up. "You did, huh?"

I nod. "Just in case you were going to be upset about it."

He strides toward me. Around me.

"Me? Upset?" He's behind me, lingering. His fingers sift through my hair, lifting the hat off my head.

I huff. "You hate when I mention him."

"That's because I hate *him*," he whispers. "And I just... if you knew, you'd hate him, too."

I spin around. I have to crane my neck back to meet his gaze. "That's just it—*if I knew*. I want a chance to know. And I need to talk to him about the Bryans."

"About them adopting you?"

"Well, it's a nice thought, isn't it?" I run my hands up and down my arms, suddenly cold. "The idea of a happily ever after."

He pauses. "Do you think you're not going to get one?"

I haven't thought that far ahead. For the last seven years, minus an odd dream or two, it was just one foot in front of the other. One *day* in front of the other. That's how we survived in the homes that sucked, in the homes that were great with an expiration date, in the group homes cramped with too many kids.

Problem kids.

I never got that official label, but I almost did. And then there really would be no future for me to hunt down.

So, no. I never thought about a happily ever after.

"I can't apply to NYU," I say. "It's outside my budget. Maybe a nice local community college—"

"Bullshit," he says.

"What?"

He motions for me to go into the kitchen. I don't budge.

"Caleb, you can't just dismiss the fact that I literally have no money—"

"I think I can," he says.

He bends down and scoops me up, an arm under my knees and the other at my back. I let out a little yip, throwing my arms around his shoulders.

"What—"

"Just let me," he mutters. "Just once, okay?"

He carries me down the basement stairs.

He's wrong. It isn't just once. He's had spontaneous moments of kindness since I returned to Emery-Rose. They were hard to recognize at first, but he really changed after finding me in the woods. Seeing me hurt by someone else's hand...

Maybe that's what this is. A premature apology for whatever damage my father's going to cause.

I hold on to him and let him do what he has to do. It'll make both of us feel better before tomorrow.

After I visit my dad, I'm either going to walk out in one piece or be broken by whatever my father has to say. Either way, I'm getting answers. I'll be changed.

This is a goodbye to the Margo I was.

Am.

Will never be again.

"Shh," he whispers. "You're crying."

"I'm not," I murmur, blinking at the ceiling. "I just have something in my eye."

"Both of them."

"Right. A bit of mascara or an eyelash or a branch..."

He coughs a laugh. He hits the light in the bathroom with his elbow, then gently sets me on the counter. This, too, is familiar. Although I'll confess—we haven't done this with clothes on before.

"Are you wearing fake eyelashes?" he asks me.

I choke on my laugh. "Yeah, Caleb, I am."

Thanks for noticing. I can't even *think* that sentence in a straight voice.

Boys are so ridiculous. The only thing they tend to notice are boob jobs, new cars, and lingerie.

Sadly, I have none of those things.

He cocks his head. "How do you get them off?"

I pinch the outside edge between my finger and thumb and slowly peel it away. It's a relief to get lashes off—not that I'm an expert or anything. Riley had to put them on for me in Ian's bathroom.

He reaches out to my other eye, which flutters closed before he can touch me. Gently, he does the other one.

"Like an unmasking," he says under his breath. "Stay here."

He disappears, returning a few minutes later with my overnight bag. At this rate, I don't even know how it got inside. Or even out of Riley's car. He finds my packet of makeup remover wipes.

"Can I?" he asks.

I squint at him. "Can you take off my makeup?"

He doesn't answer but swipes at my forehead.

I lean away, catching his wrist. "You *can*, but not like that. My face doesn't need to be scrubbed raw."

He smiles, but it's unsure. "Right."

I cover his hand with my own and guide him. His strokes become soft, and I close my eyes. Let him remove the layers of foundation and concealer, the eyeliner and eyeshadow. I take it away from him to get the mascara off, then hand it back to him.

"This shit was on your face," he says, holding it up.

"Yep."

"You're pretty without it."

I shrug. "Yeah, but it makes me feel good when I do wear it."

He hums. His hands go to my jacket, unzipping it and pushing it down my arms. My shoes are next. Then my shirt.

I raise my arms diligently.

Camisole. Bra.

I stand, and he yanks my leggings off, his expression hungry.

"Kiss me," I whisper.

He obliges. I'm not sure how he always ends up fully clothed while I'm naked, but I'm suddenly desperate to change it. Not breaking away, I unbuckle his belt, unzip his pants. Shove them down until he can kick them away. We pause to remove his hoodie, then shirt.

I run my nails down his chest, eliciting a shiver that rolls up his body.

"Bed," I say.

His chin lifts, gesturing for me to go first.

I make it halfway across the room when he grabs me, raising me by my hips and carrying me the rest of the way. My back is pressed tightly to his chest, my feet only a few inches off the floor.

"Wasn't I moving fast enough?" I joke.

I fall onto the bed and roll over, welcoming him when he climbs over me. We've had sex. We've fucked.

But tonight, I have a feeling it's going to be something entirely new.

"Am I in control?" I ask.

He shakes his head slowly, gaze going to my throat when I swallow. "Are you ever?"

"More times than you know."

A muscle in his jaw tics.

"Caleb."

"Hmm?" He's getting closer to my neck, inching down.

He's not touching me, and I'm really starting to hate him for it.

Not really. Pretty sure I don't hold an ounce of hate for him anymore.

Did I? Yes. Should I? Yes.

Do I?

I exhale when his lips finally touch my throat. His hand follows, resting there. Keeping me from moving.

"You're going to lose your innocence," he says in my ear. His breath is hot, moving my hair. "You're going to walk into that prison as you are now, and you're going to leave it as someone else."

"Maybe."

His hand tightens for a second, then relaxes.

"You're going to hold more secrets than me, and then I'm going to..." His teeth graze my earlobe.

I shudder.

"I'm not going to lose you," he says.

"How do you know?" I force him to meet my gaze. None of this running bullshit.

He's scared of the truth. He's scared of what my dad has to tell me.

And I swear, at my question, his eyes darken.

"Because if I *do* lose you, I'll go down whatever fucking dark hole you bury yourself in, and I will find you. I will bring you back."

He kisses me, silencing any other questions. His lips are rough. His tongue claims my mouth. I wrap my legs around his hips and pull him flush against me.

I don't know what my father could possibly say to make me want to run from this, but I shove it out of my mind.

That's the point.

Tonight is about us.

A hello.

A goodbye.

A promise.

Chapter 40
Margo

"Name?"

"Margo Wolfe."

"Who are you visiting?"

I clear my throat. "Keith Wolfe."

The guard on the other side of the glass is bored. There are other people—families, single people, men and women in business attire—scattered around the prison's visitor entrance.

She types on the keyboard in front of her and grunts. "You're not on the list."

"The, ah, what?"

"The approved visitors list. Wait here." She gets up and disappears into a back room.

I wait. A minute, then two. Five.

Caleb insisted on dropping me off this morning at the Bryans' house. He had to borrow Eli's truck, since his car was still at Ian's. He didn't think anything of it when I mentioned my foster parents might be suspicious. I was supposed to sleep at Riley's place, after all.

Through the night and into the morning, he was unusually... handsy. Clingy. I don't think he ever stopped touching me. My breasts, my stomach, between my legs.

I touched him right back. All over.

Until it *was* over. I climbed out of the car in front of my house, and he told me to call him later. Said he'd be waiting by his phone.

I smiled and pretended everything was fine—it *was* fine, on the surface. Underneath my skin, anxiety was gnawing at me.

And then Robert made me suffer through breakfast. He hemmed and hawed over the weather and what shoes to wear. In the end, he was stalling, too.

We drove the short distance to the prison, and he parked right out front.

"I'll be here when you're done," he said. "I'm not going anywhere."

I nodded and took a deep breath, willing myself courage.

And now I'm here—I'm doing it. But apparently only if I get... *approved.*

Finally, she returns. "Okay. I need your ID. You can put all your belongings in one of the lockers. No phone, food or gum, drinks. No purses or bags, nothing in your pockets..."

She's reading from a mental list, and I do my best to keep up. I slide my student ID through the hole. She takes a cursory glance at it then files it away.

"Take locker six. Code is seven-nine-zero-four. Then have a seat until we're ready."

"Okay." I'm so out of my league here. I collect a few sympathetic glances as I scan the lockers and finally find number six. I type in the code, and it beeps twice, then swings open.

Slowly, like I'm moving through molasses, I empty my

pockets and shut the locker. I don't have time to take a seat. Something buzzes, and a door opens.

A guard calls, "Visitors, this way, please."

I follow the group of people down the hall. I'm trembling down to my bones. But whether it's from the cold or fear, I can't tell.

This is my father's home, in a way. He *lives* here, and has for the past seven years. Or, six, I guess? I don't know where he was during the trial. I wonder if he sees it as home. If, after a certain point, he just gave up calling it anything other than *his*.

It's how I was with my foster homes, after all. The foster parents were always Mr. and Mrs. This-or-That, the home was always their house, never mine. Because it wasn't. It was temporary, just like prison.

I'm serving a sentence the same as my father, for things we both apparently did.

Our escort guard stops and presses a button. There's another deep buzz, and the guard pulls the door open. "You can hug on initial greeting," he says to us. "And goodbye. But no touching otherwise."

I force myself to nod and stuff my hands in my pockets. I'm not sure I want to hug him.

There are round tables scattered in the center of the room with attached stools, the kind you'd see in an elementary school cafeteria. It keeps people from getting too close, I guess. By the windows are two-person tables, and I automatically drift in that direction.

Visiting families are already claiming tables. Some are eager, others bored. It makes me wonder who's here on a regular occurrence.

He knows I'm here.

That thought alone has me weak in the knees.

I almost fall into a chair at a two-person table. I can't stop the bouncing in my leg. It's been seven years. Am I going to recognize him?

Is he going to recognize *me*?

Oh my God. What if he walks right past me?

Another visitor shoots me a look. "You okay, honey? You're not going to pass out?"

I take a deep breath. "I've never done this."

"They're the same guys we know," she says, shrugging. "At least they start off that way. You visiting a boyfriend?"

"My dad," I whisper.

She exhales. "Yeah, I've got a fucked-up dad, too. He finally stopped letting me come visit. Now I just see my brother once a month."

"That's..."

"Depressing as shit? Yeah." She forces a laugh. "But he passes on news of my dad, and I'll take it. We do what we have to. Remember that. To survive this place, *they* have to do what they have to, and so do we."

"Yeah."

Another buzz rings through the room, and I almost jump out of my skin.

"Inmates entering," a guard calls.

A door in the center of one wall slowly slides open on its own, and a guard walks through. He stops just shy of the door and takes a step to his left, admitting the inmates. Prisoners.

Their uniforms are khaki, their last names stitched over a breast pocket. Some scary-looking dudes come through the door first, finding their visitors and making a beeline in their direction.

The room breaks out into a low ripple of chatter as greetings are made.

I stare at the door, gripping the table like it'll save me from getting sucked underwater.

I'm convinced I'm meeting a stranger until he walks through the door.

He is exactly as I remember him. Sandy-brown hair trimmed too short, a straight nose and full lips. He has the barest hint of scruff on his face.

His eyes are dark, like mine, and they find me immediately. Like magnets.

He pauses in the entrance, and the guard removes his handcuffs. Without hesitation, he strides toward me.

"Margo," he says with all the warmth in the world.

Nothing could've prepared me for it. For the sameness of *him*. Exactly what I would've needed when I was ten. Eleven. Twelve. Hell, every year. Every occasion.

Why wouldn't he let me see him?

Tears fill my eyes, and I throw my arms around his shoulders. All my internal debating—to hug or not to hug, to smile or frown, to be happy or upset—flies out the window. *Happy. Definitely happy*.

But also... not. Also, devastated.

"Hi, kiddo," he whispers into my hair. His arms come around me more slowly, but once there, he locks on. "You're so grown up."

God, it feels so good to hug him.

We cling to each other until a guard barks at us to separate.

I shakily withdraw, swiping at my cheeks.

"Let's sit," he says. "It's been a while."

Not by my choice.

"How have you been? Your case worker was allowed to tell me a little about your foster homes... and the trouble you had. Running away." His eyebrows draw in. "I've never felt so fucking helpless."

"It's okay." I clear my throat, trying to rid my voice of the scratchiness.

"She made it pretty clear that you weren't going to come see me." Dad leans forward, into the table, and extends his hands. "You're an adult now. I can't even believe it."

I take them in my own, even though it's against the rules. His palms are calloused. He's thinner than I remember, too, but harder. I'm not sure what to think about him talking to Ms. McCaw.

Did she not relay my desire to see him? Or is he lying to save face?

He's the one who refused me. Not the other way around.

"My foster dad drove me," I tell him. "They're a really nice couple. They want to petition to adopt."

He glances down at our hands and slowly withdraws. "Oh. How do you feel about that?"

"I—"

"I'm assuming you're just here to see if I'll give up my rights."

His expression goes blank. I've seen the same thing on Caleb—it's a defense mechanism. This is not going the way I wanted it to at all.

"I came here..." I clear my throat again. The best method would be to just blurt it out, so I do. "My memory is blocked. I remember being happy, and then they were taking you away in the park. That's it. There are so many pieces missing, I need you to fill in the gaps. Just like I said in my letter."

I don't examine his expression and instead press on.

"Did you give Mom drugs? Is that what I saw that made everything blow up?"

"What?" Confusion laces his tone. "Margo, what are you talking about?"

I freeze. "Everyone said you were arrested on drug charges. Trafficking or something. I wasn't allowed to go to the trial... There's nothing about it online. All I know is what I've been told."

"Bullshit," Dad whispers. "She really told you that?"

"I'm just trying to figure out the truth here, Dad." I wipe at my face again. "If that's bullshit, then what *happened*?"

He glances at the clock on the wall. "Listen. Your social worker lied—or she masked the truth. Whatever her reasoning, I didn't get sent to prison for drugs."

"Why didn't some news outlet cover it?"

"Because the Ashers wanted it hidden," he bites out. "Lydia and her brother-in-law in particular. They want—no, they *need*—the Asher name to be pristine."

"But *why*?"

He leans forward, bracing his forearms on the table. "You saw something you shouldn't have. And you told me about it when your mother told you not to." He pauses, like he's waiting for me to magically remember.

Sorry, Dad. This is all new information.

I wish I could just freaking *remember*. "She—you—one of you locked me in my room. There was yelling. Your room was destroyed." I hold out my hands, staring at my nails. "Did you bandage me up?"

"We got into an argument," he says. "It was heated. And yes, while I was gone... I fixed you up when I got back."

I'd hate to see what a real fight looked like, if that was just the result of a heated argument.

I push that thought away. "Did you hurt her?"

He's miserable reliving this—it's written all over his face—and I almost apologize. I hold fast. I need to know. It's why I'm here, right? I can't let this be in vain.

"I didn't touch her," he says. "But... I did hurt someone else."

What?

Who?

"Can you just be straight with me?" I demand. "Why are you in here? I talked to your lawyer, but he didn't give me anything—"

"You talked to Hutchins?"

"Five minutes!" a guard yells.

Dad's face has gone white, and he grabs my wrists. I suppress a yelp and stay perfectly still, while a guard yells behind him. Dad stiffens and releases me quickly.

"You went to Tobias Hutchins?" he repeats, voice low. "Alone?"

"My friend went with me," I mutter. "We were in the city looking at NYU."

His face softens for an instant. "We'll discuss your college search the next time you come in." And then he's back to brisk. "He got me a deal. A shit one, if you ask me, but what choice did I have?"

"What deal?"

He shakes his head. "You're going to come back, right?"

Will I?

He clearly has a story to tell, but it might take some tugging to follow a single thread through the tapestry.

"Yes," I say. "I promise, I'll come back. Now tell me what deal you took. Please."

He grimaces. "I was looking at a life sentence for murder."

My eyes go wide.

Murder?

Who was murdered?

I have zero recollection.

"The deal was voluntary manslaughter. Medium security prison. I have another five years before parole is even considered."

I'm pretty sure I'm in shock. I can't move. Can't think. Dad's in prison for killing someone. That's... that's *so* not the image I had of him. I didn't think he would be capable of it.

"I didn't do it," he adds.

"Then why on earth did you accept the deal?"

He shakes his head.

"Time's up!"

Inmates around us stand and hug or shake hands.

Me? I'm locked in a staring contest with my father, trying to sort through the different emotions fluttering around inside my chest. I might throw up.

He pulls me to my feet and wraps his arms around my back. His mouth at my ear, he whispers, "I was up against the Ashers' top-notch lawyers, as well as a determined District Attorney. All I had was a shitty public defender who didn't believe my story."

I hug him back, blinking. "Why were the Ashers against you?"

He chuckles. It's the most depressing sound I've ever heard, and it drills a hole straight through my chest. In one side and out the other.

"Because according to them, I killed Ben."

Ben.

Benjamin Asher.

Caleb's dad. *Caleb's dad is dead.* All this time, Caleb

didn't mention it. He grimaced whenever I mentioned my dad, who he had loved up until... well, up until Dad allegedly killed his father.

And Caleb hates my father. He never hid that fact—because he thinks mine *killed* his. There's no way my father would hurt a fly. Literally no chance.

"Let's move it, Wolfe."

I cringe, but the guard isn't talking to me. His gaze is on my father. Steady, calm. They're not in a panic, but they're not going to let him take his time either.

Dad releases me and steps back, searching my face. I nod at him, unable to do anything more. I don't think I can speak without screaming. My throat has closed.

He and the rest of the inmates file back through the door, and it slowly slides back into place.

He's gone.

All around me, visitors stand. Some stretch, others just go right for the door where another guard is waiting.

I can't move. My knees are locked. White spots flicker in front of my vision.

"Hey, hey," the woman from earlier says, coming over. She grasps my elbow. "You okay? First time visiting, right?"

I nod.

"Yeah, first time can be intense. It gets easier. Although you look like you saw a ghost."

I force myself to smile. "Yeah, it was intense. I haven't seen him in a while."

She hums. "Well, let me walk you out."

Through the door. Down the hall. Once we're buzzed through the final door and back in the waiting area, I take a deep breath. My first one in a while.

I grab my stuff from the locker and collect my ID from the guard at the counter. I can't be in here anymore. Just visiting is suffocating... or maybe it's the impact of new truth.

He said he didn't *actually* kill Caleb's dad. But nevertheless, Mr. Asher is dead. Someone must've killed him, whether it was Dad and he's trying to preserve himself, or...

Or he was framed.

But there would still have to be motive and opportunity for the District Attorney to even get Dad arrested in the first place, right? They would've had to have evidence pointing them toward my father.

I storm outside with my emotions all over the place. I don't know whether to cry or go on a rampage. *He killed Caleb's dad.* The why is unclear.

He pled out and got a lighter sentence than *murder*.

Voluntary manslaughter.

It sounds so...

"Margo, are you okay?" Robert meets me halfway across the parking lot.

I fall into his arms, and a sob erupts out of my chest before I can stop it. Seeing my dad brings out all the ugly emotions that come with abandonment.

Fear. Longing.

Why am I not good enough?

Why didn't you want to see me?

Robert hugs me tightly, with one hand pressed against the back of my head. "Shh, honey, it's okay."

His other hand rubs small circles on my back.

I hugged Dad and it felt like home. I can't help but think that moment will forever be tainted by bars on the windows and confessions whispered in my ear.

Caleb knew I was going to come out of there as a different person. Did he know what my dad did? Of course he did! His own was killed, and he's faithfully withheld that secret.

Why didn't he tell me?

And it begs another question: what else hasn't he said?

I can't breathe over the lump in my throat. My whole face is on fire with embarrassment, shock. I slowly loosen my grip on Robert's jacket, but I don't release him entirely. I tuck my face against his chest and try to get a hold of myself.

This is fucking embarrassing.

I need to talk to Caleb.

He knows more—I know he does.

This ties into his family and my family.

My mind can't grip reality. I'm furious and sad and overwhelmed, like a tornado of feelings that refuse to unknot.

"Breathe," Robert reminds me. "It's okay. What happened?"

I take a shaky breath. When I lean away, I'm ashamed of the tear stains on his jacket.

"I just..." I can't immediately accept the truth, which means I can't say it out loud either. "It was a lot."

He guides me to his car, tucking me into the passenger seat then circling around. I watch him pass the front of the hood, bundled against the cold. He climbs in and turns on the car, and we sit there for a moment until the air gets warm.

It must've started snowing while I was inside. It falls thick and heavy now.

"Let's go home," I beg. "I could use a cup of hot chocolate."

"Len should be home by now," Robert says. "Maybe we take it easy and have a movie night?"

It sounds like the perfect distraction.

"Great idea."

He hands me a tissue, then pulls out onto the street. "You can talk about it if you want. Either to me or Len, Angela, your new therapist... There are a lot of options."

"I know." My gaze returns to my fingernails. I shredded them at some point while in the prison, either listening to Dad talk or waiting for him to come out, but I didn't notice the full extent of the damage. There's blood caked around the nail of my index finger.

"I just wanted to say, without anyone else around—you know how Len gets, hovering—that I'm proud of you. You were so against seeing your father when we first met you. It's only been a few months, but this willingness to open up—"

I bite my lip, desperate not to cry again. "I want to stay with you. And thank you for taking the time to drive—"

The SUV comes out of nowhere.

It smashes into the front corner of our vehicle, sending us flying. Robert reaches over, his arm across my chest as we catapult off the road. He tries to regain control, but in slow motion, we go off the road. The nose of the car goes down into a ditch, and momentum takes it from there.

I close my eyes, bringing my hands up to protect my face.

The car flips.

Glass shatters.

My head bangs against something, and the world flickers.

Screeching fills my ears, then the sound of wind.

And then, silence.

Darkness.

My breath in my ears.

Pain comes a heartbeat later, lacerating through me. I gasp, revived, and stare at Robert. We hang upside down, suspended by our seat belts. His eyes are closed. There's blood on his head.

Black spots form in front of my eyes.

It's hard to breathe.

"Robert?" I try to reach over, but my arm isn't working right.

I unbuckle myself, stretching up with my working arm to lower myself to the floor—the ceiling of the car. Hot liquid pours down my face, and I give in to the wave of dizziness.

Just one second, I order. Then get out.

The longer I stay still, the harder it is to keep my eyes open.

Rough hands grab at me, and I fight them for an instant.

"Stop, I'm here to help," a voice says. "It's okay, Margo."

How do you know my name?

I hesitate long enough for them to slide me out of the car. Their arm is wrapped around my chest, just below my breasts, and they manage to get me out through the broken window.

"How did you find me?" I slur. "Robert—"

"He's okay. The ambulance will take him. Come on, up to your feet." My savior hoists me up, but my legs won't hold me. After a moment, they adjust their grip and half drag me, moving backward. "You hit your head pretty good, huh?"

The voice is familiar. Distant. Talking to me through a tunnel.

"I can't leave my dad—"

A sharp inhale. Mine? Theirs?

"Where did you come from?" My heels drag across the pavement.

"You're not hard to track down."

I get a foot under me. My eyes open enough to see that we're across the intersection by now. Robert's car is almost unrecognizable. It's crumpled, upside down. Smoke pours out of the hood.

"Wait. I need to help him."

We stop, and I'm lowered into a sitting position. I stare at the car. I just need to get back there. Make sure Robert gets out. Why didn't they get him out?

"I'm sorry, Margo," the voice says. It's familiar, but their identity is just out of my grasp. Behind a wall of some sort.

It occurs to me that I could look back and see who pulled me out of the car, but I just don't care. I need to get back. It's so cold, and my neck is so stiff. My whole body is locking up. The road tilts.

"This is what has to happen," they continue. Loose gravel crunches as they kneel behind me. "You'll forgive me, won't you?"

Their hand wraps around my face. It covers my nose and mouth with a damp cloth.

I stop breathing and jerk, alarm bells ringing in my ears at the scent of chemicals. I try to get away, but I'm no match.

I can't escape. My lungs scream at me.

Finally, I have to give in.

I have to breathe.

Chemicals choke me. And a second later, I fall into nothingness.

TO BE CONTINUED…
In Wicked Promises, coming soon!
http://mybook.to/fallenroyals3

About the Author

S. Massery is a dark romance author who loves injecting a good dose of suspense into her stories. Originally from Massachusetts, she now lives in Southern California with her dog, Alice.

Before adventuring into the world of writing, she went to college in Boston and held a wide variety of jobs—including working on a dude ranch in Wyoming (a personal highlight). She has a love affair with coffee and chocolate. When S. Massery isn't writing, she can be found devouring books, playing outside with her dog, or trying to make people smile.

Join her newsletter to stay up to date on new releases: http://smassery.com/newsletter

Also by S. Massery

Hockey Gods

Brutal Obsession

Devious Obsession

Secret Obsession

Twisted Obsession

Fierce Obsession

Shadow Valley U (co-written with SJ Sylvis)

Sticks and Stones

SVU Book 2

Sterling Falls

#0 THRILL

#1 THIEF

#2 FIGHTER

#3 REBEL

#4 QUEEN

Sterling Falls Rogues

#0 TERROR

DeSantis Mafia

#1 Ruthless Saint

#2 Savage Prince

#3 Stolen Crown

Broken Mercenaries

#1 Blood Sky

#2 Angel of Death

#3 Morning Star

More at http://smassery.com

Where to Find Sara

Thank you so much for coming along on these crazy boys' journeys with me.

If you like my stories, I'd highly encourage you to come join my Facebook group, S. Massery Squad. There's a lot of fun stuff happening in there, and they're who I go to for polls about future books (fun fact: some key details in this series is decided by their votes!), where I share teasers, etc!

My Patreon is also an awesome place to connect and get exclusive content! On release months, I do signed paper-backs. Plus, get ARCs, audiobooks, and artwork before the rest of the world. Find me here: http://patreon.com/smassery

And last but not least, here are some social media links for ya:

Facebook: Author S Massery

Where to Find Sara

Instagram: @authorsmassery
Tiktok: @smassery
Goodreads: S. Massery
Bookbub: S. Massery

Made in the USA
Monee, IL
27 October 2024